BOTTLED EVIDENCE: THE COMPLETE ADVENTURES OF THE MAJOR, VOLUME 7

BOTTLED EVIDENCE
The Complete Adventures of the

Major
VOLUME 7

BY

L. PATRICK GREENE

ILLUSTRATED BY

WILLIAM M. ALLISON & HARRY PARKHURST

ALTUS PRESS

2025

TABLE OF CONTENTS

AN ILL WIND

THE HOTTENTOT'S teeth chattered violently. "I do not like this place, baas," he complained, and drew his fog soaked blanket yet closer about him.

He was answered by a feeble groan as the man he addressed also endeavored to warm his numbed body by rearranging the folds of his blanket.

The Hottentot sat up, his chin resting on his drawn up knees, his hands clasped about his ankles, and stared miserably about him. He could see nothing. The night's darkness was absolute. He looked up, hoping that the sky would give him a welcome sign of night's waning. But the thick fog which blanketed the earth blotted out the stars.

Somewhere to his right a man snored raucously; to his left a man—his sleep disturbed by a nightmare born of an evil conscience—screamed in terror and was answered by laughter and rude curses. Somewhere nearby, yet completely hidden by the pall of night and fog, men drank, gambled and quarreled.

These sounds, distorted by the fog, had an illusory, unreal quality. Only the heavy booming of gigantic Atlantic rollers on the sandy shore seemed real and, because real, menacing.

"We are all alone in an evil world, baas!" Jim, the Hottentot, exclaimed presently. "Here there is no sun, no life, only the voice of evil spirits. I do not like this place."

Another groan answered him. And then, faintly, "If you do not like this place, Jim, go back to the boat. But I stay here, gripping the earth with two hands."

"Wherefore, baas?"

"Because, Jim, if I let go, it would toss me off."

"*Wo-we*, baas!" There was a note of relief in the Hottentot's voice. "Does it take you that way, too? I dared not speak of it lest you think me mad. But I have been lurching now this way, now that, ever since we left the accursed 'house-on-water.' *Wo-we!* I tell you that the whole earth has thrown itself at me."

A soft chuckle greeted this.

"Best get back to the boat, Jim."

"Not I, baas. I prefer death to that."

A voice, speaking the vernacular as fluently as the Hottentot and his baas, bellowed, "Then die, Hottentot. But let me sleep."

The Hottentot was abashed for a moment. He continued, in a softer voice.

"I am hungry, baas. My belly is empty. I—"

"Don't, Jim! Don't talk of food. I—"

A pregnant silence followed.

The night aged. Unseen constellations rose and set. At length the fog became visible, shot with the gray of breaking day.

THERE WERE sounds now of men awakening; yawns, and querulous, sleep-filled voices. White tents loomed up gigantically in the fog, looking like sailing ships seen in a mirage.

Jim, the Hottentot, rose shivering to his feet. He twisted the ends of his blanket between his powerful hands.

"At least, baas," he said, commenting on the streams of water which came from his blanket, "no man need thirst in this place. It is only—"

He stopped abruptly, fancying he heard stealthy footsteps behind him. He turned and peered intently to the right and left, seeing vague, distorted shapes—fog shadows.

Suddenly one of the shadow shapes materialized and he looked into the face of a man who seemed to have sprung up from the ground directly before him. It was an evil face, and between parted, sneering lips Jim caught a glint of gold.

"Baas!" Jim shouted warningly for, his eyes, glancing down, had seen the gray steel of a knife in the man's hand.

The Hottentot sprang forward.

From out of the fog, behind him, something crashed down on his head with stunning force. He pitched forward onto his face and was very still.

Another dull thud and the Hottentot's baas, he had risen swiftly at Jim's first warning cry, dropped in an inert sprawling heap to the ground.

Quickly, grunting with swinish satisfaction, two dark shapes bent over the unconscious men, rifling their pockets and their packs. Then silently, swiftly they vanished into the fog which had spewed them forth.

THE EAST lighted. The fog, shredded by a gusty land breeze, was tinted opalescently by the rays of a rising sun.

The air was filled with particles of fine, flesh-cutting sand which effectively aroused to the labors, hopes and disappointments of another day the men who had joined the "rush."

And when the sun finally appeared above the horizon, completely dispelling the clouds and fog, the sands at Luderitzbucht were a-swarm with men, white-helmeted and sun-goggled for the most part, who crawled about industriously on hands and knees, prospecting their claims, looking for the stones which, when cut and polished, seem to hold something of the sun's glory.

But the Hottentot and his baas did not move. They only groaned faintly when four husky miners, on whose claim they were lying, picked them up and moved them to a place where the incoming tide would soon wash their heads.

"That'll teach the blinkin' fools not to go to sleep on our claim," one of the men said with a brutal laugh. "Come on, let's get back to work."

One of his comrades made a half-hearted protest:

"D'you think we ought to leave 'em? They look to me as if they'd been knocked out."

"What of it?" said another. "Dutch Sam's work most likely. But that's nothing to do with us. I got enough to do "babying" diamonds. 'S fact I ain't got no time to waste babying a bloomin' fool dude an' his nigger."

"But suppose they don't wake up an' gets drowned. That'll be as bad as murder—"

"Oh, don't be so bloomin' squeamish. Good riddance if they was to drown. Too many lousy fools already here. Wish we could dispose of a few more like that. My God! What with run-a-way sailors, an' cooks, an' stokers an' the gutter-scum from Jo'burg, an' Kimberley, an honest digger ain't got a chance. Look at the fools now!"

He pointed to the township, a miserable collection of corrugated iron huts clustering about three large buildings, namely: the "hotel," store and customs house. Before the latter was a pole from which hung the flag of this German West African Colony and all about it swarmed men who waited the appearance of the official who could grant them prospecting licenses.

"Oh, come on!" the first speaker said disgustedly. "No good chewing the fat here. First thing you know, some of them scuts will jump our claim, an' it's a fact we won't be able to get another."

The four moved off, returning to their claim and, caught in the grip of diamond fever, forgot all about the two men they had carried to the water's edge.

The sun rose higher. The incoming tide was but a few feet away from the senseless victims of the men who had struck in the darkness.

On the rocks not far from them sat several men, watching them intently.

"I'll betcha they ain't dead," said one. "They're drunk."

"Dead drunk; same thing."

"Bet you they ain't dead, or drunk. Bet you Dutch Sam knocked 'em out."

"You ought to know. You're a pal of his, Slim."

"Do you mean to insinuate—"

"Didn't insinuate anything, Slim. Besides I ain't interested in you, unless you want a fair gamble. Tell you what: I'll bet you an even tenner the nigger wakes first."

"Done!" said the man called Slim. "Any of you others want a little gamble?"

There was no response.

"Pikers!" scoffed Slim.

THERE WAS silence for a little while as they all watched intently. The tide was drawing nearer.

Said one, casually, "The white fellow looks like a bloomin' dude what's been caught in a rain storm, don't he. Bet he drawls an' says, 'Don'tcherknow, old chappy!' Wouldn't mind betting he wears a monocle. Any takers?"

"That's too easy, Shank. You want to gamble on sure things, don't you?"

"Well—" this was a dapper, horsey-looking man talking, with something appealing about his sharp incisive voice, and his brown eyes twinkled with kindly shrewdness—"he may be a dude, but I'm gambling he's well-bred. I don't put myself up as judge of men. Horses are my line. Just the same, when you come down to brass tacks, you can judge a man much as you can judge a horse. Look for his points—get me? All right! Look at that chap's jaw! An say, I don't care a damn if he does wear silk underwear! Look at his chest, his slim waist an' his bloomin' muscles. And he ain't muscle bound, either, I'm gambling."

"Maybe, Curt," Shank said impatiently. "But I gambled my shirt once on a bloomin' gee-gee that looked like a world beater. It had everything, as far as looks went. But I couldn't see inside the screw. It had the brains of a louse an' the heart of a jackrabbit. An' it came in last. An' I'm betting it's the same with the dude there. All looks—no guts, no brains, no good!"

"Have it that way if you will, Shank," Curt said tolerantly. "Maybe you're right. I reserve final judgment till I see his eyes. I'm betting they're gray. If they are, don't monkey with him. I'm warning you."

"They'll be baby blue," Shank sneered, "an I'll make him dance to any tune I want to pipe. What do you say to that?"

"If you let me know what flowers you like best," the other said evenly, "I'll do my best to get 'em for your funeral."

"Oh, you go to hell," Shank said, scowling fiercely as the other men laughed.

A big wave, tumbling over, spread itself out in a creamy foam and raced across the sand.

It lapped about the heads of the two men; it splashed over their faces.

The Hottentot's arms and legs moved spasmodically. Another wave followed swiftly in the wake of the first. It washed completely over the men's bodies.

With a half-strangled cry of terror the Hottentot scrambled to his feet and staggered away.

The watching men laughed uproariously.

"I win," yelled Slim. "Give me my tenner, Shank."

"How do you know the other ain't awake too. As a matter of fact, I saw his legs move a good bit before the Hottentot's did."

A noisy argument immediately commenced, the men taking sides, and the white man, still lying where the tide washed over him, was forgotten. Only the horsey man watched.

THE HOTTENTOT suddenly halted his panic-stricken flight and returned swiftly, his face gray with fear, to the aid of his baas. As he neared his face broke into a grin.

"Baas!" he cried happily. "You are all right!"

The white man rose somewhat shakily to his feet.

"Yes, all right, Jim. But my head—" He felt it gingerly.

"Mine, too, baas," the Hottentot exclaimed lugubriously.

"What happened, Jim?"

"In the gray dark, baas, just before the sun's rising, men attacked us. One, I think, I shall know again."

"You heard him speak, Jim."

"No, baas. I saw him smile," the Hottentot answered cryptically.

The white man felt in his pockets.

"They robbed us, Jim."

"Naturally, baas."

"But they left me my revolver. That is something."

"It is great wealth, baas," grinned the Hottentot.

The white man looked at him thoughtfully.

"Did they leave you nothing, Jim?"

"Not a thing, baas. But that is no matter. Before we do anything else, the baas must get himself a helmet. Let us go to the *dorp.*"

The white man nodded and the two walked slowly up the beach.

The Hottentot was naked save for a pair of white ducks cut short at the knees and his powerful torso glistened like bronze. His splendidly muscled arms were abnormally long and, despite his homely, good-natured face, there was much about him reminiscent of the savagery of primitive man. One felt that he knew and accepted the ancient law of "Kill, lest ye be killed."

The white man, his baas, was evidently a fine example of an immensely higher order of evolution, or at least of an order which had known centuries of civilization. And yet the two had much in common, Both made servants of their bodies; both had the same effortless stride—the stride which marks the experienced trekker—and the same wrinkles at the corners of their eyes. Both suggested all that is clean and wholesome.

As they passed the rocks where the gamblers still wrangled, the horsey man hailed them.

"You all right, stranger?"

They turned and faced him.

"Quite, thanks awfully," the white man drawled. "But I say, can you lend me a—er—handkerchief? I want to dry my gun."

Silently Curt gave him a red bandanna and watched him carefully dry his revolver and the cartridges it contained.

"Thanks awfully," he said as he returned the handkerchief. "I'll oil it at the first opportunity. One can't be two careful you know. It might get rusty, and rust stains the clothes most fearfully, don'tcherknow."

At that the other men forgot their squabble and turned to stare and laugh.

"What did I tell you," one cried. "He said 'don'tcherknow!'"

"An' he's got baby blue eyes."

"An' I bet he wears a monocle—don't you, Algy?"

" 'Pon my soul, how did you know? I do, of course I do." He fished in his tunic pocket. Then his face fell. "But it's broken. 'Pon my word it is. And I'm as blind as a bat without one, don'tcherknow."

"Oh gord!" one of the men gurgled. "Ain't this a treat. Beats a show at the halls any day. Go on, Algy."

"My name is not Algy—it's Aubrey St. John Major. But I'd like it much better if you'd just call me Major. *The* Major, don'tcherknow?" He beamed vacuously at them.

Two or three laughed.

"My word, if you're not off"; one cried mockingly.

THE MAJOR looked bewildered. Perhaps he was uncomfortably conscious of the ludicrous appearance he presented. He was somewhat pale under his tan—the result of the blow and the tempestuous journey he had just completed in the tub of a boat which was still at anchor in the harbor; his eyes were bloodshot, his black hair, which normally was brushed back smooth in an immaculate pompadour, was dishevelled; his water-soaked clothing— it was steaming under the sun's fierce rays—was covered with sand and clung shapelessly to his body.

He toyed nervously with his revolver.

"I wonder if you can tell me what I ought to do. You see I landed last night—couldn't stick the smell and roll of that beastly boat any longer—and I'm afraid some—er— bounder took advantage of my helplessness and robbed me."

"You mean," questioned Shank, "that you ain't got no money, no duds? You're broke?"

"Exactly. You've expressed it wonderfully."

He dramatically turned his pockets inside out.

Shank shrugged his shoulders.

"The best thing you can do under the circumstances, Mister Aubrey Major, is commit suicide. This ain't the place for dead beats. Why, you can't get a drink of water without paying for it. The condensing plant's broke down again an' the shipment in yesterday from Cape Town is as valuable as hell. Believe me, if I owned a condensing plant in the *dorp*, I wouldn't bother about prospecting for diamonds."

"Diamonds," the Major murmured. "You mean to tell me there's diamonds here?" He looked around wonderingly.

"Of course, you fool," Slim said roughly. "What else 'ud bring a crowd of men to this lousy hole. Diamonds! Why they say this place is going to make De Beers take a back seat."

The Major's smile was indicative of great relief.

"Oh, topping! Absolutely priceless! That, as it were, takes care of all my worries. I'll just wander around with Jim— that's Jim over there you know. He's pointing to his head like that, not, as you might at first suppose, to indicate that he's—er—slightly lacking, as it were, but to impress upon me the fact that I need a helmet. Great lad, is Jim. But, as I was saying! All I have to do is look around, keeping my eyes open for diamonds sparklin' in the sun—and I'm rich."

"Why—there's one!"

He leaped forward excitedly, and, bending down, picked up a smooth glittering pebble which stuck out of the sand almost at Slim's feet.

"What luck!" he exclaimed rising slowly. "The first time I look— Oh, I say! *Why* did you do that?"

The man Slim had pounced on him as he rose and had wrested the stone out of his hand.

"That's mine, you know," the Major continued indignantly, and made ineffective attempts to regain it.

BUT SLIM—HIS nickname was a misnomer— warded him off with his brawny, hairy hand, laughing contemptuously as he examined the stone.

"Here, dude," he said presently, "you can have your pretty stone. It's only a *bandtom*—the beach is covered with them." He tossed the stone to the Major who stared at it incredulously.

"You mean," he stammered, "that it's not a diamond? That it's not worth anything?"

"You wouldn't get a cent for a thousand of 'em. But let me tell you this, dude: it ain't safe to go a-picking up stones anywhere about here, see? All this ground—'s far as you can see, an' further—is laid out in claims. See? An' supposing that *bandtom* had been a diamond, it 'ud have belonged to me. Get that?"

"You mean you own this claim?"

"Exactly. An' furthermore, before you can do any prospecting you've got to get a license."

"How funny! An' where do I get that?"

"Up there." Slim gestured toward the customs house.

"I see. Thanks! Then I'll be toddling along. Toodle-oo!"

He turned away and joined Jim who had been squatting on his haunches listening to the conversation, yet not understanding—Jim's knowledge of English was confined to a few parrot-like phrases. But even if he had not understood the talk, it had afforded him much amusement; he was always amused when his baas played a game, feigning ignorance of things—*his* baas who knew diamonds as few men knew them, his baas who could do all things, and do them well.

"What game do we play, baas?" he asked now.

"I'm not sure, Jim. I only know that my head aches, that I will not trust myself to a sailing-boat again and that, in some way, this place must render us justice. We landed with much equipment, we are now empty handed."

"The baas forgets his revolver and the cartridges," Jim said.

The Major looked at him and smiled.

"You're a regular little sunshine chappy, Jim," he drawled in English.

"My word yes, baas. If I don't see you, s'long, hullo!" Jim replied with an air of portentous gravity.

The Major laughed. Then, in the vernacular, "Wait here a minute, Jim. There is something I must ask those men."

He ran back to the little group on the rocks. They were arguing violently as to who had won the bet. They looked up as he came to a breathless halt.

"I say, you laddies, can one of you tell me where I am likely to find Dutch Sam?"

They stared at each other.

Then Slim said suspiciously, "Do you know him?"

"Oh, no, never met the dear soul. Wouldn't know him from Adam if I saw them together, except"—he giggled—"I suppose Mister—er—Dutch Sam would be wearing the most clothes."

There was a laugh at this. Slim continued, "If you don't know him, what do you want to see him for?"

"Well—er—the fact is, a little bird told me it was a man named Dutch Sam who banged me on the head and helped himself to my equipment."

"What do you mean, a little bird told you?"

THE MAJOR'S hands fluttered. It seamed a helpless gesture, yet, whereas his right hand had been empty, it now held his revolver.

The man Curt laughed softly. He was enjoying this, especially as the others had not, apparently, sensed the significance of the dude's lightning draw.

"What do you mean, a bird told you?" Slim repeated truculently.

The Major gaped inanely.

"Well, perhaps it wasn't a bird. I only used that as a—er—figure of speech. No. Of course it wasn't a bird. Probably the waves whispered it to me. Mysterious thing, the sea, you know. It's responsible for all sort of—er—upheavals and outpourings, and what nots. Ha-ha! I speak, feelingly, as one who knows."

"Aw, stow your gab. Answer my question. Who told you about Dutch Sam?"

"I'm afraid you did, old dear. Surprising how well your voice carries! You see, I was reclining there, gazing up into the—er—eternal blue, waiting for the tide to come up and give me my morning bath, when I distinctly heard a voice, your voice, dear old boy, say: 'Bet you Dutch Sam knocked them out.'"

Slim scowled. For the moment he was speechless.

"An' did you hear anything else?" Curt asked, grinning.

"Why, yes, now you mention it, I did. Another voice—I think it was yours"—he turned to the man called Shank—"said: 'You ought to know. You're a pal of his, Slim.' Of course I heard other things, but that's all that's important. And so—"he beamed at Slim—"because you're a friend of his I came back to ask you where I might find him. And, having asked, I—er—pause for a reply."

"And what are you going to do, dude, when you see him?" Slim asked.

"Why—I shall—er—just point to him the error of his ways, and I shall demand the return of my kit."

"An' suppose he refuses?" Slim was grinning now.

"Why, he'd never refuse, surely? Not when I've explained things. But should he refuse, I'm afraid I'd be compelled to—er—chastise him."

Slim howled with glee, and the others joined him.

"Dutch Sam," Curt explained, answering the Major's look of bewilderment," is the bully of Luderitzbucht. He stands six foot six, an' he's as strong as an ox. An' there's no rules but his, when he fights."

THE MAJOR nodded thoughtfully. When he spoke again the vacuous look had vanished from his face—it was almost as if he had removed a mask—and his eyes were steel gray. He spoke sharply to Slim.

"I asked you where I would find Dutch Sam."

Slim sobered suddenly.

"You'll find him, most like, up at the store. You can't miss him. Head and shoulders above everybody else; an' he's got red hair and a red beard. He—"

"Ah, thanks," the Major drawled. The mask was on his face again and Slim, angry at himself for his momentary panic, said jeeringly, "Don't slap his wrist too hard, dude."

The Major nodded absently and moved away toward Jim.

Curt came running after him, and he waited expectantly.

"Don't rush things, Major," the horsey-man warned. "Dutch Sam's the boss of a big gang of cut-throats an' if it came to a fight you wouldn't have a show."

"Thanks," said the Major. "I'll be very careful. But tell me: how does he earn his living?"

"He calls himself a prospector," Curt replied bitterly. "But he prospects pockets, that's all. The pockets of honest miners."

"And they do nothing?"

"What can they do? He's on the right side of the German officials. Besides, he's got his gang, and it's organized. The miners ain't." He looked around cautiously and started as his eyes met those of Slim's.

He turned away quickly, first whispering, "Don't forget my warning, Major."

Rejoining the group at the rocks, Curt said breathlessly, "I was sounding him out, Slim. I thought, for a time, he wasn't the fool you thought him. But he is. His eyes are blue. You said they would be, didn't you, Slim?"

"Yes. And yours'll be black if you ain't more careful, Curt," Slim snapped vindictively.

And then the squabble over the bet recommenced.

THE MAJOR and Jim the Hottentot did not halt again after leaving the men at the rocks, but made their way directly up the long, sandy beach, heading for the township.

They passed through hordes of toiling blaspheming men, men who crawled about their claims on hands and knees, turning over the sand with pocket knives and sieving it through bleeding, nail-broken fingers, men whose clothes were black with sweat, whose eyes were bloodshot and whose lips were cracked and bleeding. Some of them, men who had ventured to "wash" for diamonds, standing knee deep in the sea, were covered with painful sores. All of them had a haunted look of avarice in their eyes and regarded their neighbors with open suspicion.

A few looked up as the Major and Jim passed, some laughed jeeringly, some scowled and mouthed a threat. But most of them seemed unconscious of their passing. Most had eyes only for the sand beneath them and labored with feverish industry as if there was a time limit set to their operations, as if impelled by an urge to locate their fortune quickly so that they could have more time to spend it.

It was a depressing sight.

Coming at length to the township, the Major and Jim turned into the street which led to the store. It was ankle deep in dust and littered with empty bottles: champagne bottles, beer bottles, whisky bottles and a few, a very few, water bottles.

As they passed the customs house a mob of men surrounded them; white collared men, fat gross-living men whose eyes twinkled with cunning and false *bonhommie*. Be-ringed hands, unsoiled by labor, pawed at the Major. Grimey, money-loving hands waved packets of paper in his face. Shrill voices "touted" him.

"Here you are, Mister! Buy shares in the Golconda. It's a second Kimberley! It—"

"Don't you listen to him. Look here. I represent Sharp and Stye—London Stock Exchange, doing business—"

"At the Old Bailey! Hi, mister! Don't deal with sharks, deal with the old firm. I got a few shares—"

"Shares, hell! Listen, mister: You want a claim of your own, ain't that best? An' you can't get a license. They ain't issuing any more. Now I got a claim. Don't want to make a cent in it. It's a good claim. I'm only selling because I've made my pile an' I am going home. Five hundred quid, an' the claim's yours. Cheap enough—"

"Yah—as cheap as the stuff in it—"

Smiling, the Major pushed his way through the shouting crowd of men who preyed upon the gullibility of others. But it was not until he exhibited empty pockets that their deafening clamors ceased, and they hastened away to swarm like hornets about a miner who was dancing about, excitedly proclaiming to the world that he had struck it rich.

"Bah!" Jim exclaimed in disgust. "They are not men, baas. They are hyenas."

The Major nodded absently.

He was unloading his revolver as he walked. The cartridges he put into his pocket, then re-loaded the weapon with cartridges from his belt.

"Best put those others in your belt, baas."

"Why, Jim?"

"*Au-a,* baas. The place for an egg is in the nest."

"Or in a man's belly, Jim."

"Some eggs, yes, baas," Jim agreed with a grin. "But see that they are given to the right man.

"I don't quite follow you, old lad," the Major drawled in English, "But I'll do as you say."

HE TOOK the cartridges from his pocket and fitted them into the empty loops of his cartridge belt.

As they neared they heard a noise as of two men wrangling. A voice, clear and insistent, another, coarse, bullying, sounded above the hum of conversation.

The Major quickened his steps, ordering Jim to efface himself as much as possible. Wise in the way of the men who flocked to the diamond or gold fields, he knew that a wordy quarrel nearly always developed into a fist fight which, as the onlookers took sides, eventually became a general mêlée. And in such a rough and tumble a native became the target for every man's hands and feet.

Jim dodged behind one of the tin huts, content to watch from there. But, "Take care, baas!" he said.

The Major nodded and went on alone. His eyes gleamed; his lips tightened. Already there was the thudding sounds of blows and the jeers of onlookers. He had no doubt that Dutch Sam, or one of his henchmen was one of the fighters. If that proved to be the case, he, the Major, meant to take a hand in the case.

"He broke my bloomin' monocle," he muttered, "and if I get sunstroke—the sun's getting frightfully hot—that will be his fault too."

He stopped abruptly as the door of the store opened violently and a man reeled out, collapsing in a heap in the middle of the road.

Another man came to the door of the store; a big, red-headed, red-bearded giant of a man. He filled the whole doorway with his massive bulk. The Major could see other men attempting to peer over the giant's shoulders and between his straddled legs.

"You!" bellowed the redhead. *"Ach sis!* I will teach you not to call Dutch Sam names. You pig's offal! You swine! Here! Take your trappings."

He flung a helmet at the man in the road. A revolver and belt thudded into the dust close to the prostrate man's head. Then followed a bulky kitbag. And as it hurtled through the air the lashings closing it came undone and its contents were littered on the road.

"Swine!" Redhead said again, spitting contemptuously, then turned and closed the door of the store.

The Major heard cries of:

"Good old Sam!"

"That's the way to treat snivelling greenhorns—!"

Cries of sychophantic admiration, laughter and the clinking of glasses.

The Major went to the man in the road and knelt beside him.

HE WAS badly dazed. His eyes were puffed up, one almost closed, and the flesh about them was stained by blows. His mouth was bleeding. He had the appearance of an untrained man who had been sparring with a brutal prize fighter.

The Major gently raised him to a sitting position, supporting him with his knee and, beckoning to Jim, ordered that worthy to pick up the man's goods which littered the road.

"Steady, old lad. Steady, now," the Major said soothingly as the man—he was really quite young, barely out of his teens—struggled to rise to his feet.

"Let me go," he gasped.

"Where, old chap?"

"Back there to finish what I started with Dutch Sam!"

The Major smiled whimsically:

"Better wait a little," he advised. "You're in no condition to finish anything at present. What was it all about?"

The other groaned.

"You ought to know. You're one of his crowd, aren't you?"

"Well, no, not exactly. I don't know the man. Never been introduced officially, though I have reason to believe I was—ah—honored by a call from him in the early morning hours. At least, he presented his calling card in the shape of a nasty blow on the head."

The other smiled. It was a painful effort.

"If common misfortune means anything," he said, "we ought to be friends. At least," he continued with a sudden surge of rage, "if we join forces we'd be in a better position to get even with Dutch Sam."

"And how do you propose doing that."

"Damned if I know," was the listless reply. "I suppose the best thing I can do is beg a passage back home and confess myself a failure."

The Major looked at him intently. He recognized that this youth was a type not entirely foreign to the diamond fields. A well-bred youngster, straight out from home, with no knowledge, no experience that would enable him to compete with the sharks that swarm around the "fields." Courage, yes. But courage alone is not enough. The Major's mind went back through the years. He thought, "I was like this youngster when I first came out." And aloud, he said, "What's your name, youngster?"

"Hilton—John Hilton. I—say, I think I can get up now."

He rose to his feet but would have fallen had not the Major held out a steadying hand.

"Thanks," said Hilton with a wry laugh. "He must have punished me pretty severely. There was no room, you see, to box him. The men crowded about us, and they made me toe a line. I—"

"Don't talk," the Major interrupted curtly. "My name's— but never mind that. You can call me Major. Have you any money?"

"Not a copper. I gave it all to Dutch Sam for a claim that's worth exactly nothing."

"How do you know? No, don't answer. We'll talk about that later. Have you anything else? Anything, besides your claim?"

"A rotten, worm eaten bell tent that I bought with the claim, and a few stores. That's all."

"My word, it's a lot. You're bally rich old lad. Now—it's a bally awkward question and all that—but do you think you can trust me?"

Hilton looked at him in silence for a moment. Then, "Absolutely," he said with evident sincerity.

"Thanks, old man!" The Major almost stammered. "Then we'll be partners, what?"

He held out his hand and Hilton took it willingly.

"Now," said the Major, "you trot along to your claim. Jim, here—you don't speak the vernacular, do you? Ah! of course not. And Jim knows no English, at least his vocabulary is slightly limited. But never mind. You'll find Jim very clever at making himself useful. Put yourself in his hands. "Jim!"

"Yah, baas!"

"You will go now with the young baas to his claim. And take care of him, Jim."

"Yah. There is much about him that makes me think of you, baas."

"Ah! So you see that too, eh, Jim?" the Major commented. And to Hilton, "Toodle-oo for the present, old chap and worthy partner. I'll see you anon.

"But where are you going, Major?"

THE MAJOR laughed lightly. He seemed of a sudden to have been transformed into the complete dude.

"I have a very boring duty to perform, dear lad. Social amenities are always a bore, aren't they? But one must recognize them. And so—I'm going to return Dutch Sam's early morning call. Toodle-oo!"

The next moment the doors of the saloon had closed behind him.

Hilton stared thoughtfully after him, then made a move as if he intended to follow the Major into the store. But Jim barred the way, his white teeth flashing in a broad grin.

Hilton made an impatient, half angry gesture.

"I must go too," he said in a loud voice as if by shouting he could overcome the barrier of language. "Dutch Sam will kill him."

Jim's grin was reassuring.

"No," he said in the vernacular, shaking his head. "My baas—he said I must go with you to your claim. We go there now." Jim thought a moment. Then added triumphantly, completely exhausting his parrot-like stock of English phrases, "All right! Golly-damn me yes. No? If I don't see you. S'long! Hullo!"

Hilton laughed and Jim, shouldering the kit bag, waited expectantly.

Said Hilton soberly:

"I don't like running away and leaving another man—a stranger at that—to fight my battles. Still, somehow I think that's what I must do. I think the Major knows things. He strikes me as being very efficient. And he's my partner. So—" he looked whimsically at Jim—"you can't understand a word I'm saying, can you? Oh, well! Come on!"

He turned on his heel and led the way to his claim which was situated at the foot of some sand dunes beyond the township.

THE STORE was a big barn of a place, crowded with men, most of whom, even at this early hour, were in various stages of drunkenness. Many were seated about a long trestle table playing banker; others lined up at the counter at the far end of the room purchasing supplies from the wall-eyed storekeeper. Yet others were grouped about the red headed giant, laughing at his coarse jokes, grossly flattering him.

One or two stolid-looking, uniformed Germans wandered aimlessly about, stopping here and there, gravely accepting the drinks proffered them. They apparently regarded this invasion of their territory with an amused tolerance tinged with contempt. And, certainly, the character and conduct of the majority of the diamond diggers was not worthy of respect.

AS THE Major made his way through the smoke laden atmosphere, one or two sharp featured men looked up at him appraisingly. But their interest quickly waned. He was so evidently *not* a claim they could work. His wrinkled, sea-stained clothes, his vacuous look of bewilderment, told the tale all too plainly.

Said one with a laugh, "He's already been babied."

A rat-faced, black-garbed man jostled against the Major and his long agile fingers swiftly explored his pockets.

"Blymme!" the rat-face man complained as he returned to his seat. "He's cleaned out. He ain't got the price of a drink on him. All *he's* got—" he swore viciously and sucked the middle fingers of his right hand—"is some pieces of broken glass in his pocket."

And the Major, apparently unconscious that he had just been honored by a very clever pickpocket, made his way to where Dutch Sam was holding court.

"I say," he bleated plaintively, waving his hand above his head like a schoolboy seeking to attract his teacher's attention. "I say!"

The men immediately before him turned and laughed in his face.

"What do you make of this, Sam?" one of them cried.

Dutch Sam rose ponderously and walked slowly toward the Major. The other men parted to the right and left, exchanging winks, grinning anticipation.

"And what do you want?" Dutch Sam demanded.

The Major stammered, "Are you Dutch Sam?"

"Almighty, yes. And there is no other like me. Ma-an! Do you know I could take you up in my two hands and break you across my knee?"

"No—could you really?"

"Do you doubt my word?"

"Oh, no! Wouldn't dream of being so—er—rude. But, look here—" the Major's tone was meant to be admonishing—"if you are Dutch Sam I must ask you to return my property at once. It isn't done, you know. Really it isn't."

Dutch Sam looked genuinely mystified.

"What are you talking about, dunderhead? What isn't done?"

"Why—er—I am given to understand that it was you who—er—knocked me on the head and helped yourself to my equipment and whatnot. Of course, if you can give me your word that you are not guilty of such a caddish act, I'll apologize and—er—say no more about it."

Dutch Sam's eyes twinkled with hoggish cunning.

"Oh, you will, will you?" he said heavily. "And who, may I ask, gave you to understand that I knocked you on the head."

"A chappy named—er—I think, Slim. He—"

"Oh, he did, did he?" Dutch Sam growled, and it was evident from this that Slim was booked for an uncomfortable interview. "Well, supposing I say that Slim spoke the truth, what are you going to do, eh?"

"That depends," the Major drawled. Sitting on the edge of a table, the Major looked singularly ineffective.

"Depends on what, you dumkopf!" Dutch Sam roared.

"On whether," the Major said slowly, examining his finger nails, "you are prepared to return my property."

"And if I don't?" The question was a challenge, the laughing, sneering challenge of a bully.

"If you don't," the Major drawled, and his posture slumped still more, "I shall, in my own way and in my own time, be compelled to chastize you."

IT SEEMED as if the walls of the store rocked with the laughter which greeted this. The gamblers looked up from their cards; Dutch Sam and the Major were hemmed in by a crowd of grinning men.

"Almighty!" Dutch Sam roared and looked down at the Major. "Almighty!" he said again, wonderingly.

The Major's pose had suddenly changed. He was standing erect now, his shoulders squared.

Dutch Sam no longer topped him by head and shoulders, but by three or four inches only. And some of the more observant among the onlookers saw further than that; they realized that Dutch Sam's mightily muscled body was softened by fat. Even in a rough and tumble fight, fought under Dutch Sam's peculiar rules, the result would be in doubt. That is, supposing Dutch Sam refrained from calling his followers to his assistance. But that was too much to expect. They were already crowding behind their leader.

Still, if fists only were used, and no blackjacks, knives or knuckle dusters, the stranger ought to put up a good fight before weight and numbers overwhelmed him.

There was a tenseness in the room. Tables and chairs were pushed aside. Men hastily drained their glasses which the storekeeper's men put behind the bar; the counter was cleared. One or two voices were heard offering to bet that the stranger wouldn't last two minutes. There were no takers and the voices died away into an abashed silence.

All eyes were on Dutch Sam. It was his move and *his* eyes were fixed on the Major, who stood swaying easily on the balls of his feet, smiling provocatively.

Dutch Sam was worried. For the second time this morning a man had stood up to him instead of cringing, instead of running for safety. And that was something entirely foreign to his experience! That was something which caused him most furiously to think.

True, the first one had been only a stripling who had stung Dutch Sam with a blow to the jaw and had bewildered him with many strange appeals to play the game, to fight like a white man, to be a sport. And that one had been very easy, once Dutch Sam had got to close quarters.

But this one! *Ach sis!* This one was something else again, and Dutch Sam's little soul lost itself in his big frame. This one was a man who, despite the fact that he was the shorter of the two, made Dutch Sam feel small and insignificant.

Dutch Sam noted his powerful shoulders, his slim, tapering waist, his resolute jaw, clear gray eyes and the fact that one strong, sunbronzed hand was resting on his hip very close to the butt of a revolver. Something told Dutch Sam that the man facing him could use that revolver. And Dutch Sam, in common with many of the men who flocked to the South African diggings, had no time for revolvers. A knife stab, a blow in the dark—that was Dutch Sam's metier.

He started to bluster, realizing that something was expected of him. His eyes shifted from the Major to those around him.

"*So-a!* You would chastise me—*me,* er? It is to laugh. *Vrachtig!*"

"And yet," the Major countered softly, "I do not hear you laugh."

HE SEEMED to be looking *through* Dutch Sam, into the mirror at the back of the bar and, simultaneously with a look of triumph which flashed into the redheaded man's eyes, the Major side-stepped swiftly and, half turning, caught the upraised hand of a man who had crept up behind him. That hand gripped a bottle which, in another moment, would have crashed down on the Major's unprotected head.

The next moment, and things happened so swiftly that no one could afterward say how it was done, the bottle wielder hurtled through the air, dropping at Dutch Sam's feet. The bottle crashed on the floor, splattering the Dutchman with its contents.

"Almighty!" Dutch Sam bellowed, and kicked his henchman in the ribs. "Get out of my way fool, before I your brains kick in."

Yelping, the man tried to crawl away but was frustrated by a ring of kicking feet.

"He was clumsy," the Major said casually. "Will you permit me to hand you another bottle." He snatched one from the table behind him and offered it to Dutch Sam with a courtly bow.

The onlookers roared with mirth as Dutch Sam knocked it from his grasp with an angry curse. But their laughter was at Dutch Sam, not with him.

He looked around at them angrily and most of them sobered uneasily. Only one or two, bolder, less dominated by him, laughed. Yet those who were silenced seemed to be considering their final verdict, were waiting to see how he would meet this challenge.

"You swine!" he said hoarsely. "So you would me chastise eh? You think I take your equipment. *Ach!* And you think truly. Yes! So now what?" He crouched slightly, his big hands contracted and the blue veins showed prominently amid the red hair which covered the back of his hands. "Hans!" he said. "Pete!"

Two men came forward grinning, and stopped either side of him. They were big, loose-limbed fellows; their faces were brutal. Each carried a heavy, knobbed stick. The men behind Dutch Sam crowded nearer.

"What is it, Sam?" Pete asked.

"Watch the *roinek*, fool. You see he has a gun. Take it from him. And do not be too gentle. He is no friend of mine."

Pete and Hans looked at each, then at the Major. They were no longer grinning. They took a tentative step forward, then halted, evidently dismayed at the speed with which the Major drew his revolver and levelled it at them.

Dutch Sam, too, flinched. His hands shot above his head.

A burst of laughter greeted his gesture of surrender.

Dutch Sam scowled furiously and ventured to lower his hands again. He realized that he was in danger of losing prestige, and the prestige of a bully, once lost, is hardly ever regained.

HE DECIDED to try craft, to try to catch the Major off guard and, if that failed, to give the signal that would let loose all his men on this one lone stranger.

He said grandly, "I am tempted to thrash you, *roinek*, but I have already disciplined one fool this morning. Besides, I do not fight with girl-faced dudes. So put down your little pop gun and you shall Hans fight."

This suggestion evidently pleased the crowd. Hans and the Major were perfectly matched as far as height and weight went, and everything pointed to a good fight.

But Hans, apparently had other views. Above the shouts of approval and the confusion of shuffling feet as a ring was hastily improvised, his voice could be heard violently protesting to Dutch Sam that he wasn't going to fight and that no one could make him.

But after a whispered consultation with the red-headed giant, and an exchange of knowing nods and winks with the members of the gang, Hans' attitude changed and he stripped to the waist, boasting loudly.

A smooth shaven, clerical looking individual sidled up to the Major.

"I will be your second," he said smoothly. "Much as I detest violence, I realize, that sometimes we cannot escape it."

He barely opened his lips as he spoke.

"Good of you," the Major murmured absently. He was watching Dutch Sam and the men who crowded about him.

"Here, drink this," the oily voice continued. "It will buck you up."

The Major raised the glass the other had put into his hands.

Then someone—it was the horsey little man, Curt, who had just entered with Slim and the others—jostled against him and the glass fell from his hand with a crash to the ground.

"Oh, I say!" the Major exclaimed in tones of consternation, but his eyes were still fixed on Hans and Dutch Sam.

"You pig!" swore the man who had offered to be the Major's second. "Curt, I'll cut your liver out for that!"

There was a rasp in his voice now and, as his lips parted in an explosive curse, the Major saw that a number of his teeth were gold-crowned.

"I wonder if that was what Jim meant?" he mused.

"Nothing to get mad about, Holy," Curt was saying. "Here's the price of another drink." Then in a whisper Curt added, "Don't you drink anything Holy Joe brings you, Major. He—"

"Hi, you! Curt! Come here!"

The dapper little man slunk hastily away at Dutch Sam's roar.

"And now," continued that man, addressing the Major, "give us your popgun and strip to the waist, so's you an' Hans can get busy."

The Major returned his gun to its holster.

"I'm not going to fight Hans," he said. "My goodness! Why should I?"

"Because—" roared Dutch Sam, now confidently truculent—he was sure he had seen an expression of fear in the Major's eyes—"Because I order you to. Because— Almighty! If you won't fight him, you shall fight me!"

There was no mistaking the fear in the Major's eyes now as he looked desperately around the room.

"But I don't want to fight," he stammered. "I only came here to ask you to return my—er—kit which you had— er—borrowed. I—"

"Almighty!" shouted Dutch Sam. "You would of me make a game," And he rushed at the Major, his arms swinging wildly.

The Major, pushed by someone behind, lurched forward, recovered and leaped to the left just in time to avoid Dutch Sam's devastating rush and, before the red-headed one could turn, the Major, head down, his fists swinging like flails had made his way to the door. He had met little opposition, his move had been so unexpected.

There was a wild rush for him, headed by Dutch Sam.

With a frightened yell the Major opened the door and fled. After him, laughing, yelling obscene taunts and threats, pelted the men from the store.

But the chase soon waned. The sun was very hot, the Major fleet of foot.

"Let the *roinek* go," Dutch Sam growled. "Another time I will get him."

And boasting loudly, confident that his prestige had been increased, he led the way back to the store. "Slim'll buy the drinks," he added. "And—" this was after the gold-toothed man had whispered in his ear— "Curt'll dance for us. Almighty, yes!"

HILTON LOOKED unbelievingly at the Major. The two men were seated on the sand in the shelter of one of the enormous sand dunes which hemmed in Hilton's claim.

The sun's shadows were lengthening and the approach of night enveloped Hilton's camp with the mystery of the desert. Luderitzbucht seemed vaguely remote, although its murmurs were occasionally wafted to their ears by an ocean born breeze.

"I'm damned if I understand you, Major," Hilton blurted petulantly.

"All through the day I have been worrying about you, thinking that Dutch Sam had killed you, or at least had beaten you very badly. And then you come here, laughing as if at some great joke, refuse to say anything until we've had *skoff,* and now tell me, as if it were something to be proud of, a most amazing tale!"

"Oh come, laddie. Nothing amazing about it surely. I—"

"I could give it a harder name, Major. I thought you were going to stand up to Dutch Sam. But you ran from him like a licked cur."

"Yes," the Major said softly. "I ran from him and I *hope* he thought I ran like a licked cur." He laughed. "And, my word, how I ran!"

"I don't see that that's anything to laugh at, Major," Hilton said frigidly.

"Don't you? Strange that you don't. You didn't run, and—pardon me for referring to it—as a result you have two lovely black eyes; lucky you didn't suffer worse. On the other hand, I ran and I live to fight another day. Also, I gained much useful information."

"I'm afraid—I feel sure—I'm a fool, Major," Hilton said apologetically. "But I don't see what you are driving at. Won't you explain."

"Ah! That's better, old lad. Well, in the first place, you must admit that there's no sense in butting one's head against a brick wall. And that's what tackling Dutch Sam on his own battlefield amounts to. And, so, I contented myself with sounding out his weak points and then—er—vamoosed. He's a coward, dear lad, that's understood. But a coward who can dictate the conditions under which he will fight is a dangerous foe. And so I resolved to leave Dutch Sam alone until I can get him where *I* can dictate the terms. My word, yes."

Hilton nodded dubiously. Young, impetuous, he was not able to concur with the wisdom of the Major's scheming. Nor, as his next words proved, did he think that it would be possible for the Major ever to be in a position where he could dictate terms to the bully of Luderitzbucht.

"You won't be able to get Dutch Sam alone. He's always got two or three thugs in attendance. And, if you did get him alone, he wouldn't fight fair. You don't know his reputation, if you think that."

"But I do know his reputation," the Major replied calmly. "I've met many Dutch Sam's during the course of a more or less-er—varied career. They're all cut to one measure. Know one, and you know them all. Now tell me something about yourself?"

HALTINGLY AT first, more fluently as the Major's sympathetic attitude reacted on him, Hilton told a story which has a thousand parallels: of an only son adventuring to mend the fortunes of an impoverished family; of a girl at home who was waiting for him to make good.

"Not," he explained carefully, "that Grace cares about money. She was ready to marry me before I came out. But of course that couldn't be. She agreed with me that I owed it first to the family to make enough money so that they'd never be worried again by tradesmen's bills. And last week I wrote home that our fortunes were made. That was just after I had bought the claim from Dutch Sam." He was silent until roused by the Major's gentle prompting question as to why he had felt so optimistic about his fortune being made.

"Because," he continued, "before I closed the deal I came out here with Dutch Sam and I found diamonds on the claim myself."

"Did he let you keep them?"

"No, of course not. Why should he? I hadn't bought the claim yet. But after finding the 'stones,' I was only too anxious to buy. It didn't occur to me to wonder why he was willing to sell his claim so cheaply. I was a fool. I thought I was getting wealth. Instead I was paying a high price for experience. Five hundred pounds, practically every penny I have in the world, for a worthless claim and a rotten tent!"

"And when did you discover the claim was worthless, Hilton?"

"This morning, for sure. But I'd began to doubt several days before that. It struck me as funny that I should have found diamonds without difficulty when Dutch Sam took me out to see the claim, but not a trace of one after three day's back-breaking toil by myself. And I wondered why some of the miners looked pityingly at me, why some laughed. I asked Dutch Sam why I was finding no diamonds. He said the wind had probably blown them away. My God! And I almost believed him."

"Why not?" the Major commented. "It has happened."

"Really!"

Hilton laughed sceptically.

"Anyway," he continued morosely, "that isn't what happened here. This morning three or four miners came here and told me the truth. All of them had owned this claim at one time or other. Dutch Sam had 'salted' it and sold it to them. Then, when they were at the end of their resources, he had bought it back from them. He—" Hilton spluttered wrathfully—"offered me half a bottle of whisky for it when I went to him this morning and demanded my money back."

"But you didn't sell him the claim, did you? You still own it?"

Hilton nodded. "Yes," he said bitterly.

"I thought I might as well keep it. It's the graveyard of my hopes. It'll be the graveyard of my body."

"Ah!" the Major said in tones of stinging contempt. "Now you're talking like a melodramatic young ass."

Hilton flushed.

"What else is the claim good for?"

"You never know," the Major said cryptically. "The wind that taketh away sometimes gives. And—" he cocked a knowing eye at the sky—"it looks as if it will blow bally hard tonight. You know—" this seemed an afterthought— that Dutch Sammy is a frightfully unpopular Johnny. I've been spending the day talkin' to no end of lads who have been bilked by him. Oh, well! You turn in. You need a good night's sleep. I'm goin' to have a chat with Jim. Toodle-oo! Don't worry. Let your partner do that for a change. And I'm your partner—eh, what?"

Hilton nodded.

"Let's shake hands on that." He jumped to his feet. "Good night, Major. You're a good egg. Just the same," he added wistfully, "I wish you hadn't run from Dutch Sam."

He went into his tent.

"Jim!" the Major called softly.

The Hottentot came and squatted on his haunches close to the Major.

"Yah, baas?"

"What think you now of the young baas?"

"Au-a! He is the makings of a man, baas. He needs aging, baas. That is all."

THE MAJOR nodded absently and both men were silent for while. They understood each other, these two, could read each other's thoughts.

For a little while there was great darkness and a wind howled over the dunes. Then the moon rose, illuminating the desert with its white light.

"And what game does the baas play?" Jim asked suddenly.

The Major had taken several cartridges from his belt and, extracting the bullets—they were strangely loose—emptied the contents of the cases on to a handkerchief which he spread on the ground.

"What are these worth, Jim?" The Major indicated the stones on his handkerchief.

"Tears, baas. Much labor, great wealth, happiness, sorrow. Who shall say?"

"What are they worth to you, Jim?"

"No more than this, baas?" Jim picked up a handful of sand which he tossed contemptuously up into the air.

"And to me what is their worth, Jim?"

"Little more, baas. The joy to you is in the seeking, not in the finding. Your joy is in the hunt, not in the kill."

"The old lad is right as usual," the Major drawled in English. "A bare handful of stones, picked up in the desert. The naked children of bushmen play jackstones with better ones. Yet civilized men would commit murder for one tenth of their value. Women would exchange their dearest possession for only one. But to the youngster in there they mean happiness. And so—" He reverted now to the vernacular, "Jim—we are going to play a game."

"Good, baas." The Hottentot grinned. "And the game?"

"We play with these—" he indicated the stones—"and with men. Now listen."

They talked and planned, these two, until the moon was blotted out by a dense, wind created wall of sand.

"*Au-a,* baas!" Jim complained. "The wind which blows in this place must come from the cavern of evil spirits. The sand blinds my eyes, fills my mouth and stops up my ears.

The Major's chuckles sounded weirdly in the darkness.

"It is an ill wind, Jim," he said. "But I think it is laden with wealth for the young baas."

IT WAS noon the following day. Despite the scorching heat of the sun, Hilton prospected his claim with a feverish newborn hope. Fired with the Major's stories of diamonds deposited during a sand storm he had commenced work early that morning and had, almost immediately discovered a stone which, said the Major, "might be a diamond."

"Let me have it, old chap," the Major had continued, "and I'll go along to the *dorp* and find some honest chappy who'll tell me what it's worth and so on."

Since the discovery of that stone Hilton had worked like one demented, and Jim, the Hottentot, though inwardly protesting against the role his baas's plans called upon him to play, had ably seconded the white man's endeavors. Three other stones were discovered after the Major's departure and at each discovery Hilton had danced a wild fandango, he was so sure they were diamonds, so sure that a miracle had happened.

He straightened himself at a shrill coo-ee and saw the Major running toward him. His elation left him. Perhaps his rejoicings had been premature. It was incredible that his luck should have so suddenly changed. Of course they were not diamonds, they looked like worthless fragments of discolored glass.

But the Major was smiling and waving his helmet—a battered one of Hilton's—excitedly.

With a calmness he was far from feeling, Hilton waited his arrival.

"It's all right," the Major gasped as he came to the claim. "It's a diamond, and a good one. Found any more?"

Unable to maintain his pose of nonchalance any longer, Hilton exhibited the other stones. They compared them with the one the Major had taken to be appraised then danced and sang and patted each other on the back like men mad with joy.

It was the Major who sobered first.

"That's enough young fellow my lad! Come and sit down in the shade an' we'll have *skoff*, an' then we'll sleep. No more work till the sun's down a bit."

"Food—sleep!" Hilton scoffed at the idea. "Do you think I can eat or sleep now? I'm not going to rest till I've prospected all over—"

"Don't be a fool," the Major said sternly. "Come and sit down."

He dragged Hilton into the shade.

"But Major, another wind might blow it all away again."

"It might, but, somehow, I don't think it will. At least not till we've prospected it thoroughly!"

"At least," said Hilton, struggling to release himself, "let me finish 'babying' the stuff. I've just shoveled in." He looked longingly toward the rickety "baby" he had bought with the claim.

"No, not even that," the Major said sternly, and Hilton finally submitted. He found, later, that he *was* hungry and, after the tasty meal Jim concocted, very sleepy.

But before he slept: "Listen, youngster," said the Major to him, "the chances are you won't find very many more diamonds in this claim. Perhaps there are no more. So I want you to promise me something. If somebody offers you a good price for the claim, you'll sell it and let me do the bargaining. And, when you've got your money, you'll take the next boat home. You promise?"

"Yes, Major. Here's my hand on—" A snore prematurely ended his sentence.

THAT AFTERNOON Dutch Sam made his way to the claim of young Hilton. By his side, panting in an endeavor to keep up with the redheaded one's giant strides, walked the gold-toothed man, Holy Joe.

Once Dutch Sam halted undecidedly.

"I don't like this, Joe, I tell you ma-an. This is a time for sleep, not for trekking over the *verdoemte* sand, I will go back and wait until the cool comes."

"Don't be a fool, Sam," the other pleaded. "This is the best time to make a deal—before the others get wise."

"I am a fool if I go on," Dutch Sam growled. "There are no stones on the claim. *Ach sis!* I should know—I who have 'salted' and sold it so many times."

"But the diamonds *are* there," Holy Joe insisted. "Last night's dust storm carried them. I myself saw the one the dude stranger had. I told him it was a worthless 'bort.' And the fool believed me. He knows nothing of diamonds. You know what Slim said. How he thought a *bandtom* was a stone? And I watched young Hilton and the nigger working the claim until I saw the dude coming back. They found other stones. I tell you the claim's rich, Sam. And we can get it for a song."

"Maybe, Joe," Dutch Sam said heavily. "But I wish—" he looked around furtively—"I had brought four or five of the boys with me. I do not like this silence. I think I will go back for them."

Holy Joe clutched the giant's arm.

"No, don't, Sam. You don't want to share the pickings with anybody."

"No, that's the truth," Dutch Sam chuckled. "I had forgotten that. No. I share with no one."

"You will not forget the bargain you made with me though, Sam, will you? I'll get my share, won't I?"

"*Ach sis,* yes, ma-an!" Dutch Sam said impatiently. "You will, what is coming to you, get."

He moved swiftly forward again, forgetting the heat, ceasing to regret that he had come upon the venture practically alone, with hoggish anticipations of the rich claim he would easily acquire.

The two men threaded their way between enormous sand dunes and so came, finally in sight of Hilton's claim. They stopped for a whispered conference, then triumphantly went boldly forward.

Hilton and the Major were both fast asleep, sprawled in the scanty shade of the tent, snoring loudly. Jim, the Hottentot, also slept, sitting propped up against the "baby," his mouth wide open. His hands were closed lightly on a shovel which rested across his knee. Apparently he had fallen asleep over his task of shoveling sand into the "baby."

Silently the two men crossed the intervening ground and, bending over the "baby," ran their fingers through the sand it contained.

Presently Dutch Sam tensed slightly.

"I've got one," he whispered hoarsely. He showed Holy Joe the stone he had just discovered.

"What did I tell you," the other replied exultantly. "What are you going to do, Sam? Wake 'em up and close the deal?"

They started violently at a lazy, drawling voice:

"I say you chappies, what do you think you're doing here?"

WINKING AT each other the two men turned slowly to face the Major. They were sure they had nothing to fear from that man.

Then their faces fell and their hands shot above their heads in answer to the menace of the revolver he aimed at them.

"Almighty!" Dutch Sam ranted. "This is no way to treat a ma-an. For this you shall pay! For this—"

The Major yawned.

"Oh shut up, Redhead. Hi! Hilton! Wake up, old chap. We have callers."

Slowly Hilton struggled to wakefulness, blinked, stared round vacantly, then, seeing Dutch Sam and Holy Joe, sprang to his feet with a yell of rage.

"Steady, steady, lad," the Major cried. "That is no way to treat guests. You should be more courteous. Specially as Mister Dutch Sam has been prospecting for us. He took something from the 'baby'—come to think of it, that's so deucedly appropriate to him. I imagine that is how he started his distinguished career. Taking things from the baby, you know."

"You dunderhead! For this you shall pay. Almighty! Must I much longer keep my hands up like this?"

"We came to talk business," Holy Joe said smoothly. "We were sorry for young Hilton. We—"

"You'll finish up by being very sorry for yourselves," Hilton snapped. "Let me have a go at him, Major," he added pleadingly, anxious to wipe out the memory of the thrashing he had received yesterday.

"You sit down, youngster, and keep quiet. *I'm* going to handle these pretty gentlemen. Sit down," he repeated sternly, "and don't get in front of my revolver again. It might be disastrous."

Hilton obeyed reluctantly.

"Jim," continued the Major.

"Yah, baas?" The Hottentot's voice sounded very sleepy.

"Get a rope."

"I have one, baas."

"Then tie those two—but first, redhead, throw me the thing you took from the 'baby.'"

Cursing, Dutch Sam threw the stone to the Major who glanced at it casually and gave it to Hilton.

"Only a *bandtom*," he said lugubriously. "That is what you call them, I believe, Holy Joe?"

TAMELY THE two men submitted to being bound, hand and foot, then, at the Major's invitation, sat down, side by side, on the burning sand.

"You'll pay for this," Dutch Sam vowed grimly. "And as for you, you—!" He turned loose a string of invectives upon Holy Joe who cowered and whimpered inarticulately.

"What pretty fellows you are," the Major said in tones of deep disgust. "What shall we do with them, Hilton?"

"Shoot 'em, Major. They deserve it."

"I think you're right," the Major said slowly, and his trigger finger contracted.

There was a report and sand spurted up into the men's faces.

Holy Joe screamed. Dutch Sam swore.

"Don't be a fool, *roinek*," he continued. "I came out here, like I've said, because I was sorry for the way I treated the young one there. I came to offer to buy this claim back from him. A hundred pounds I'll give for it. An' that's generous."

"Very," the Major said dryly. "He gave you five hundred for it, I believe."

Dutch Sam gulped.

"*Ach sis!* I'm a soft fool. I will the five hundred pounds return to him. And all shall be as it was. The money his, the claim mine. Eh?"

The Major and Hilton whispered together. Then, "My partner does not trust your generosity, old dear," the Major drawled. "If you are willing to pay five hundred for the claim, then it is worth that to us. The view's magnificent."

He rose to his feet and stretched himself lazily.

"Because I am soft," Dutch Sam said sulkily, "I offer five hundred. Not another penny will I give."

"In that case, then, there's nothing to discuss. So we will work. Yes—rather. But let me see—" the Major stroked his chin thoughtfully—"Yes, I think so. You are a strong an experienced miner. So you shall help us. Yes. You shall 'baby' for diamonds. Free his hands, Jim."

Jim obeyed.

"And the other, baas?"

"No. He shall be an honored, more or less, spectator. Get up, Redhead, and rock the baby."

With ill concealed eagerness, Dutch Sam stumbled to his feet and, hopping clumsily to the 'baby,' manipulated the rocker as Jim shovelled sand on to it.

HIS EYES bulged excitedly. Long experience on the diamond fields had sharpened his vision and, presently, on the rocker he saw five, six, seven stones which he *knew* were diamonds.

He gaped as the Major picked them out and tossed them carelessly at the Hottentot.

"*Roineks!*" he panted. "The heat is too much for me. Almighty! If you keep me here much longer I shall die. Listen: one thousand pounds I will give you for the claim."

"You talk too much," the Major said curtly and, picking up another stone out of the 'baby,' shied it at an empty can laughing at his poor aim, for the stone dropped into the almost empty water barrel.

"One thousand five hundred I will give you." Dutch Sam stammered.

The Major and Hilton conferred together.

"We accept that," the Major said. "Where's the money?"

"Almighty! Do you think I carry so much on me?"

"Then go and get it."

Dutch Sam shook his head.

"You would work the claim while I was gone. You come with me."

"No. We do not trust you, old lad. I'll tell you what. You shall write a letter to your—er—banker telling him to pay bearer the sum of one thousand five hundred pounds. Hilton shall take it in and you and I shall sit here and—er—watch each other."

Dutch Sam nodded.

"Give me pencil and paper," he said.

DUTCH SAM smiled contentedly as he watched Hilton vanish behind the dunes, heading for the *dorp*. He felt that he could afford to smile for had he not concluded a deal which made him sole owner of a fabulously rich claim?

True, he was paying more than he had figured but he would even matters up by seeing that Holy Joe—he scowled at that unfortunate man—received no share of the takings.

And as for the dude sitting opposite him, there would be plenty of time to settle with him. *Ach sis!* What a settling that would be! One blow under cover of the darkness of the night would write paid to that account. Or he might even thrash the man in broad daylight.

"Only," Dutch Sam mused, "he wouldn't stand up and fight. So—I think the other way would be best."

He lolled full length on the ground, shut his eyes and indulged in an orgy of pleasant day dreams.

For a little while he slept.

His awakening was sudden. Some one prodded him in the ribs: A voice said sharply, "Get up, hog." With a snarl he opened his eyes and saw the Major standing over him.

"Ach sis!" he stammered blinking owlishly. "What is it, *roinek?* Has the youngster returned?"

He lurched heavily to his feet. During his sleep, some one had cut the ropes which bound them.

He wondered at their lightness, wondered that the sand should burn. Looking down—he saw that he was bare-footed. And—Almighty!—the dude was barefooted also. Furthermore, the dude was stripped to the waist, his white skin gleaming in the red tinted rays of a sinking sun. *"Ach sis!"* Dutch Sam exclaimed. "Have you mad gone." He did not like the mocking light in the Major's eyes.

He saw that he was standing in the centre of a roped space.

He stared open mouthed about him and broke out into a cold sweat of fear as a number of men emerged from behind one of the dunes.

They were dourly silent as they lined up about the roped enclosure.

"Gentlemen," the Major said with a flourish of his hand, "allow me to introduce to you Dutch Sam, the pride of Luderitzbucht."

They looked at Dutch Sam; their eyes glinted savagely.

"What game are you playing, *roinek?*" the redhead growled.

"Game! This is no game, Sammy lad. This is a more or less formal reception. I have invited these gentlemen to meet you and to—er—as it were, renew an old acquaintance."

"Almighty!" Dutch Sam looked around as if meditating flight. But the line of scowling faces quelled him and he moved nearer the Major as if seeking his protection.

The Major laughed.

"Shall I introduce them to you, Dutch Sam, or do you already know them."

"He knows us all right," an aged man shouted in a high, shrill voice. "He'll know us better when we're finished with him."

"Such loving friends you have," the Major murmured. "But you are quite sure you know them all? I am insistent on that point because, you see, this is a very exclusive affair. We don't want outsiders butting in."

DESPERATELY DUTCH Sam looked at the men, hoping to find one or two he could call upon for support, hoping to spot a weak place where he could burst through and escape from the retribution which, he sensed, was so close at hand.

He started suddenly as the Major's hand closed about his wrist.

"You do know them, don't you?" the Major insisted. "Look; that gray-haired, toothless laddie in the corner is 'Sundown' Hawley—you beat him into unconsciousness because he accidentally spilled your beer. That youngster next to him is Tom Smithers—you killed his brother."

"I didn't-it was *Holy Joe!*" Dutch Sam protested.

"At your orders. You were present. You laughed. You held Tom back so that he couldn't go to his brother's assistance. Look; that thin fellow is 'Shanks' Stoner. You left him to die in the desert. The one next to him is 'Fat' Morten—you jumped his claim. That sandy mustached chap with one eye—he had two before he made your acquaintance—you sold this claim to, after you had salted it."

Dutch Sam gurgled incoherently.

"What's that?" the Major asked sharply.

"Almighty, mister! I only asked what your game was."

"You'll see, presently." And the Major continued to call out the names of the men around the ring, reciting, sometimes at their prompting, the evil they had suffered at Dutch Sam's hands.

It was a frightful indictment.

"Well," the Major asked sharply, "how do you plead, prisoner?"

Dutch Sam was silent.

"He's guilty."

"Guilty as hell."

"We ought to hang him."

"Hanging's too good for the dirty dog."

The Major held up his hand and the shouts of the miners ceased.

"The jury finds you guilty, prisoner."

Dutch Sam scowled.

"They can't prove none of them things against me. And if you kill me— Almighty! That would be murder!"

"Yes: I'm afraid it would be, in the eyes of the law. And so, Dutch Sam, the sentence of the court is—that you fight me."

Dutch Sam laughed. His courage flowed swiftly back. He would kill the dude *roinek,* and afterward he would deal with those others.

"I am ready, *roinek,*" he said. He remembered how this man had fled in terror from Hans.

"Wait!" the Major said evenly. "There are conditions. We will fight as white men fight. There will be no kicking, no wrestling, no biting; none of your dirty foul tricks. The jury will see that you fight fair. If you foul, they will shoot you like a dog. You understand?"

"Almighty, yes! I do not need tricks to deal with you. But what happens after I have thrashed you?"

"Nothing. No one will molest you. But if I thrash you— and I shall, you know—you will pay back to these men all that you have stolen from them. Is it agreed?"

"No! I will not fight. You would trick me. You—"

THE MAJOR shrugged his shoulders and turning walked slowly away. "Then I leave you to the—er—tender mercies of the jury—"

There were loud, menacing threats as the men who surrounded the ring converged on Dutch Sam.

"Wait!" Dutch Sam shouted desperately, "I agree."

The Major turned, the men returned to their places.

"But," Dutch Sam continued, "will they let me go, after I have thrashed you?"

"Don't you worry about that, Dutch Sam," they cried. "We'll keep to the agreement."

The Major smiled.

"So, you see, there's nothing else to wait for, is there? Strip to the waist."

"But—" Dutch Sam still played for time—"I have no one to second me. I—"

"I have arranged for that. Holy Joe came with you, you know. He will do. And we have one or two others of your gang present. They did not come willingly and so they must be, more or less, passive spectators. Bring on his supporters, boys."

There was a commotion beyond the ring of men, then some dragged tightly bound forms to the front. And Dutch Sam recognized many of his gang.

"Take out their gags so they can cheer their champion," the Major ordered.

As this was being done, Holy Joe timorously entered the ring and went to Dutch Sam, whispering.

"Out of my way, fool," the red-headed man yelled and, swinging wildly with his fist, knocked Holy Joe across the ring. He fell to the ground, and was content to remain there.

"Strip," the Major said curtly.

A moment Dutch Sam hesitated, then, heartened by the hoarse shouts of his followers, pulled off his shirt.

"Now then, if you're ready! And remember the rules!"

The words were hardly out of the Major's mouth when Dutch Sam rushed savagely, hoping by the suddenness of his attack to overwhelm his slimmer opponent.

But the Major was too experienced to be rushed off his feet in that way. He side-stepped, and, as Dutch Sam lurched by, slapped him on the back with the palm of his hand. And that, in the furious fight which followed, was the only time the Major indulged in the light banter which came so natural to him. From that time on he fought in deadly seriousness and with a certain measure of vindictiveness entirely foreign to his real self. He had deliberately set himself the task of completely "breaking" the bully of Luderitzbucht, of reducing him to a state of impotence.

So when Dutch Sam turned and rushed again he was staggered by a right and left to the jaw. He shook his head and waded in. The Major backed slowly before the impetuous rush, his arms moved in and out like pistons.

He boxed coolly, with the assurance of a trained athlete, avoiding Dutch Sam's wild swinging blows with ease.

The big Dutchman was bewildered. The air seemed full of flying fists. They stung him, goaded him to a panic of rage.

DUTCH SAM had only weight and brawn. His powerfully muscled arms lacked a cool directing brain, and his belly was soft, flabby. His skin was mottled, lacking the sheen of good condition. Already he was breathing noisily. One eye was badly swollen; blood streamed from his nose.

He stood stupidly now in the center of the ring, mouth agape, his hands outstretched before him.

"Come here, *roinek*," he panted. "Don't dance. Fight!"

Swiftly the Major accepted the invitation. A left jolt to Dutch Sam's middle brought the man's chin forward; a right uppercut, landing flush on the point, sent him over backward to the ground.

He rolled over on his belly well content to remain where he was.

He could hear the shouts of the onlookers, the jeers of his own men. Let them shout! Let them jeer. *Ach sis!* He was one big ache.

It was the Major's voice which finally roused him.

"Get up, you big oaf. I haven't begun to hurt you yet. Are you going to part with all your filthy money so easily?"

"Almighty, no!" Dutch Sam rose slowly to his feet.

And now the Major surpassed himself, showing most amazing speed and footwork. He left himself open in order to tempt Dutch Sam into swinging wildly and then, stepping inside the flailing fists, punished him before dodging back again out of reach.

A look of cunning came into Dutch Sam's half-closed eyes. He had heard the shouted advice of one of his men and when next the Major closed with him he brought his knee up sharply. It caught the Major in the groin and he dropped to the ground, horribly nauseated.

With a shout of triumph Dutch Sam threw himself down on the Major, his fingers closed about the Major's throat—

"Back! Back you, swine. You've fouled. You—"

Dutch Sam looked up and saw that three miners stood over him, covering him with their revolvers. He rose sulkily to his feet.

"You dogs!" he swore. "You will keep your agreement. A fair blow knocked him out. A—"

"It was your knee. We are not blind."

"Get back to the ropes. This is not finished yet." At the Major's voice the three men looked at each other uncertainly.

"But the fight's over, Major," one protested. "He fouled you. And—"

"He fouled me, yes. But get back. I haven't finished with him yet." They looked at Dutch Sam. "Stand back," one said to him. "And you don't touch him until he's on his feet. Understand?"

DUTCH SAM nodded and licked his lips hungrily. He was sure of victory now. He could afford to abide by the *verdoemte* fool rules.

He stepped back a couple of paces. The miners returned to the ropes.

The Major raised himself slowly, his face white and contorted with pain. He was on one knee now, his hands resting on the ground.

His sight gradually cleared; the black specks which had floated before his eyes vanished; the color was coming back to his face. An active life, years of clean living, had endowed him with marvelous powers of recuperation.

But Dutch Sam was not aware of that. He thought his opponent beaten; thought him too feeble.

The Major's hands were off the ground. Suddenly he was on his feet. As suddenly Dutch Sam rushed and, meeting no resistance, was carried halfway across the ring before he could check himself and turn to face the Major who had cleverly stepped aside and was now right at his heels.

The Major did not attempt to fight at close quarters now, but boxed at long range, getting in blows which cut and bruised. They reduced Dutch Sam to a condition of helpless futility. He staggered around, bellowing with rage and pain and presently his legs no longer functioned. They felt like lead. He could not move them. He was now a helpless chopping block, and the Major, remembering the man's evil crimes, did not spare him, until, blubbering, *"Ach sis!* Enough. I have had enough!"* Dutch Sam whined, and dropped to the ground.

The Major turned away. Now that it was all over he felt strangely weak. He had been punished too. He had not avoided all of Dutch Sam's blows. His upper lip was cut, one eye completely closed. The flesh covering his ribs was an angry red. He felt as if he had been pounded by a steam hammer.

"I am all right," he said to the men who ran to assist him. "Leave me alone, there's good fellows."

He laughed aside their compliments and thanks.

"I leave the rest to you," he said. "See that he keeps to the agreement. And you keep to yours."

"We will, Major. Sure you don't need help?"

"Quite. I'm going to duck my head in the barrel, dress, and join my partner. You go and look after Dutch Sam. I think he will give you no trouble."

TWO HOURS later, the Major joined Hilton down on the shore. Jim was there too.

"I got the note you sent by Jim," Hilton began. Then, in tones of deep concern. "But what have you been doing?"

"Had a little set-to with our friend, Dutch Sam. But never mind that. Did you get the money."

"Yes."

"That's good. And the stones—did Jim give them to you."

Hilton nodded.

"Splendid. And you've arranged for your passage to Capetown on that tub of a boat."

"I've obeyed all the instructions in your letter, Major."

"Good lad. Then you'd better be getting on board. Good-by, old lad."

"But, Major. Aren't you coming too?"

"Oh, no—rather not. Too much fun here, eh, Jim?"

"Then we must divide up, here and now. We're part-ners and—" as he spoke Hilton started to open his kitbag—"partners share and share alike."

"Nonsense," the Major said curtly. "What you have is your share. I have mine—really I have. And no end of fun into the bargain. Give my regards to Regent Street, and all that. Toodle-oo. Come along, Jim."

DUTCH SAM groaned. He was ruined. The miners had departed, their claims satisfied. Around him sprawled the men who, in the past, had obeyed his orders. They were still bound. He was glad of that, for they all eyed him malevolently. In order to satisfy the miners he had been obliged to deplete the funds of his creatures.

Dutch Sam looked at the envelope he held in his hand. It had been handed to him by one of the miners. He opened it and, for a moment, the world seemed brighter. The contents of the envelope gave him the possession of the claim. This rich claim. *Ach sis!* The dude had overlooked that. But had he? There was a letter. He read:

> *Dutch Sam:*
>
> *I'm not sure about the ethics of this little deal, but I think they are quite all right. After all we never claimed to find any diamonds on it—and you insisted on buying it, didn't you.*
>
> *You know, somehow I don't think you'll find any diamonds. Diamonds are funny things aren't they—specially on this claim. They are at the sport of every wind that blows, if you know what I mean. Here today and gone tomorrow, eh what?*
>
> *But you won't mind buying a worthless claim, will you? I hope not. After all, you've sold it yourself so many times.*
>
> *And you must be filled with a sense of happy contentment. Think of all the men you've made happy this afternoon. Righted wrongs, and all that.*
>
> *Oh, well. I'm getting rather long winded. But not altogether an evil wind. I fancy I have, in my own little way, blown a number of men a little good.*
>
> > *Toodle-oo!*
> >
> > THE MAJOR.

Dutch Sam swore miserably.

One of the men, a puny undersized Cockney who had the courage of a rabbit and was the butt of all, rose to his feet. He had succeeded in freeing himself—the miners had purposely bound him loosely.

A knife glistened in his hands. He bent over one of his companions, intending to cut him free.

"Almighty!" Dutch Sam shouted. "Do not cut them free yet, ma-an. Wait—"

The little Cockney straightened and turned angrily.

"An' who the hell do you fink you're talkin' to, you bloomin' big hulk? Get out of there before I cut yer up."

He took a menacing step forward and Dutch Sam took to his heels.

The bully of Luderitzbucht was no more. He was running like a whipped cur, spurred by fear, pursued by derisive laughter.

BOTTLED EVIDENCE

"**HANDS UP!**" Trooper James cried exultantly. "I've got you!"

Jake Shiners, the bartender at the Bodega, cringed and winked a message at the men who backed precipitately away from the young policeman. The stocky, blackhaired man who stood at the bar slowly finished his drink and wiped the ragged ends of his mustache with the back of his hands.

"Hands up!" James repeated impatiently. "And don't try any tricks. I've got you covered, and I've got all the evidence I want. Hell—" a note of boastful triumph crept into his voice—"you've been playing a *slim* game. But this is where it ends. And you'll be a bit slower on the trigger after a ten years' sentence on the Breakwater. Come on, now. Put up your hands!"

The black mustached man raised his eyebrows and, straightening himself, thrust his hands in his coat pockets.

"Meaning me?" he questioned sarcastically.

"Yes, meaning you!" James retorted. You're under arrest and I warn you—"

"Ah!" the other interrupted. "I never warn. It gives the other bloke an advantage."

A shot punctuated his sentence. James stared at him for a moment, blank surprise on his youthful face. Then his revolver dropped from his hand with a noisy clatter to the ground; he lurched forward, a red stained hand pressed to his side, and slumped in a huddled heap at the feet of the man who had shot him.

"Drinks round, Jake," that man ordered, looking with annoyance at a scorched jagged hole in his coat pocket from which a coil of blue smoke slowly drifted. "Drinks round, then the boys can cart this fool out on the veld somewhere—the further from here, the better."

Jake, leering sycophantically, swiftly filled the orders which were shouted at him and presently the men were all drinking to the good health of their hero, the man who had killed so expertly, so callously.

They were the scum of the diamond diggings; men without honor, banded together for mutual protection and gain. Totally unmoved by the killing, their only emotion was one of abhorrence of the labor which would be entailed in carrying the body away from the saloon. Killing was, to them, a pretty crime. Their victims rarely escaped as lightly as had Trooper James. They were generally tortured first, and these scoundrels' methods of obtaining information from victims—the hiding places of diamonds, for example, would have done credit to an official executioner of the Middle Ages.

THE DRINKS finished, two men picked up James and, supporting him on either side, others crowding round them, walked with him out of the bar, just as if they were escorting a drunken comrade home: So it looked to the town policeman whom they met just outside and who wished them "Good night," adding, "I thought I heard a shot."

"You did," one replied with a laugh. "*He's* been shooting off the tops of bottles again."

The policeman nodded, and grumbled.

"Well, I wish he'd choose some other time for target practice: That's all I can say. It's getting to be so a fellow can't snatch a wink of sleep on his beat nowadays."

"Better go in and tell him that!" a man jeered.

As the little group of men passed on, singing maudlinly, reeling, the policeman muttered, "They're all as tight as owls an' that one they're sort of leading looks so drunk he's paralyzed. God! I could do with a drink myself. But I can't afford it. I'm honest. I'm no crook. An' it's a sure thing I'm not going to put my head inside Jake Shiner's place. He ain't what you'd call hospitable to policemen. Not this time of night, he ain't."

IN THE veld, not more than two miles from the *dorp* and on the fringe of the newly-opened diamond diggings was a white man's out-span: A small, bell-tent, and a wagon with a canvas hood. Twelve mules, knee-haltered, grazed nearby; apart from them, as if contemptuous of her half-bred relations, was a chestnut mare in excellent condition, her skin shining like silk.

Reclining in a deck chair, set in the shade of a wide-spreading tree, was a white man. His riding breeches were spotlessly white, so was his silk shirt. His brown riding boots were highly polished; and the box spurs he wore gleamed golden in the yellow glare of African sunlight.

Little was visible of the man's face, for his helmet was tilted forward, but that little gave the lie to his dude-like attire and general air of inefficiency; the chin was strong. It belonged to a man of action and of justified self-confidence.

Just beyond the white man squatted a Hottentot, naked from the waist up, washing dishes. His back was scored by the marks of a recent *sjamboking*. Occasionally he looked at his baas and smiled knowingly; occasionally he looked across the veld toward the township. His attitude then was of a man listening.

"Baas," he said presently, in a low penetrating voice. "Baas! They will be here soon. They ride fast."

The white man looked at the native; a light of merriment appeared for an instant in his blue eyes. Quickly the mirth faded and the blue changed to a cold, steel gray.

"And are they policemen, as you said, Jim?" he asked, and he spoke the vernacular as purely as did the Hottentot.

"Yah, baas."

"But I cannot see them, Jim."

"That, baas, is because now they ride along the bottom of a *donga*. I think it is their plan to take us by surprise."

"But they won't," the white man said in English, drawling his words affectedly. "It's easier to catch a—er—weasel asleep than to catch you napping, old lad!"

"Golly, damn, yes! If I don't see you, hullo," the Hottentot agreed, his whimsical face breaking into a smile of pride at his fluent command of the English language.

THE WHITE man laughed and taking a cigarette from the heavy silver case which was on the table before him, lighted it and smoked luxuriously.

"Ah!" he exclaimed presently. "Now I think I hear them. And so does Molly."

The chestnut mare had nickered softly and was now standing in an attitude of expectancy, looking across the veld.

"Yah, baas," said the Hottentot, "They are very near now. Is all safe, baas?"

"Safe, Jim?"

"Yah, baas. When men come so secretly it is because they hope to discover something. Have you nothing that you do not want them to find?"

"Plenty, Jim. But it is hidden. It will not be found."

"Good, baas," Jim exclaimed, and concentrated once more on his dish washing, singing one of the barbaric songs of his people.

The white man tilted his helmet still further over his face and seemed to sleep.

The Hottentot's singing blended with the monotonous drone of flying insects; overhead the sun blazed in a sky of fathomless blue. Dust devils, evidence of the passing of some errant breeze, gyrated madly over the veld, and, in the far background, range after range of purple-shadowed hills trembled in the heat haze.

Everything was strangely peaceful; civilization and its attendant ills had no place here. This was Africa, black, damned, Africa, in the disguise, which is not a disguise, of a fair enchantress.

The white man snored; a refined, affected snore like a soft, deprecating sigh. The Hottentot chuckled appreciatively and then, as three uniformed horsemen rode suddenly into view, sprang to his feet with a warning cry of: "Baas! Baas!"

At a growled command from one of the policemen he then went toward them, silently, a sullen expression on his face, and meekly suffered himself to be handcuffed to one of the wheels of the wagon. Two of the policemen had dismounted to perform this task, while the third, who wore a corporal's stripes, also dismounted and covered the sleeping man with his revolver.

HE WAS joined by the other two and the three, revolvers in their right hands, handcuffs in their left, crept cautiously nearer.

And then the sleeper awoke, yawned, and stretched himself lazily.

The policemen tensed.

Suddenly conscious, it seemed, that he had visitors, the Hottentot's baas jumped to his feet with a show of confusion, doffed his helmet and, "Good morning, dear defenders of our firesides," he drawled. "I regret that I should—er—appear so inhospitable, but your visit is, to say the least, quite unexpected. Quite!"

"It was meant to be," the corporal growled. "And I don't want any of your lip. Get that?"

"Get that?" the other repeated vacantly. "I don't quite—er—understand. You mean?"

"Oh shut up," the corporal snapped.

"Oh, quite!" the other exclaimed helplessly and dropped back into his chair. As he did so, his right hand reached out furtively for the silver cigarette case which glistened in the sunshine. His long fingers closed over it and he was about to replace it in his pocket when the corporal continued:

"And leave that case alone. Quick now. Take your hands off it. You needn't think you can fool me, Major. I've heard all about you."

"Ah, really! Extraordinary! Of course I don't pretend to know what all this is about, an', to tell you the truth, I am not at the moment particularly interested. But you will be, before I'm finished with you. My word, yes. I shall report you to your superiors; I shall sue you for damages an' what not. You tie up my servant! You wake me from sleep. An' now you dare to prevent me from helping myself to a cigarette."

"Oh, shut your mouth," said the corporal. "An' you leave that cigarette case alone. Go an' get it from him, Wilkins."

One of the troopers took the case from the table and gave it to the corporal.

"Watch him close now, boys," that man said, "while I have a look-see what sort of cigarette he smokes."

He opened the case.

"My God!" he exclaimed, sniffing noisily. "I believe they're scented. My word!"

"They're not, really they're not," the Major protested. "It is not likely you would appreciate their delicate aroma. But I say—what do you bally well think you're doing?"

The corporal was crumbling the cigarettes, one by one, between his fingers.

"I'm alookin'," he said heavily, "for the aroma."

"But, my dear man, you can't *see* an aroma. You smell it, you know. You—"

"I smell a rat," the corporal said, and the two troopers chuckled at his humor. "And I'm a damned good rat-catcher. See?"

"Not quite." The Major was evidently bewildered. His hand went to the breast pocket of his shirt.

"Watch him, boys!" the corporal ordered sharply. And, to the Major. "Don't you try any shooting tricks on me."

The Major's hand came hastily away from his pocket.

"I was only fishing for this," he said meekly, holding a monocle up for inspection.

"Bah!" exclaimed the corporal.

"Exactly," said the Major and, with much facial distortion, fixed the monocle in his eye; it heightened his resemblance, to a silly ass. He looked now the complete brainless dude.

ONE OF the troopers laughed derisively. "Blimey!" he observed, "if he ain't a stage door 'Haw-haw Johnny,' I'll eat my bloomin' hat. Thought you said he was clever, corporal?"

"You keep your mouth shut and watch him, Smith. When you've served as many years as I have, you'll learn that you can't tell how deep a river is just by looking at the surface."

"Oh! But that's capital, dear old lad," the Major chortled. "And just how deep am I?"

"I got you sounded out all right, Major, an' don't you think different. Besides, I've been reading a full account about you in a report sent down from headquarters at Kimberley. No. You can't pull wool over my eyes. I'm on to all your little games."

"Splendid! But won't you let me join you in the game you're playing now? I can spoil cigarettes just as you're doing."

"There's only one left," the corporal replied. "Now there's none." There was a note of disappointment, of despondency, in his voice.

"You don't seem happy, dear lad," the Major commented.

"No. And I ain't. By all rights, according to my deductions, there ought to have been diamonds hidden in them fat cigarettes of yourn."

"Diamonds!" the Major exclaimed incredulously.

"Yes, diamonds. An' don't try to come the innocent with me. I know your reputation an' how you pretend to be a fool while all the time you're as *slim* as the devil. Why, I've laughed myself sick over some of the tricks you've played on the diamond detectives down Kimberley way. But, let me tell you, you don't get away with any of your tricks on me."

"No, of course not. Wouldn't dream of attempting to trick you, Corpie dear."

The policeman glowered at him.

"Well," he continued, "knowing your reputation as an I.D.B., an' knowing how crafty you are, I'm betting you hide your stones in a place right out in the open. And, from certain observations of your actions, I was ready to swear that you'd got 'em hidden in your cigarettes. But I drew a blank."

He frowned at the case, turning it over and over.

THE MAJOR held out his hand for it. "Then you can let me have it back, eh, corporal? It's a family—er—heirloom; full of sentimental attachments an' all that sort of thing, you know."

"I suppose so," the corporal grumbled. He rather prided himself on his deductive powers, and, because they had failed him, was now at a loose end. "But I'm betting you've got diamonds hidden somewhere around and I'm not going to leave here until I've searched every stick an' stone."

"You're so brutally thorough, dear boy," the Major murmured. "Go ahead with your search. I'll call 'hot' and 'cold' if you like. But, in the meantime, I'd like to have my case, please."

The corporal was about to hand it over, but looking up sharply he saw something which caused him to hesitate. For one unguarded moment, it seemed, a little gleam of triumph showed in the Major's eyes.

"On second thoughts," the corporal said, grinning, "I think I'll have a little closer look at this case. My! It's heavy an'— Say! Wouldn't it be funny if I discovered it had a secret hiding place an' found diamonds in it!"

"Very funny!" the Major agreed, somewhat sourly. "I suppose it's no good assuring you it contains no diamonds?"

"Not a bit." The corporal held the case to his ear and shook it. He heard a slightly rattling noise.

"Now," he said heavily, kneeling down and placing the case on a boulder, "either you tell me how to get at the hidden pocket or I smash it open."

The Major shrugged his shoulders.

"You slide the monogram to the left—it's a little stiff— and presto! But, I give you my word you won't find any diamonds."

"NO!" THE corporal exclaimed. He had acted on the Major's directions, and had discovered the false pocket inside the thick heavy lid of the case. "No!" he said again, sarcastically. "Then what are these?" He emptied out on to the palm of his hand five fair sized stones.

"Those?" the Major said helplessly. "Those—why they're bits of—er—specimens I picked up in the desert. Brought them along as curios, if you know what I mean. They're quite charming, aren't they? But quite worthless."

"You're going to find 'em damned expensive," the corporal said with heavy humor. "They're going to cost you a few years on the Breakwater."

"But I don't understand, really."

"Oh, yes, you do. You know the penalty for having unregistered diamonds in your possession."

"But they are not diamonds, old horse. If you examine them closely—"

"Oh, stow it!" the corporal interrupted. "Hell! I'm disappointed in you. I thought you were *slim*—and you try to tell me a kid's yarn like that. Well, this is an end to *you*. You're under arrest, and I warn you—"

"Don't, don't! Please! I know it all so well. Anything I say may be used as evidence against me. Well, use this: I tell you those stones are not diamonds. If you'll give them to me I'll show you—"

He stopped, confused by the laughter of the policemen.

"What do you think of him, boys?" the corporal gasped. "As if I'd trust him with these stones in his hands. Why, he'd chuck 'em where we'd never find them, an' we'd have no case." To the Major he said, "You got to try something smarter than that. Well, now! Are you coming quietly, or do we have to handcuff you?"

"I'll be very good," the Major said earnestly. "Give you my word of honor. I'll not try to escape."

The corporal nodded.

"I'll accept it. The records say your word's as good as your bond."

"Pity you won't take it about the stones."

"Ah!" the corporal laughed knowingly. "That's something different."

THE MAJOR shrugged his shoulders and rose to his feet. "If you will release my Hottentot, he will saddle my horse an' we'll be on our way. I'm rather anxious to see your captain."

"You're in a hell of a hurry, all at once," the corporal growled.

"Of course. Why not? The sooner I've had an interview with your captain, the sooner—"

"You'll be on your way to the Breakwater," the corporal finished.

"Have it that way if you like," the Major drawled.

Ten minutes later Jim the Hottentot brought the Major's mount, saddled and bridled, up to him.

"I'm ready, my noble escorts," the Major said as he swung up into the saddle.

"Baas!" Jim exclaimed anxiously. "Did they find them?"

The Major nodded.

"Au-a!" Jim's tone was sorrow-filled.

The corporal beamed.

"Say good-by to your baas, Hottentot. You won't see him again for a long long time."

"It is not a long time to sundown," the Hottentot said cryptically.

The corporal stared at him; doubts were beginning to pester him.

"Come on!" the Major exclaimed impatiently, tightening his hold on the reins. Then, just as they were about to move off, "Wait!" he cried. "My coat, Jim. It would never do," he explained to the scowling corporal, "to appear before your captain in my shirt sleeves. Such deuced bad form, don't you know."

He put on the coat Jim brought him. It had been hanging from the back of his chair. It was a khaki tunic and was adorned with a number of large, leather buttons.

And Jim, grinning happily, returned to his dish-washing and his singing.

"AND," THE corporal concluded his report to his commanding officer, "I accordingly arrested prisoner and warned him."

"Um!" Captain Murray looked at the Major, then down at the silver cigarette case which was on the desk before him. His strong brown fingers toyed idly with the stones the case had contained. "And did the prisoner make any statement, corporal?"

The corporal grinned.

"He only said—on his word of honor—that they wasn't diamonds, sir."

Captain Murray looked up at the Major.

"And have you any statement you wish to make now— er—prisoner?"

"My word, yes!" the Major exclaimed indignantly. "I want to protest against this highhanded proceeding. I intend to make it hot, very hot indeed, for the indignities to which I have been subjected. I've been treated like a common felon. I—"

Captain Murray interrupted.

"You can go into that later. Do you want to explain, or try to explain, these?" He indicated the stones.

"My good sir!" the Major expostulated. "I refuse to go into such trivial matters. I—"

"You will find it anything but a trivial matter, Major. You were arrested with illicitly purchased diamonds in your possession and the penalty for that—"

"You need go no further, dear lad. I know the penalty and, if you can prove your case, I'm quite willing to pay it. But where's the evidence?"

Captain Murray indicated the stones on his desk.

"Those!" The Major nearly choked with mirth. "Oh, really! This is too much. They are not diamonds. I suggest you examine them closely. Look here!"

Before anyone could stop him he stepped quickly forward and taking up a heavy brass paper weight dropped it on one of the stones.

"There!" he said patronizingly. "Now are you satisfied?" He lifted up the weight and showed that the stone had been ground to a fine powder. "You will find the others respond in the same way to similar treatment. And diamonds wouldn't, would they?"

He smiled confidently.

"No—they wouldn't," Captain Murray admitted slowly. "I might have known, Major, that you were too smart to allow yourself to be so easily caught.

"Corporal!"

"Yes, sir?" The corporal looked very sheepish.

"You are a fool! Don't you know what's a diamond and what isn't? Don't you—oh, get out!"

And the corporal, regretting that discipline would not permit him to point out that his superior, also, had not known the stones were not diamonds, got out.

AS THE door closed behind his subordinate, Captain Murray sighed with relief and said, "Sit down, Major. We can revert to the normal now, but, for a moment, I thought your career had come to an end."

"But that, surely, would not grieve you," the Major said as he seated himself.

"It would," Captain Murray assured him. "You know your arrest and sentence to the Breakwater would be a great loss to us all. It would take away one of our chief recreations. We all want to catch you with the goods, but—well, it's hard to explain. Look at it this way: every good sportsman is glad when a game fox succeeds in running away from the hounds. Of course, you're a frightful thorn in the flesh of the mine magnates but I'm inclined to think that a few more thorns like you would be good for them. And that, of course, is rank heresy."

The Major smiled and the two men were silent for a little while. They were old acquaintances and had crossed wits many times.

"You know," the Major observed, "I've never been guilty of half the exploits you laddies lay to my charge. Really," he insisted as the captain smiled. "I'm telling you the truth, old dear. You chaps call me an I.D.B. You have a sneaking belief that I buy stolen stones from natives. You think— Oh, I know what you think! And it hurts—really it hurts."

He shrugged his shoulders as the captain's smile expressed incredulity.

"I am wondering," said that man presently, "just why you allowed the corporal to arrest you. Why didn't you show him that these weren't diamonds."

"I told him," the Major protested in injured tones, "and, as he wouldn't believe me, I let him bring me in. I thought he needed a lesson. As if I would ever be such a bally criminal as to indulge in such—er—reprehensible an undertaking as buying diamonds illicitly."

CAPTAIN MURRAY smiled sarcastically. "Major," he said hesitatingly, "I think that you will admit that we have always been good friends. I do not like to stress this, but it's a fact, that you will admit, that on the whole the police have treated you like a white man."

"My word, yes! Oh, quite!"

"Well, then, Major," Captain Murray said, "I am going to appeal to you for help. See here: ever since this place has been proclaimed a diamond field we've been swamped by the gutter scum from Kimberley and Jo'burg. They've made the place a hell. They rob, and booze, and bully. They're all guilty of beastly crimes. Every last man is an I.D.B., but there's nothing I can do. They arrange perfect alibis, and it's impossible to get Court of law proof evidence against them. I want you to help me to get that."

"You mean you want me to join them—then turn informer?" The Major made a grimace of disgust.

"If I thought that the best plan, yes. There is no dishonorable way of trapping rotten swine."

The Major nodded.

"I regret my exhibition of squeamishness. Go on, old dear. Why can't I pretend to be one of them and get information that way?"

"Because," Captain Murray said heavily, "before you can be one of them you have to prove your rottenness by committing some beastly crime in the presence of two witnesses."

"Phew! Sounds like a close organization. But do you *know* this is so?"

"No proof. Only well founded rumor."

"Then how do you suggest I go to work?"

"As a policeman."

"What!"

"Exactly—*and* uniformed."

"Oh, my giddy aunt! But why?"

"Because three of my men detailed to the duty have been murdered.

"The last one, a youngster named James, was found on the veld this morning, a bullet through his heart. He, like the other two, was on the point of discovering something, I think. He was boasting before he went out yesterday morning that he expected to make important arrests before the day was over. He even told us the name of the man he suspected was the ring leader of the gang."

"And you have done nothing."

"WHAT COULD I do? I had the gang up here—but they all had hole-proof alibis. I couldn't hold them. I had to let them go. Yet I knew the murderer was among them. And James—he was such a decent lad. Keen as mustard; straight as a die."

"I still don't see," the Major said after a short pause, "why you advocate that I investigate disguised as a—er—bobby."

"Because, from what I have been able to deduce, the swine are so sure of themselves that they deliberately led the other three along up to a certain point—I believe they deliberately gave themselves away and then shot them. And I think they will lead you on, too, if you go to them openly as an investigating officer. And they will attempt to serve you as they served the others."

"This is a bally nice mess you're throwing me into, old dear," the Major murmured.

"It's a damned nasty mess, Major. But, because—well, because of your experience, I believe you will find a way of avoiding the end which James and the others met. Well—

there it is. And if you want to withdraw your offer of assistance I shan't blame you one bit."

"It'ud be difficult, maybe, for me to pose as a policeman," the Major observed, ignoring Murray's last sentence. "I imagine some of the merry swine know me."

"You'll find a uniform a good disguise, Major. And men are so accustomed to seeing you with a monocle and your hair brushed back in a pompadour that if you omit the monocle and part your hair on the side you'll look entirely different. Then, if you forget your drawl and your silly assisms—"

"You're asking me," the Major interrupted, "to throw on one side the traits which I have so industriously cultivated that they have become, as it were, a part of the real me. 'Pon my soul, sometimes, I'm beginning to think, I'm as big an ass as I look."

Captain Murray laughed softly.

"You couldn't be, Major!"

The Major shook his head.

"Do you think you can find a uniform to fit me?"

Captain Murray nodded.

"It'll be a tight fit. You're six foot, aren't you? And, I should say, a 42 chest."

"Forty-six, I'm afraid," the Major said apologetically.

"Good God! You dwarf Hercules. But that tunic you wear now will do, if you replace those buttons with police ones."

"Clever of you, very," exclaimed the Major and taking a sharp paper knife from the desk he cut off the buttons. "But you will take care of them for me, won't you?" he added as he pushed the little pile of buttons over to Captain Murray.

"They are, as it were, quite priceless and I should not like to be without them."

Captain Murray swept the buttons into his desk drawer.

"I'll take care of them for you," he said. "So I take it that you are going to help me?"

The Major nodded. "Yes," he said slowly. "I was going after them in my own way. They caught and thrashed Jim."

"And when will you report for duty?"

The Major rose to his feet, his heels clicked together and he stood rigidly at attention.

"Reporting now, sir," he said.

THE HABITUES of Jake Shiners's saloon bar were boasting loudly of their exploits of cruelty, of bloodshed and rapine! That a policeman was present seemed no sort of a deterrent. Indeed, one would have said that their boastings were meant for his ears, for, each time a man concluded an account of his ill-doing, he would glance provocatively at the uniformed man as if expecting, and hoping, that he would make some comment.

But he, seated at a table against the distant wall, seemed deaf to all their boastings seemed chiefly interested in the beer he was slowly sipping.

A man swaggered over to his table.

"Say!" the stranger said thickly. "I'm a newcomer to this *dorp,* but I got an idea I've seen you some place before. What's your name, bobby?"

"Trooper Thompson. But my pals call me Major."

"Major, eh. You ain't *the* Major by any chance, are you?" He knocked off the policeman's helmet. "No, I see you ain't. He wears his hair in a pompadour. And he wears a monocle. Cripes! He's a dude if there ever was one—which you ain't. Not by a long shot! So they call you Major, eh?"

"Yes. Any objections?" Major's voice was crisp, in keeping with his smart, soldierly appearance.

"No, I ain't got any objections. Except— See here: my name's Swift, Jim Swift, and you can take it from me that I ain't slow, not in any way. I'm Swift—swift to take offence when a bloomin' bobby tries to be funny with me. So, stand up when you talk to a gentleman."

The Major stood up, completely dwarfing the other.

"And now what?" he snapped truculently. "If you're looking for trouble you can have it."

Swift giggled.

"Say, ain't you the little fire-eater?" he said banteringly. "Course I don't want no trouble. Here—finish your drink and I'll buy you another."

As he spoke, he picked up the half-filled glass of beer and, when the policeman held out his hand for it, threw it in his eyes.

Roaring with rage, rubbing his eyes with one hand while his other fumbled at the flap of his revolver holster, Major made a bull like rush at Swift only to find his way barred by a circle of jeering men.

"Let me get at him," he bellowed.

"Get at who, ducky?"

"That Swift. I'll teach him to throw beer into my face. I'll—"

"You're crazy drunk," they told him. "Nobody threw beer in your face. You was balancing your glass on your forehead and spilled it, that's how it happened. At least, that's how all of us say it happened. And what are you going to do about it?"

The Major scowled at them.

"Nothing," he said finally in subdued tones. "If you say that's how it happened, that's all there is to it. But I warn you fellows: I can stand a bit of horseplay as well as the next one. But don't goad me too far, that's all!" This was greeted with another outburst of laughter as the men returned to the bar and, their glasses replenished, resumed their vicious boasting.

THE MAJOR sat down again in his chair and stared moodily before him, mentally reviewing the things he had discovered in the week which had elapsed since he had donned the uniform and authority of a police officer.

"My word," his thoughts ran, "I wish now I hadn't sent old Jim away. I don't know though—perhaps it's just as well. As it is, one or two of these laddies suspect I'm not quite what I seem. And if I had Jim here, they would be more suspicious. A uniform wouldn't be much of a disguise for him. Just the same, I miss him."

A noisy, quarreling argument suddenly broke out at the bar. The Major looked up just in time to see a man bring down an empty beer bottle on the head of another with skull breaking force. The man dropped like a log. The others callously rolled him to one side and the incident, apparently, was closed.

"My word!" the Major muttered. "I wonder if that was a staged knock out with the object of forcing me to action? If so, they're going to be bally disappointed. I'm seeing nothing—not a bally thing."

Then, his thoughts continued: "I've seen a lot and heard a lot, but for all they know I'm blind and deaf. And, for the matter of that, I might just as well be. For what I've seen and what I've heard would be useless as evidence for the prosecution. Perjury means nothing to these blighters.

They'd give the lie to anything I said, and I'd be laughed out of court. But I have an idea—and it's only an idea—that if I could get the—er—goods on the ringleader, the gang wouldn't hold together very long.

"And tonight's the night—perhaps.

"I wonder where the blighter is? It'll be most annoying if he doesn't show up. Wish I had my monocle—it's deuced hard to be without it! I've grown to rely on it more than I had realized. And I wish I had not let old Murray rush me into investigatin' in uniform. I don't appear at my best substituting for a police chappy. I have to expend too much energy playing my role! Besides, I've spent so many bally years running from a uniform that I feel, as it were, like a fish out of water in one.

"No, I don't like the job at all. But I must go through with it. There's one thing in my favor: If I do any killing, my hands'll be clean. Not that I want to shoot to kill, that's not my style. To threaten death is a much more efficient way—not that threats would stop rats. My word, no!"

HE SLUMPED down still further in his chair; his chin rested on his chest; his eyes were half closed. With lazy fumbling fingers he unhooked his collar and unbuttoned his tunic coat. His movements were those of a sleepy man who has surrendered to heat and feeling of lassitude.

"I wish," his thoughts ran on, "I wish they wouldn't keep turning round to look at me. Makes me feel like a bally ass. Oh, quite. And they keep grinning. Wish I knew the joke although I have a feeling it is not a nice one. My word, no!

"You know—they think I'm a nice little bit of meat for a pack. But they'll find it poisoned; they'll find the bait's on a barbed hook, as it were. Abso-bloomin'-lutely!

" 'Pon my soul, though, this won't do. I oughtn't to let my thoughts run on like this. I'll be talking that way, an' then the game would become more complicated. My role is that of a thickheaded blundering trooper who can't see evidence when it's put before his nose. And I'm a very heavy drinker—specially," he chuckled softly, "as there's a large flower pot so handy."

He rose to his feet and walked heavily over to the bar.

"A whisky this time, Jake," he ordered, scowling at the men who crowded round him.

The door at the other end of the room opened, but the Major seemed unconscious of it and the others tried very obviously to appear as though they were unaware of the presence of the black-mustached man who stood framed in the doorway.

"Careful!" the bartender said suddenly, just as the Major was about to drink. "There's a worm or something in your glass. Look!"

With an angry curse the Major held his glass up to eye level, turning slightly as he did so.

The next moment he was staring stupidly at the splattered fragment of glass he still held between thumb and forefinger.

Then—and it seemed as if he had taken these few minutes to connect cause and effect—the revolver shot and the shattered glass he held—he threw the broken glass from him, wiped his whisky splashed hand on the seat of his trousers, and turned angrily to face the man at the door. As he did so he fumbled with the flap of his heavy, revolver holster.

"What in hell do you think you're doing?" he yelled, adding swiftly in softer placating tones, "Oh! It's you, is it, Bottles?"

"Me it is," agreed the black mustached man, somewhat sinisterly, coming forward to the bar. His hands were empty. He carried no visible weapon. The speed of his draw, the shot and the return of the weapon to its original hiding place had all been done with such astonishing smoothness and speed as to suggest months of steady practice.

THE OTHER men, whispering together, drew away from him and he and the Major were left standing face to face.

"You can shoot straight, no doubt about that," the Major said, breaking a silence which seemed well nigh unendurable.

"Yes—I can shoot," agreed the man called Bottles.

The Major nodded. He seemed somewhat fuddled; not drunk exactly, but, evidently, the liquor he had been imbibing had slowed up his motor and mental reactions.

"It's one thing," he observed heavily, "to do fancy shooting at fancy targets. But how do you shape when your target's a man with a gun in his hand? Tell me that."

Bottles laughed.

"I've been known to miss with my first shot," he said.

"Ah! That's bad."

"Not so bad. My second shot is on its way before the other feller has a chance to let off his first."

"Not so good," the Major commented, "if the other man happens to be as quick on the trigger as yourself."

"Not so bad," Bottles said and laughed confidently. "That man ain't been born yet."

"But he will be born some day," the Major persisted with a drunken-like gravity, "an' when he's grown up—"

"I'll be retired an' a respectable law abiding citizen, so he won't bother me," Bottles countered lightly.

"And you're not now? Not a respectable citizen, I mean?"

Bottles laughed contemptuously.

"You ought to know. You've been dogging my footsteps long enough. Have you found out anything?"

"Not a damned thing," the Major said promptly. "But," he added quickly, "I've got suspicions."

Bottles's eyes narrowed; his thin lips drew back exposing yellowed teeth in an ugly snarl. He tensed, poised on his toes like a boxer. For a moment the hissing intake of breath from the other men was the only sound. Then he relaxed and laughed with an affectation of good humor.

He said. "Why don't you arrest me?"

"Because—hell! Suspicion ain't no sort of proof. Of course it'ud be different if I could get one of these rats of yours to squeal, or—"

"His first squeal would be his death rattle," Bottles interposed. "So you won't succeed that way. But you hadn't finished. Or—"

"Or if I could get proof of something you'd done. Get you on one thing so's we could lock you up out of harm's way—and then we could soon rope up the rest. But—" the Major shook his head sorrowfully—"it looks like a pretty hopeless task. From what I know of you, you're just a chap with a funny hobby."

"Yes?"

"Yes. An' I can't arrest a man just because he goes around collecting empty champagne bottles to use as targets."

Bottles laughed.

"So you ain't discovered nothing?"

"Not a damned thing. I'm pretty sure you're a big I.D.B., for instance. But I can't prove it: I can't discover who hands you the stones, or how."

"That's too bad. And yet it's done right before your eyes, bobby."

"I know. You've said that before. And I've searched you, God knows how many times, but not a 'stone' have I discovered. You know—" the Major's tone was ludicrously confidential—"I'm half a mind to frame you."

"Try it," taunted Bottles, "and I'll show you some shooting that'll open your eyes, an' then damn quick close 'em for good."

AGAIN THERE was a pregnant silence. Jake Shiners licked his fat red lips and passed grimy, beringed fingers over his oily hair. The other men watched covertly, secretly anticipating a well known climax—a mistaken, hasty move by the policeman—a shot—a man slumping lifelessly to the ground, and Bottles saying callously, "Drinks round, Jake—then some of the boys can carry this offal out on to the veld."

Bottles looked a killer now; evil emanated from him. He was as deadly as a snake poised for striking.

But a wild pig's tough hide makes it practically immune from snake bite; and the Major's seeming lack of sensitiveness protected him from the death which was held in readiness for him. Nothing that Bottles had said or done had stung him to heated retorts.

Bottles was nonplused. Even a snake will not strike unless it has a grievance—real or fancied. He looked at the Major's blank, expressionless face and shrugged his shoulders helplessly.

"About this shooting, now," the Major said, once again breaking the tension. "I'm not a bad shot myself."

"You shoot! Don't make me laugh."

"It's a fact though. I'm rated a first class shot with a revolver."

"Call that a revolver," Bottles gibed. "It's a young cannon. I know all about them service revolvers. They kick like a mule, throw off to the right, and if you miss your target the breeze flattens it."

"An' that's useful," the Major commented soberly, glaring round savagely at the men who laughed. "But I don't miss. See them bottles—" he pointed to a row of empty champagne bottles on a shelf behind the counter—"let's go to the other end of the bar an' fire alternate shots—aiming at the tops. The one who misses first, stands the crowd to champagne."

"They're my pet targets," Bottles demurred. "I was going to take 'em home with me and set 'em up on a stump outside—"

"Just as you like," the Major said casually, "only I'm sick of hanging around doing nothing. Thought it might be a bit of excitement. Besides, I wanted to show you you ain't the only marksman about."

Bottles hesitated a moment then, "Come on," he said. "Let's see what you can do."

HE WALKED to the other end of the room, the Major following him. Jake vaulted over the bar and joined the men who had lined up along the side.

They were very noisy, all wishing to bet on Bottles's success and finding no takers.

"You," said Bottles "start with the bottle on the right an' I'll take the left of the line. We'll fire six shots each as fast as you please. If you fail to knock six tops off, you buy the drinks."

"An' if I hit 'em all?"

"We'll try something harder."

"An' if you miss—?"

"I shan't," Bottles said shortly.

And as he spoke he went into action.

Six shots following in swift succession; so swiftly indeed that it seemed impossible that a man could have drawn his weapon in that time. Six shots, and six neckless bottles. Six shots—and the marksman lounged lazily against the wall, his arms folded, a mocking smile on his face. And no weapon was visible.

There were sycophantic shouts of applause.

"Beat that, policeman," said Bottles.

The Major shook his head. "No good me trying—not as regards speed. But I don't expect to miss."

He undid the flap of his holster and drew his heavy revolver.

"The light's bad," he muttered. "An' I'd like to have a sighting shot. But here goes."

Slowly—his style labored and very patently acquired on a range under the eagle eye of a military instructor—standing slightly aslant to his target, his left arm behind his back, his revolver went up, came down slowly on the mark—

Six shots in as many minutes and five more neckless bottles stood on the shelf. The sixth shot had been a little low and had shattered the bottle to fragments.

"Not so bad for a bobby," Bottles said patronizingly. "But hell! A man could run out of range before you got in your first shot."

"That's true!" the Major admitted. He was industriously cleaning the barrel of his weapon with a piece of red-striped two-by-four. "Well—" he returned his revolver to its holster, fastened the flap and returned to the bar—"who's drinking? The treat's on me."

For a little while there was no sound but the popping of corks and the gurgle of liquid down over thirsty throats.

The Major seemed obsessed by the failure of his last shot.

"The light's bad in here," he insisted thickly. "Tell you what, let's take the rest of the bottles out on the veld somewhere—back of the old mine, say—an' try again there."

Bottles looked at him keenly.

"All right!" he said and winked at the others.

They laughed. There were a number of open shafts, they knew, at the deserted working. And here was a victim prepared to carry his own body out on to the veld!

HALF AN hour later the Major and Bottles arrived at the deserted mine. Six men accompanied them. They all carried six bottles each.

And there, at the back of a slag dump, the man Bottles gave another astounding exhibition of shooting. The Major's shooting was also good, but painfully slow.

At last, "I've got one more shot left," said the Major. "Stick up a bottle and I'll put a bullet down its neck."

"There ain't no more bottles," Bottles said. "Find another target."

"There must be," the Major insisted with a gravity that was suspiciously like that induced by too much drink. "There's eight of us—" he counted gravely—"an' we brought six bottles each, an' six eights are forty-eight. You've smashed twenty-four an' I've smashed twenty-three. So there must be another."

"There isn't, I tell you," Bottles said coldly. "Do you doubt my word?"

"No, course not, old feller. Me and you are good friends. Wouldn't think of doubting your word. But I wanted another target, that's all, an' I felt sure there was another bottle."

There was a stupid expression on his face, as he turned his pockets inside out, looking for the bottle.

Failing, he said:

"Must have another target."

"Tell you what," said Bottles thoughtfully, looking at the long gray ash on his cigar. "Let's try your nerve. Trim the ash off my cigar for me. Then I'll return the compliment."

The Major demurred.

"I don't know as I'd care for that. It's too risky. I might hit you."

"God help you if you do."

"God help you, you mean. But hell, no, I don't like it."

Putting his cigar between his teeth, Bottles took his stand at fair shooting range, standing sideways to the Major.

"At that," the Major muttered, "it's an easy shot." He went through his elaborate preliminaries, then fired.

"Missed!" he exclaimed and threw down his empty revolver with an expression of disgust.

The men wondered at the crash of broken glass.

BOTTLES, THE long ash of his cigar untouched, felt gingerly of his hip-pocket. It was full of broken glass—the shattered fragments of the forty-eighth bottle! He viciously spat out his cigar.

"You fool!" he snarled, advancing a few paces. "Think you are clever, don't you? Pretending to be deaf and blind to the things which have been goin' on under your nose."

"What the hell!" the Major exclaimed in wondering tones. "God knows I'm sorry I missed. But that's no reason for you to raise a row. I might have hit you."

"You didn't miss. You hit what you aimed for: The bottle in my hip-pocket. Well—you know too much. So you're goin' to be my target. You're goin' to die like James and the others died."

"They hang men for murder, old dear," the Major drawled. He had dropped now the pose of a stolid thinking policeman. In effect, he had placed a monocle in his mental eye which converted him into an inane dude.

Bottles stared at him wrathfully.

"They won't hang me," he boasted. "I've got witnesses that'll swear you shot yourself accidentally."

"Nice of them," the Major commented easily. "But I wonder if you feel inclined to let me into your little secrets. You've done a lot of boasting, but I'm inclined to doubt. You haven't the guts to do the things you claim to have done."

Bottles's face was convulsed with wrath.

"I haven't, eh? Listen: you've heard rumors. Well, now I'm goin' to quote you chapter an' verse."

Words flowed from him in a vicious stream as he recounted boastfully of his and his gang's evil doings. He dilated on the methods he had used; he gave names and places. He made so complete a statement that his henchmen looked at each other uneasily; they realized that it would be possible for the leader's rash statements to be checked up and their crimes brought home to them.

Bottles came to a final sneering conclusion.

"You're a rotten beast," the Major said slowly. "You're— My word! It's impossible to give you an appropriate name. But you're also a fool. You've said too much. You're finished."

Bottles laughed.

"Finished, eh? You're finished, you mean. You don't think what I've told you is goin' to do you any good? Besides, you ain't goin' to live to—"

"You bore me," the Major said, stifling a yawn. He added in a sharper tone, "You're under arrest—all of you. Put up your hands."

"You dolt!" Bottles snarled. His hand moved swiftly. But swifter still was the Major's draw and the shot which splintered the bones of Bottles' wrist.

SCREAMING CURSES the man swiftly shifted his revolver to his left hand. There was another shot and his revolver dropped to the ground. He stood looking at the blood which streamed from his wrists.

"You would be wiser," the Major advised him icily, "to keep quite silent. You others, put up your hands."

They obeyed him swiftly. They looked in awe at the smoking automatic the Major held in his hand. None had seen him draw it; none had suspected he possessed one.

"You can't get away with this," Bottles whimpered.

"I can get away with murder," the Major replied. "I have witnesses."

As he spoke he stepped away from the door of the shack. It opened and four policemen, revolvers in hand, stepped out and, without any hesitation, handcuffed the men together.

"What charge shall we hold them on, Major?" one asked.

"Oh," that man said airily. "I.D.B. will do. They're all buyers, I imagine. That's the least of their crimes. And Bottles is the receiver. You'll find the evidence in his hip pocket. But be careful. It's mixed up with broken glass. You see, no one ever thought of examining the bottles he used to take away from Shiners's place. Very simple and very clever, yes. But now—oh, well! Take him away. I have a righteous horror of I.D.B.'s."

THANKS TO you, Major," said Captain Murray, "We've got that gang of cut-throats safely under lock and key."

"There's no fear of a slip-up?" the Major asked anxiously. "I mean it would be bally rotten if that man Bottles, for instance, had to face no other charge than that of I.D.B."

"He'll face graver charges than that, Major. He boasted too much in the hearing of witnesses and already we've been able to check up as true a great deal. He'll go to his appointed doom. And so will the others. Thanks again to you."

"It was nothing, old dear. I was—er—reasonably sure that I could shoot just a little quicker than he could. I might have finished the business several days ago. But, you see, I have a natural abhorrence of I.D.B.'s and I wanted to catch him with the—er—goods. And I got him. Right in the seat of his—er—trousers, as it were. Well, I must trot along. Jim will be expecting me."

He rose to his feet, gallant, debonair, monocle gleaming in his eye, his jet black hair brushed back in an immaculate pompadour. He was dressed in his normal garb; a finished dandy save that on his tunic—he had removed the police insignia—there were no buttons.

"I say," he said. "May I have my buttons back? Almost forgot them."

Captain Murray took them out of his drawer and handed them to him.

"Thanks," said the Major. "Wouldn't lose them for the world. And so now I can resume my own—er—interesting profession."

"Not I.D.B., Major," Murray said warningly.

The Major looked reproachfully at him. "Come, come, old horse! I am so open and free from guile. Where, I ask you, could I conceal diamonds?"

The door closed and he was gone.

THAT NIGHT the Major and Jim sat by their fire out on the veld. The Major was carefully cutting up his leather buttons and disclosing the fact that each button was the hiding place of a good sized diamond.

"Come to think of it," the Major chuckled softly, "this affair had its humorous points."

"Golly, damnme, yes, no. If I don't see you, s'long, hullo!" Jim agreed eloquently.

THE FOOL, THE
VILLAIN, THE
HERO

THE LURE of diamonds brought two of them
to the Kalahari Desert; joy of adventure the third.
A stinking water hole in the heart of South Africa's Great
Thirst Land was the magnet which drew them together.
Three white men, outwardly as definitely cast as three
masked characters in an old time Morality Play.

The first came from the north. His colossal strength was
sapped by the furnace heat, the shifting, powdery sand and
the burden he carried in his arms. At his heels, their ears
pricked up at the scent of water, two heavily laden pack
donkeys ambled.

Coming to the water hole, the big man lowered his
burden in the shade of a gigantic sand dune, bent over it
anxiously and men, frowning slightly, climbed carefully
down the slime-covered sides and filled his water-bag.

He tasted the water, his fatigue-lined face expressing
disgust at its flavor, and returned to the top. As he did
so the bundle he had placed in the shade moved fitfully,
disclosing itself to be a man—a bushman; naked, dirty, his
coarse hair matted with grease, his bones threatening to
burst through his yellow skin.

The white man ran to him, knelt beside him, carefully
raised him to a sitting position and held the water-bag to
his lips.

The bushman's eyes flickered open for a moment as he swallowed greedily, then he returned to the death-like coma from which the smell of water had roused him.

Whistling softly the white man took the packs off the donkeys and turned them loose to feed on the *t'samma*, the melon-like desert plant, which grew in a measure of profusion near-by.

That done he made camp—lighted a fire, filled his billy-can with water which he put on to boil—and sitting down with a weary sigh, smoked a well-seasoned pipe. He looked occasionally toward the bushman as if meditating what course to pursue in order to revive life in the man he had carried for so many weary, waterless miles.

Presently his eyes closed, his pipe dropped from his mouth and, for a time, he found easement from his bodily aches in sleep; so sound a sleep that he did not observe the approach of the second man.

THIS ONE came from the south.

He was a wizened, rat-faced little man; his upper teeth were abnormally long and protruded unpleasantly.

In a holster strapped to his thigh was a revolver—his right hand rested on its butt—and in his left hand he carried a *sjambok* with which he menaced the pock-marked bushman who, walking between two boney pack mules, led the way. The bushman was almost at the point of exhaustion, and when the mules, scenting water, quickened their pace to a jaded trot, they dragged him off his feet for his wrists were firmly bound to their packs.

The little man laughed as he hurried after his mules and prisoner. Catching up with them he brought the animals to a halt and scouted ahead—first giving the bushman

harsh instructions to keep himself and the animals hidden behind a near-by dune.

He came almost immediately in sight of the first man's camp beside the water-hole. Dropping to the ground, he wormed his way cautiously forward. His revolver was now in his hand, his eyes glistened.

Right to the very edge of the water hole he crept, his presence unsuspected by the sleeper. He helped himself to some water from the first man's canvas bag—evaporation had cooled it but had not destroyed its stench!—and swallowed greedily.

Then he fired a shot into the air.

THE FIRST man awoke with a start; his hand dropped to his revolver holster.

"None of that," said the second man.

The first one laughed; he saw that the little man had him covered.

"Of course not," he said. "There's no need for anything like that, is there? Only you startled me. Why did you fire?"

"That was a signal for my nigger to come up with the mules," the other replied.

"I see!" the big man looked meditatively at the other. "But I don't understand your exaggerated caution. Put away your revolver and let's be friendly; there's enough water for us all and plenty of *t'samma* for our animals.

"You're the first white man I've seen since I came into the desert—and that's three months ago. My name's Handley, Richard Handley; Dick to my friends."

"And mine's Snape—generally known as Rat Snape. And I ain't putting away my gun, mister. I'm keeping you covered—see? Just now, water an' a good meal means a damned sight more to me than a bushel of diamonds—an' I ain't taking any chances."

HANDLEY SHRUGGED his shoulders.

"Just as you like. I was going to suggest, though, that we pool our resources, Maybe we can concoct a good meal—"

"What I want of yours, mister," Rat snapped, "I'm going to take—and don't you forget it."

"Why take when I'm ready to give you," Handley said gently. "However—"

He broke off and looked keenly at Rat's mules which now came lumbering up to the water hole, dragging the bushman between them.

"That's no way to treat a nigger!" he exclaimed. "You've been thrashing him with a *sjambok*. The poor devil's back is—"

"It is and I have," Rat said grimly, "and it's no business of yours, mister, how I treat a nigger. An' let me tell you, that one 'ud be dead if he had what he deserved.

"An' say," Rat continued, looking keenly at Handley, "since you're so bloomin' kind hearted, suppose you untie that nigger of mine, take the packs off the mules an' let 'em out to graze? Go on! Hop to it!"

Handley hesitated and then answering the threat of Rat Snape's revolver, obeyed. But he obeyed in such a way that it was evident that he had no intention of continuing to accept this invidious situation.

Snape, realizing this, scowled uneasily.

"Don't you try any tricks, mister," he warned. "I'm watching you all the time, an' there's no call for you to be so blamed interested in them packs of mine. There's nothing in them, nothing for you to see."

His face reddened angrily as Handley straightened himself with a contemptuous shrug of his shoulders.

"An' furthermore," Snape ranted as Handley bent over the bushman and spoke to him in a low voice, "you leave that nigger of mine alone. He's my pilot—that's what he is. He's going to lead me to—" He stopped short. "Anyway," he added gruffly, "you leave him alone. See?"

"I was only asking him if he wanted a drink," Handley said smoothly. "Don't you understand the vernacular?"

"No, I don't. Why in hell should I? I ain't no bloomin' dog ape—an' that's the language he talks, blast him. But he understands the sort of English I talk to him, an' that's good enough for me."

FOR A little while there was silence. The sun, although near its setting, blazed with undiminished fierceness; the mules, too tired it seemed to eat, huddled together in what scanty shade they could find. And the two white men— their common lot should have formed a bond of friendship or, at least, of companionship—glared at each other suspiciously.

Snape's bushman crawled to the shelter of the sand dune and sat beside his prostrate fellow tribesman; silent, hate-filled.

Snape looked toward them and cursed. For the first time, it seemed, he was conscious of the other bushman's presence.

He strode over to them and looked at the man Handley had carried to the water hole.

"Your own nigger don't look any too healthy, mister," he said with a leer.

"No, poor devil. I found him back there in the desert, starving and half dead. I carried him here—"

"Quite a hero, ain't you?" Snape jeered. "But let's eat; what you got?"

"Flour, a tin of bacon. What have you?"

"Nothing. At least nothing I'm going to use. Hell, no! I'm an invited guest; you're going to be hospitable and feed me. See? So get busy an' cook grub."

AGAIN HANDLEY hesitated and seemed on the verge of a violent refusal to act as slave to the rat-faced little man; again the menace of the revolver calmed him.

"But look here," he said protestingly. "Why do you act like this, old fellow? Here we are, two white men, met by chance in the desert, miles from civilization, and you act as if I was your deadly enemy."

"And how do I know you ain't?" Snape countered. "See here—I'll put my cards on the table. I'm on the track of diamonds—maybe you are, too. You must be, or you wouldn't be in this damned hell on earth. Right then. I've seen men murdered for diamonds. I've seen 'em murdered by men they thought their best friends, in a *dorp*, where there wasn't one chance in a hundred of the murderer getting away. Well, if men'll murder there, it's a sure thing they would here where there ain't one chance in a thousand of their being found out."

"A sane man," said Handley, "wouldn't take one chance in a million of being hung for murder."

"Men ain't sane when they're on the track of diamonds, mister," Snape retorted. "So me, I ain't taking any chances. If so be one of us is going to commit murder—that one'll be me. I certainly ain't going to be the one murdered. So put that in your pipe an' smoke it. I'm looking out for number one, me, Rat Snape, all the time."

"You're next door to a villain," Handley said shortly and then, without further comment, busied himself preparing a meal—coffee, *veld-briks* and grilled bacon.

He was conscious that Snape was watching his slightest move, and presently Snape moved closer to him.

"I've heard," Snape said craftily, "of blokes being poisoned. Don't you try any monkey business like that with me, mister."

Handley laughed shortly, but made no reply. He was searching amongst his pack for condiments to add to the flour.

"Yes," Snape continued, as if proud of his forethought, "it's easy to poison a man in this country an' a damn sight safer than shooting. Say, I've heard of blokes being killed through eating powdered glass. They die damned painful, so I've heard. An' then there's a lot of poisons the niggers know about. But I'm too damned smart to be caught that way. I've heard—"

"Have you heard this one?" Handley asked swiftly as he blew a cloud of pepper into Snape's eyes.

The little man screamed, his revolver exploded harmlessly—Handley had thrown himself to one side—and the next moment his feet were knocked from under him. He rolled over and over, panting, clawing and cursing.

Handley rose to his feet, a triumphant, self-complacent smile on his face.

He drew his revolver and stood over Snape.

"We'll change places for a bit," he said suavely. "I don't know what sort of a crook you are—but I'll be watching you closely. You won't have a chance to poison me!" He laughed at that, "I'll be watching you all the time—but not too close!"

Snape sat up and frantically rubbed his red, inflamed eyes with his dirty hands; tears streamed down his cheeks.

He groped blindly for his revolver which he had dropped after the first panic-inspired shot, and swore viciously as one of Handley's nailed boots came down heavily on his hand.

"Blimme!" he exclaimed in a whining voice. "No call to act like that. We're white men—alone in the bloomin' desert. An' white men ought to stick together. That's what I always say. Ow! My bloomin' eyes burn like hell!"

"I say! I hope I'm not intruding!"

AT THE sound of the slow, cultured drawl, Handley turned with a start to face the third white man to arrive at the water-hole. He had come up unobserved during the struggle.

And then Handley laughed—loudly, derisively. Snape blinked and peered suspiciously before him. What he saw in the way of outfit was sufficient to make him forget his anger toward Handley and the smarting pain of his eyes. And he too laughed—laughed until the tears flowed again, bringing further easement to his eyes, washing out the black grains of powder.

The newcomer looked at him, looked at Handley, mouth agape, a bewildered expression on his clean-shaven face.

"I say!" he stammered. "Have you Johnnies gone mad or what? Maybe the sun has affected your—er—brains, the way you are laughing."

Snape was about to make a boisterous retort when Handley interposed.

"You must excuse us," he said smoothly. "Perhaps as you suggest, the sun has affected us. On the other hand, you must admit your appearance is a trifle incongruous in the heart of the desert," and he once more examined the newcomer from head to foot. The man, who was mounted astride a donkey, wore a white silk shirt, open at the neck, white drill riding breeches and highly-polished polo-boots. A white helmet disguised the shape of his head and cast a shadow over his eyes. A monocle gleamed in his right eye. It twinkled when it reflected the rays of the setting sun.

"Don't you think," drawled the newcomer, "that introductions are in order? My name—sorry I have no card—is Aubrey St. John Major. I'd be charmed if you'd call me Major—*the* Major, you know!"

He smiled.

"Pleasure's all mine!" Snape said with an elaborate bow.

"My name's Handley," said the big man. "And this is Rat Snape."

"Ah—you are partners, I presume?"

"No, far from it," Handley replied.

"You bet your life we're not," Snape echoed.

"Really?"

"Yes—really!" Snape mimicked. "We just met by chance, not an hour ago. Tomorrow we goes our own ways again—an' nobody is going to go *my* way. See?"

THERE WAS a threat in Snape's voice.

"Poor lad," the Major said feelingly, "so you're all alone in the world. And that's why you were crying. Never mind. I'll come with you."

"By God, you won't," Snape shouted, then grinned self-consciously. What was the use of losing his temper with a fool dude? Muttering under his breath he turned away and attended to the *veld-briks* just in time to save them from being hopelessly burned. He raked them out of the red embers and dusted the ashes from them.

Handley frowned. The Major puzzled him. The man looked like an utter fool! "Take out your monocle, Major?" he said abruptly.

The Major obeyed wonderingly and Handley, coming closer, stared keenly into his face.

"My word!" the Major murmured, "I do hope you're quite all right. Or is it that you think—er—you saw some green in my eye?" he laughed self-consciously.

Handley shook his head.

"I wonder," he said, "if you *are* such a fool as you look?"

" 'Pon my word—!" the Major began indignantly, but Handley, ignoring him, continued as if talking to himself.

"It hardly seems possible; and yet his eyes—even without the monocle—are an innocent baby blue. And his jaw seems slack; he holds himself as if his muscles were flabby and he looks as if he's got a tub of a belly. I wonder? At that he's taller than I am—at least he would be if he held himself erect."

Handley's black eyes were now focused thoughtfully on the revolver the Major carried in a holster at his waist.

"What do you want?" he demanded, his tone suddenly changing. "How did you come here? Where's the rest of your outfit?"

"It's a long story, mate," the Major began in a mock tragic voice, "but—" and he pointed to the west—"here comes my partner; he can tell you better than I."

HANDLEY AND Snape both turned and looking in the direction the Major indicated saw a white tented-top wagon, drawn by eight mules, slowly approaching the water hole.

A Hottentot walked beside the leaders, his squat muscular body gleaming like burnished copper.

"Hi!" Snape yipped excitedly. "There ain't enough *t'samma* for all them animals. An' it's a damned sure thing there ain't enough water. So you can move on Mister Monocled Major. You ain't going to camp here tonight."

"But really!" the Major expostulated.

"Snape's right," Handley agreed reluctantly. "First come, first served. There's another water hole thirty miles or so on, they say."

"But where, where?"

Handley shrugged his shoulders.

"That's for you to find out," Snape said. "All I know is, you ain't going to camp here an' drink my water."

"I didn't know it was your water, old chap."

"Well I say it is—so what are you going to do about it?"

The Major appealed to Handley. "At least you'll let me fill my water kegs?"

"What can I do?" that man asked in mock mournful tones. "Snape was here first—that gives him control over the water. The best I can do, if he permits it, is give you a bagful out of my supply. And I'm willing to do that."

"Kind of you, dear lad. Kind of you—very. But I am distressed. It is impossible for us to go on—really! We shall die of thirst in the desert. Oh, I say! Don't do that."

Snape, retrieving his revolver, had fired a shot in the direction of the oncoming wagon. A little cloud of sand spurted up just ahead of the foremost mules, showed where the heavy bullet had hit.

The mules were halted.

"That's just a warning shot, Mister Major," Snape said. "Now you tell your nigger to keep away from here or I'll let daylight into him and your mules."

"But where are we to go?" the Major asked helplessly. "It will be dark very soon and—"

"You can go to hell for all of me," Snape said. "But you don't camp here."

"Better go, Major," Handley said softly. "He's within his rights. Anybody who knows the desert'll tell you that."

"I'm not likely to go to law about it, old horse," the Major replied. "If you think I'd better go—"

HE CUPPED his hands to his mouth. "*O–he*, Jim!" he shouted. "Wait a bit."

"Yah, baas," the Hottentot replied.

The Major turned to Handley.

"That's all the vernacular I know," he said with a self-conscious grin. "I'll have to tell him the rest by signs."

He gestured wildly, his arms swinging like windmills.

Snape and Handley looked at him, laughing contemptuously at his antics.

And then, suddenly, they no longer grinned. Handley reeled back, staggered by a blow on the jaw; and at almost the same moment Snape's revolver dropped to the ground, his arm almost paralyzed by a chopping blow, delivered by the edge of the Major's palm, on his wrist.

Before either man could recover, the Major was standing close to the water hole. In his right hand was a revolver with which he covered Snape and Handley.

"What the hell!" Snape demanded.

And Handley, nodding sagely, "I thought you weren't such a fool as you looked, Major. But there was no need of this. You ought to have known we were only having a game with you. As if we'd turn a white man away from the only water hole for miles!"

"Of course we wouldn't," Snape added swiftly. "We was only having a lark."

The Major laughed affectedly.

"A rippin' joke, rather. I'm glad you laddies have a sense of humor. Perhaps you will better appreciate my little joke. I'm going to teach you a new desert rule. And that is—possession is nine points of the law. In other words, for the present, the water hole—and all that it contains—is mine. In the meantime—permit me."

He stooped and picking up Snape's revolver handed it to its owner. Then he returned his own revolver to its holster and turned to watch the approach of the wagon.

Snape and Handley exchanged meaning glances. It was evident that they considered the Major a colossal fool. Having gained his objective he had immediately thrown it away; had, by returning Snape's revolver to him and turning his back, put himself in the power of the two men.

Snape's eyes glistened, and his grip tightened about the revolver. There was no questioning his intentions. But Handley frowned and shook his head imperatively; his lips framed the words:

"No. Too risky. His nigger would get away and tell the police. Wait."

And at the same moment the Major—he had been polishing his eyeglass—turned sharply on his heels and said playfully, flourishing his monocle, "You have no idea what a lot it's possible to see in this. It's, as it were, quite a third eye. Helps me to see what is going on at my back if I hold it just so. Oh well, don't be so downcast, dear old Snapey. A better opportunity will doubtless present itself. I'm such an utter fool, you know."

What else he would have said was interrupted by the arrival of his wagon, the mules expertly handled by a squat, muscular Hottentot who evidently considered that his baas was supreme and walked with the gods.

SWIFTLY, IGNORING the scowls of Snape and Handley's running fire of good humored conversation, the Major and Jim the Hottentot outspanned. In an incredibly short time the mules were hobbled and turned out to graze; a white bell tent was erected; and in it were placed a collection of camping luxuries—cot bed, with linen sheets; mosquito netting, water filter, uniform cases, a chair, a table and a hanging lamp.

Snape's eyes bulged greedily at the sight of them, and Handley was frankly envious.

They were both completely astounded when the Major presently appeared in full dress clothes—looking as if he were prepared for an evening at the opera. And they could be excused for gaping openly. The Major's appearance was decidedly incongruous in that bizarre setting; the yellow shifting sands, the weirdly shaped dunes which were melting now into the falling curtain of darkness; the flickering fire flames—and the other two white men, unkempt, unshaven, their clothes shapeless and ragged.

But the Major moved with a complete assurance which made the incongruous congruous. So much so indeed that Handley openly apologized for his appearance and requested the loan of the Major's razor, while Snape endeavored to comb his tangled hair into a semblance of order with his grimy fingers.

"I hope," said the Major, and there was a touch of formality in his tone, "I hope you two gentlemen will dine with me. You will find Jim, I think, an exceedingly good cook."

"The pleasure's all mine, guv'nor," Snape said with a smirk.

"Delighted," exclaimed Handley.

"Then that's that," said the Major. "Please make free of whatever you need in the way of toilet articles."

He bowed them into the tent then went over to where the two bushmen were lying and, squatting on his haunches—native fashion—talked with them in the harsh, spitting dialect of their tribe.

His face was stern when he returned to the table which Jim had set just outside the tent.

II

THE EVENING meal was over. The three men were leaning back in their camp chairs, sipping their coffee and smoking contentedly.

"That," vowed Snape, "was a meal as was a meal!"

"Your nigger is a wonderful cook," said Handley. "He can give a west end chef points."

The Major waved his hands deprecatingly. Then, his face was stern, he leaned forward.

"I don't like to talk of unpleasant things—but haven't you gentlemen been treating your bushmen a little harshly?"

"That's a good 'un," Snape chortled. "How'd you expect a white man to treat a nigger? Kiss him? Say, mister, listen; I found that nigger way back in the desert. He was bad with fever an' just about fit to die. Well, I nursed him well an' because he told me he knew where there was diamonds, brought him along with me. It seemed he wanted to come, else he could have gone to find his people for all of me.

"Well, what do you think the ungrateful devil did this morning? He tried to stick me with a knife—an' so I thrashed him. Do you blame me? He tried to do a bunk then but I made him come along. An' now the blighter says he don't know where there are diamonds. He's a liar—they all are—but I know a way of dealing with lying niggers. He'll take me to this Bushman's Treasure afore I'm done with him."

"Ah!" the Major said softly. "You don't speak the dialect do you?"

"No, I ain't no bloomin' ape. But that nigger I brought along speaks a bit of Zulu—an' I know that."

"An' he talked about Bushman's Treasure, did he? Well, somehow, I'm not too sure you'll like it when—and if—you find it."

"Not like diamonds, mister?" Snape exclaimed incredulously. "Say, it ain't possible for me to lay hands on too many of them. Diamonds, hell! Diamonds mean heaven, London, home for a chap like me."

"Then," the Major said tentatively, "Bushman's Treasure may be even more precious to the Bushman than to you."

Both the men laughed derisively, Snape adding, "You don't know much, do you, mister? What good, I ask you, is diamonds to a bushman? They don't mean no more, if as much, to him as a handful of colored beads."

"Maybe you're right, dear lad," the Major drawled. "But about this other matter—of ill-treating the bushman I mean. I dislike—oh most profoundly—anything which even remotely approaches brutal treatment of natives by white men. I—er—set my face resolutely against *sjamboking* an' all that sort of thing. But in this case, if one is to believe your story, the *sjamboking* was deserved. Oh, quite!"

"Thanks for nothing, mister," Snape said sarcastically. "Didn't know you was a sky pilot; but you can preach all you want after feeding me like you done."

The Major turned to Handley.

"Your bushman seems to be in even worse plight than Snape's," he said quietly.

Handley laughed softly.

"You don't expect me to say anything, do you? You've been talking with the bushman. You know his story. There's nothing for me to say."

The Major nodded thoughtfully.

"Just the same—I'd like to hear your story. It is so rare that one hears of such heroic self-denial as you have shown."

HANDLEY LOOKED at him sharply, frowned, then in the self-conscious voice of one who attempts to decry his own good deeds, he said:

"Oh—I only did what any real white man would do. It's not worth talking about."

"Perhaps not," the Major agreed, "but there are few white men, I think, who'd quarrel with his partner over—a—nigger."

"Tom used to go mad almost," Handley murmured. "He'd beat the nigger till he couldn't stand. I stood it as long as I could. I warned Tom plenty of times what would happen if he didn't change his manner of treating our nigger. But it was no use. Yesterday morning he lost his temper again—the nigger spilt some coffee on him. I wasn't in camp at the time. When I arrived he'd got the nigger on the ground and—well, we had a fight, Tom and me did. After it was over, we divided up our goods, tossed to see which direction we'd go—and parted company. Knowing about this water hole, I headed for it, hoping to fall in with some of the nigger's tribe."

"And you carried him—?"

"Well, I couldn't leave him alone to die, could I?"

"Some men would," the Major observed.

"An' so he would have," Snape growled, "only, I'm gambling, he wants to get something out of the nigger."

HANDLEY SHRUGGED his shoulders.

"That, Snape," said the Major reprovingly, "is the classic attitude of the villain toward the hero."

"He's no bloomin' hero," Snape said fiercely, "and I'm no—hell, what's the good of talking to a fool like you!"

"Oh, finish it!" the Major's lips smiled, but not his eyes. "You were goin' to say you were no villain. Is that it?"

"Something like," Snape replied sulkily.

"But you must be," the Major laughed. "You look exactly like one." He turned to Handley again. "And you're after diamonds, too?"

Handley shook his head.

"No; I've had enough. I'm on my way out of the desert—and nothing will bring me back again. How about you? You've asked us questions enough. Why are you here? What's your game?"

"I'm hiding from the police, dear lad. They want me for murder."

"Murder!" Handley echoed.

"Murder!" Snape exclaimed. "Do you mean to say I've been *skoffing* with a bloody murderer?"

"You're joking," Handley protested, his hand to his eyes, veiling the hard light which came into them.

"No—it's a fact. Read for yourself if you have any doubts." And the Major passed over a fragment of a police circular. On it was a portrait of himself and a full description of the man and the crime for which he was wanted.

"I don't think it flatters me, do you?" he drawled. "The portrait, I mean. And as for the description—still, I'd like to have it back. It's an interesting—er—souvenir."

"So you're *that* Major, are you?" Handley said slowly as he returned the circular to the Major. "You're the I.D.B.; the man who pretends to be a fool; the man—"

"And you," said Snape indignantly as he rose to his feet, "have the bloomin' cheek to try an' call me down for *sjamboking* a nigger! Hell! And you're after the bushman's treasure, ain't you? You're after diamonds, too."

"Diamonds—my word, yes. Look."

From his pocket he took a handful of uncut, unpolished stones and tossed them carelessly on the table.

The other men pounced on them excitedly, examining them with the shrewd appraisal of experts. As if by some secret agreement they divided the stones into two equal piles and pocketed them.

The Major laughed. "I'd like them back, please."

Snape tried to look innocent.

"Have 'em back," he echoed. "Why, mister, you gave 'em to us. They're our reward for not givin' you away to the police. An' what's more," he added excitedly, "it's my belief you've found the place of the Bushman's Treasure my nigger talked about. Well—you're goin' to take me to it."

"I'll be delighted—really—but you won't be. And in the meantime—" he held out his left hand—"I want my stones back."

The others made no move.

"If you please," the Major insisted quietly, and his right hand moved with a lightning rapidity.

Handley and Snape jerked into action, answering the threat of the revolver in the Major's right hand.

"After all," Handley sighed regretfully as he returned the diamonds he had taken, "I don't suppose we have any right to them even if you are a murderer."

"*Wanted* for murder," the Major drawlingly amended. "There's a world of difference. But I'm glad you realize you have no right to the stones. I find a revolver a powerful advocate. Thanks, Thank you, too, Snapey."

"Oh go to hell," Snape growled. "I'm returning these stones because they don't amount to a damn. What do I want with five or six—"

"You shouldn't forget the old proverb, Snape," the Major interrupted. "A bird in the hand—and all that."

"Five or six stones," Snape continued doggedly, "don't mean nothing to me. You're goin' to take me to where I can pick 'em up by handfuls. You promised—an' I'm goin' to see you keep it. It ain't murder when you kill a murderer."

"Oh—I'll keep my promise," the Major said hastily. "I'll take you to the place of the Bushman's Treasure. But you'll be disappointed—really. And now, after I've had a few words with Jim, I'm going to turn in. Bally tired, don't you know. Oh, by the way, I think we're goin' to have the deuce an' all of a blow tonight—at least so say the two bushmen.

And they *know*. So you'd better make all things fast. I'm having Jim inspan my mules—it's safer. Good night!"

III

FOR A time Snape and Handley did not move. They saw Jim the Hottentot enter the tent; they heard, but failed to understand, the conversation he had with his baas. They saw him emerge again, heard him inspan the mules.

The light in the tent was extinguished. The candles on the table—hitherto they had burned steadily—flickered and danced unsteadily before a sudden upspringing breeze. A stronger gust extinguished them. Sparks from the fire whirled upward and were lost in the black dome of night. The sticks were scattered, the fire ceased to be. The darkness was intense.

"He's a fool," muttered Snape. "What did he want to give himself away like that for?"

"Yes—he's a fool," Handley agreed and rose to his feet.

"Where you going?" Snape asked, sensing the other's movements and stretching out for him with a groping hand.

"To see to my kit." Handley's voice sounded from some little distance. "The Major was right. It's going to blow hard."

Cursing, Snape shuffled forward, fighting his way against a wall of darkness. He stumbled and fell heavily to the ground.

He called to Handley, to the bushman, to the Hottentot and, finally, to the Major.

There was no reply. The wind drove the words back into his throat.

The darkness became even more material; the air was filled with grains of needle sharp sand which stung the flesh. Snape could not face it. He crouched low. The wind's fury increased. The desert was filled with the sound of shrieking wind devils. No stars were visible.

Mules neighed in terror. There was a rattle of wheels, the thunder of hoofs, the rifle like reports of a driving whip wielded by an expert—then silence.

Snape grinned. That would make things easier; easier to handle the Major now that his nigger had gone into the night with the stampeding mules.

He moved slightly, experimentally, then desperately; alarmed by the weight of sand which shrouded him. With an effort he wriggled free and rose to his feet, bending to the wind's force, turning his back to the driving sand.

HE CONCENTRATED his faculties in an endeavor to orient himself—a difficult task in this hell's darkness. Succeeding, he dropped on hands and knees and crept slowly toward the tent. He smiled grimly. He was acting on a suddenly conceived plan. A bird in the hand, the Major had quoted. And now Snape was on his way to make sure of the diamonds the Major had on him. If he resisted—Snape grinned. There was no need to be squeamish when dealing with a murderer. Besides, no one would ever know. This blasted sand would take care of that.

He came at last to the tent fly and, locating the lacing which closed it, cut through it with his knife. A moment later he was inside the tent enjoying its shelter from the wind's hard buffeting.

For a few minutes he sat motionless, endeavoring to quieten his breathing; nerving himself for the next move.

He listened intently, detected the sound of a sleeper's measured breathing and crawled stealthily in that direction. He halted at a low chuckle.

"It's bally dark," the Major's voice said, "but I believe I have you spotted. Oh, rather. 'Specially as I've been expecting you. Now I'm goin' to count three an' if you're still here at the conclusion of my count I shall fire. One—very amusing this, isn't it? Blind man's 'bluff' with a vengeance. Two—"

There sounded a dull thud, a gasp, the noise of a falling body.

"Hey! What the hell? Major!" Snape shouted. He jumped to his feet and lurched forward.

Something had descended on his head with stunning force and, slumping to the ground, he wandered for a time in a darkness which far transcended that of night.

SNAPE AWOKE to the brightness of another day's sunrise. His head ached and, sitting gingerly erect, he tenderly fingered a big bump on the back of his head and wondered vaguely what had happened.

He stared about him and groaned. Apparently he was alone in the heart of a desolate and unknown waste. The water hole had vanished—so too had the queer shaped dune which had been his landmark. The Major's tent, the bushmen, the mules, Handley—all had vanished. There was not one thing visible to indicate that at this place, only last night, three white men had outspanned.

Weakly, Snape staggered to his feet and looked around despairingly. He understood now. Last night's sand storm was responsible for everything. It had filled ravines and shifted hills. The water hole was buried, beyond recovery, most like. The familiar landmarks had all been blotted out. Overnight the face of the desert had been changed.

Overhead the sun blazed with a fierce intensity in a cloudless sky; the heat, although the morning was young, was oppressive, thirst creating.

Snape licked his dry lips. A worried light came into his eyes. He knew the desert well enough to appreciate the peril of his situation—without food or water; alone.

Then, remembrances suddenly flooded him, and he commenced to dig frantically in the sand with his hands, hoping to uncover the body of the Major. He hesitated presently, greatly puzzled.

"It's funny," he muttered. "Why wasn't I buried in the sand, me lying there unconscious all through the night? An' I wonder who it was knocked me out. Wasn't the fool dude Major, that's sure. I'm betting he was knocked out first. Might have been the bushmen or—Handley. Yeh! Reckon it must have been Handley. It's a fact he's nobody's bloomin' hero.

"Oh hell! This thinking don't get me anywhere. I got to do something—get somewhere. But what? Where?"

He rose to his feet and stared moodily about him, rocking uncertainly.

THEN HE stiffened, and stared unbelievingly at a black shadow on the yellow sand—the shadow of a man. He looked to its source and saw the Major, carelessly debonair—clad in pajamas and sun-helmet, come from behind a sand dune.

Snape gasped with relief.

"My God," he exclaimed, "I thought you was buried down under about thirty foot!"

The Major smiled. "And you were worried—"

"Of course," Snape said shortly. "But never mind that. I want to know what it's all about."

"Natural enough, so do I. I'm afraid I'm very much of a fool. You see I was expecting a visit from one of you last night and had no intention of being caught napping. I greeted you quite warmly, didn't I? But I wasn't expecting Handley too. I rather misjudged him. I thought he was too clever for straightforward robbery with violence. And so he won the game. He knocked us both out and—er—decamped with the takings."

"Do you mean to tell me he's got your diamonds, Major?"

"Exactly. Is that what you were digging in the sand for?"

"Hell no! I thought you was buried under there. Killing by way of business is one thing but I'm damned if I can stand by and see a man buried alive. So I started to dig."

"It would have been a long task," the Major commented. "What made you stop?"

"I used my brain. It stood to reason that if you was buried I ought to be buried too. An' I ain't."

"No," the Major agreed softly. "You—er—ain't. An' you can thank me for that. You see Handley was a little too cocksure last night. He didn't make a thorough job of things and I recovered quicker than he expected. Even so, it was almost too late. That was a deuce an' all of a sand storm which blew last night. I was nearly buried—"

He shrugged his shoulders.

SNAPE STARED at him.

"So I got you to thank, have I?" he said. "If it wasn't for you I'd be buried down there somewhere. Life's funny. Here I was ready to knock you out last night and—"

"But you didn't," the Major interrupted lightly. "And this morning you started to dig for me in the sand with your naked hands. That, I imagine, about squares things."

They were both silent for a little while. Then said Snape, "Hell, but I'm dry. What do we do next?"

"What do you want to do?"

"Why, drink until I bust. But small hope of that! We're in a hell of a hole, Major. As far as I can see—our bones'll be bleaching here afore long."

"Nasty imagination you have—very!"

"It's no good shutting your eyes to the truth. We ain't got a dog's chance of getting water—we don't know where water is. It's the end for us but afore I go, I'd like first to have a quiet talk with that Handley."

"Maybe he's gone to get help," the Major suggested.

"Don't be a fool!" Snape said bitingly.

AGAIN THERE was a silence, broken this time by the Major, who said briskly, "Well—come on, old lad. Let's trek."

"Trek where?" Snape asked dully. "What's the good of trekking? We've got to die, so might as well die here."

"But that's silly. Why die; at least we might find Handley, you know."

"I'll trek till I drop in hopes of that," Snape said fiercely.

"Good. That's the spirit. Now follow me an' don't talk—talking makes one dry. I have an idea that Handley made for the place of the Bushman's Treasure. We'll go there. An' so I shall keep my promise to you."

"To hell with the Bushman's Treasure," Snape said. "I'd trade all the diamonds in the world for a drink. However—lead on. If I can have a word with Handley afore I peg out I'll die happy."

IV

IT WAS high noon. The heat of the desert had increased beyond the limit, it would seem, of human endurance. Yet over the blinding white sand the Major walked with easy, effortless stride, despite the burden which he carried on his back. A burden which cried and cursed; now begging to be put down and left to die; now urging his human steed to quicken his speed. The desert had utterly defeated Snape. Added to the blow he had received over night, it had reduced him to the verge of insanity.

But the Major was deaf alike to his tears and curses. Not once since the time he had by force restrained Snape from eating the briny crust of a salt pan—Snape's fevered mind insisted that it was snow and he had fought viciously to escape from the Major and indulge in it to his heart's content, and death—had he eaten. He was conserving his strength, his eyes fixed on a queer shaped *kopje* which danced fantastically ahead of him.

TIME PASSED. Snape relaxed, his head lolled forward and he forgot his misery in sleep. And there was no sound save the measured crunch of the Major's feet on the shifting sand.

And so he came presently directly under the lee of the queer shaped *kopje*, encircled its base and passed on amidst a welter of rocks. There he halted, lowered Snape to the ground and gently shook him into consciousness.

Snape sat up with a start.

"Blimme!" he croaked. "Where are we?" His lips were cracked, bleeding. "I thought— Do you mean to say you carried me?"

"Quiet," the Major silenced him. "We're at the place of the Bushman's Treasure—and Handley's here. Listen."

As he spoke the man Handley came into view. He was almost naked—the few clothes he wore hung in shreds about him and at them he tore with nervous, plucking fingers.

Snape jumped to his feet with a savage curse. "Let me get at him," he gasped, then collapsed under the Major's restraining hold.

"He's been punished enough," the Major said. "He's lost—and he's thirsty. Leave him to me."

He stepped forward.

"Handley!" he shouted. "Handley."

The man peered suspiciously about him.

"More voices," he muttered. "They mean nothing—nothing." Then he saw the Major and Snape. He dropped to the ground, hiding his face between his hands, rocking back and forth.

THE MAJOR walked over to him and touched him on the shoulder.

Handley shivered, yellow with fear, then clutching hold of the Major's legs pinched them and finding them real gave way to a frenzy of relief—jumping to his feet and capering about excitedly.

The mood passed and he looked sullenly from the Major to Snape, then back to the Major again.

"You're real—you're alive!" he said.

The Major nodded.

"Small thanks to you," Snape said bitterly.

Handley laughed insanely.

"What's it matter? Soon we'll all be dead. But I don't care much now. I didn't want to die alone. It's been hell. There were voices that—"

"Of the man you had killed?" the Major asked.

Handley nodded.

"Yes. Of my partner—I killed him back there as soon as I'd found out where the Bushman's Treasure was. He died easily. He didn't know what thirst was. And I heard your voice—and the voice of that little rat."

He pointed at Snape.

"But you're not dead," he resumed, a puzzled light in his eyes.

"No, we're not dead," the Major said calmly.

"Then the voices— Hell! Was I mad? No, of course I heard them—and you're dead. I killed you both last night and the sand storm buried you. I came here with the bush-men. All through the storm I trekked. They led me to this place, holding my hands. But in the morning I was alone— all alone. And the water in my flask was turned to brine. And I've been searching for years—looking for diamonds."

"There are no diamonds here," the Major said sternly; and there was that quality in his voice which sobered Handley, destroyed his thirst-created delusions.

"No diamonds here!" he echoed. "But they told me this was the place of the Bushman's Treasure. They—"

"Come!" the Major said. "I will show you the Treasure. We all need it."

He led the way forward amidst the chaos of rocks, climbed the lower slopes of a *kopje* and halted presently before a triangular shaped cleft.

"Come!" he said again and passed into the cleft, passing along a narrow tunnel-like passage which opened out presently into a large cavern. And the floor of that cavern was a pool of crystal pure water fed by a subterranean spring.

"This," he said, "is the Bushman's Treasure."

The two men heard no more. They had flung themselves into the life giving fluid—drinking it through their thirsty pores.

Complete sanity quickly returned to them.

"We can search now," said Handley, "for the diamonds. We'll forget our little differences. What do you say?"

"There are no diamonds," repeated the Major.

"I don't want any," said Snape. "I only hope I'll never be that thirsty again. An', as for you, Handley, I ain't forgetting what you did last night or what you said a bit ago."

"What—?" Handley began viciously.

"Let us go outside," the Major said smoothly. "We can talk better in the sunlight. And there is something else I want to show you."

THEY FOLLOWED him meekly enough outside and there halted, gaping in amazement.

For there was the tented-topped wagon, and the Hotten-tot—grinning contentedly—and the mules, and the two bushmen; and seated comfortably on a camel, a policeman.

"Hands up, Handley," he said. "I arrest you for murder of your partner."

"How do you get that way!" Handley exclaimed. "He died of fever. He—say, if you want a murderer, there's one." He pointed at the Major.

Before he could say more Snape felled him with a shrewd blow to the point and, wheeling, the little man drew his revolver and aimed at the policeman.

"Put up your hands," he yelled. "And, you, Major, get on your way, quick. I'll hold him here till you've got a good start."

The Major looked at the policeman who nodded.

"Thanks, Snape, old top," the Major drawled and climbed onto the driver's seat of the wagon. "The bushman's got the diamonds Handley pinched from me. They're yours. A hero's reward, you know. So long."

The Hottentot flourished the long driving whip, the mules broke into a canter and, in a few minutes the wagon had passed from sight.

HALF AN hour passed. Snape lowered his revolver.

"I reckon you won't catch him now," he said.

"No," agreed the policeman. He was bending over Handley, handcuffing him securely. "Thanks to you."

"I had to do it," Snape said. "He saved my life. He's a bloomin' hero, if you ask me."

"Don't have to. I've met the Major before. He's a white man."

Snape looked puzzled.

"I don't understand. If you know he was the Major, why didn't you arrest him for murder?"

The policeman laughed.

"That circular was an old one. We thought once he'd committed a murder but it was afterward discovered that he purposely made it look as if he were guilty to shield a woman. No; the Major doesn't commit murder. Say, don't you understand what it's all about yet?

"I was trekking with him across the desert when we run across the body of a white man. He'd been shot, no doubt about that, but it 'ud have been a hard thing to prove he was murdered. It 'ud have been impossible for me to have proved it on the murderer working in the ordinary police way. So the Major takes the trail and catches up with you and Handley. He guesses one of you's the murderer, but don't know which for sure. First he suspects you, then he suspects Handley. Then you again. Then after a talk with Handley's bushman, he's sure it's Handley. But that ain't proof. So he shows you the diamonds he's got—he *does* know where there's more; not that getting rich interests him—and fixes up with the bushmen to lead you to this place. It's a long story—you'll have to figure it out for yourself."

"You mean," said Snape slowly, "he deliberately offered himself and the stones for bait?"

"Yes. He reckoned that a man mean enough to murder his partner wouldn't boggle at another murder or two—'specially with a sand storm in the offing to cover up his crimes. 'Specially when there was a couple of bushmen ready to lead him to a good hide-up and—as he supposed—more diamonds. And Handley took the bait."

"So did I—nearly," Snape confessed. "What a fool I was. An' it's a good job for me Handley was a bigger one. An' you' an' the Major's nigger Jim was waiting here all the time, eh?"

The policeman nodded.

"We were here when Handley came with the bushmen—they hid from him right away—and, believe me, as soon as he discovered he was all alone, an' without water, an' lost, he talked a lot to himself. He's a dirty villain if there ever was one."

"It's a fact he ain't no hero. But look here—why did that hushman of mine play a double game with me? First he told me he knew where this place was, then he said he didn't."

The policeman laughed.

"He said he knew where the Bushman's Treasure was. You thought he meant diamonds. And when he said he couldn't take you to diamonds—you lost your temper and thrashed him. He got sulky after that."

Snape grinned. "I reckon I'm a blamed fool."

"And a bit of a villain; a bit of a hero, too, by all accounts."

"A damn' small bit," Snape spat in selfcontempt. "I thought I was doing a big thing by giving the Major a chance to get away. He must be laughing at me."

"Not he," the policeman said decisively. "That's not his way. And now, if you'll give me a hand, we'll see if we can't bring a bit of life into the real fool and villain. It's funny, isn't it, for he looks like a bloomin' hero!"

THE MAJOR'S PRIVATE BANK

"**JIM**," **SAID** the Major, "from this time on I play no man's game but my own. I tread my own trails."

"Yah, baas!" Jim the Hottentot grinned and, standing up, his feet wide apart, flourished his long driving whip. The lash recoiled with two vicious reports and the eight mules which pulled the light, canvas topped wagon broke into a gallop. For a little while neither man spoke. The white man concentrated on steering the mules across the veld, swinging them around thorn scrub and boulders. Whenever the pace of the mules slackened, the Hottentot flourished his whip and the mad gallop was continued.

"That is enough, Jim," the Major said presently. He pulled the mules to a walk, handed over the reins to the Hottentot and sat hunched up, his face resting on the palms of his hands, staring morosely at the range of rocky *kopjes* which seemed to bar the way to the country beyond.

He fingered a bleeding scratch which ran from his right eye down his cheek to the corner of his firmly moulded jaw.

"I have been a fool," he said morosely. "All my life I have been a fool. But now—it may be too late—wisdom has come to me."

"And that wisdom is, baas?"

"Never to interfere with the affairs of others, Jim. If evil is being done—I will close my eyes to it. But when payment is due to me—I will see that payment is made."

"That is great wisdom, baas," said Jim and chuckled softly. "Does it hurt, baas? Does the scratch hurt?"

THE MAJOR scowled.

"The hurt is not there, Jim. But they, they laughed at me. *Wo-we!* The man *and* the woman laughed at me! That is what hurts."

Said Jim sententiously, "A man does not hunt for eggs in a hyena's burrow, or look to fools for gratitude." And he added, "Also a wise man does not interfere between husband and wife—that was your folly, baas."

"But the man had half killed her, Jim; he was beating her with a *sjambok*. A frail woman—and he a giant of a Boer."

"So you thrashed the man, baas—and the woman who was half dead—" Jim could hardly speak for laugh-

ter—"thrashed you. They are hard women, these frail wives of the Boer folk!"

The Major smiled wryly.

"Well—I have learned my lesson, Jim."

"Maybe, baas. Maybe not. I think now your pride is hurt, but, presently, you will laugh and the lesson will be forgotten."

"Never, Jim!" And in English he added, his voice an affected drawl, his expression vacuous, " 'Pon my word, I'm through. I've been a bally knight errant and a wanderer, as it were, upon the face of the globe, long enough. I've feathered other people's pockets, and now I'm going to feather my own. 'Pon my word, yes! Eh, what, Jim!"

And Jim, whose knowledge of English was about equal to that of a sailor-trained parrot, answered glibly, "Damme, yes, no. No bloody fear. If I don't see you s'long hullo."

"Exactly!" agreed the Major, continuing in the vernacular, "Oom Paul Andries lives hereabouts, Jim?"

"Yah, baas. Behind Lion's Head Kop." The Hottentot pointed with his whip toward a hill which, to one gifted with a vivid imagination, bore a vague resemblance to a lion's head.

"We will go there, Jim."

"Yah, baas." Jim swung the mules on to the new course. And he said, "Wherefore, baas?"

"Two, three years ago we did Oom Paul a service—a big service if all that he said was true."

"We saved his life, baas, and the honor of his womenfolk."

"And that was worth—what, Jim?"

The Hottentot shrugged his wide, powerful shoulders.

"He offered the baas an old wood brake-block for the wagon. And the baas—*Au-a!* The baas did not know it was offered. The baas had no thought of reward. The game he played was the baas's reward. It was always thus. So it will always be."

"No, Jim," the Major said flatly. "My eyes are open. And now I go to Oom Paul for my reward. And it will be a big one. The old man is rich. If he offers me a brake-block I'll smash his head on it."

The Hottentot grinned.

"Oftentimes," he muttered, "the baas has need of a brake to stop him from rushing into danger." And aloud he said, "And if Oom Paul values his life and the honor of his

women-folk at no more than a worn-out brake-block—
what then, baas?"

"We will ford that river, Jim," the Major said shortly,
"when we reach it."

Jim chuckled and urged the mules to a faster pace.

"We will be there in a little while, baas."

THE MAJOR nodded and climbed into the rear
of the wagon where he changed from his travel-stained
clothes.

When he rejoined Jim again on the driver's seat he was
dressed in white duck riding breeches of exaggerated cut,
a white silk shirt—open at the neck and sleeves rolled
back—and highly polished, brown riding boots on the
heels of which glistened polished spurs. The flow of blood
from the scratch had been stopped and the scratch itself
almost hidden under an application of iodine. The color of
that application blended, so as to be almost invisible, with
the sun-tanned bronze of the Major's skin.

They were travelling now in the grotesque shadow cast
by Lion's Head Kop, following a course which would take
them round the western spur under the nose, as Jim put
it, of the lion.

Here their pace slackened—first to a sedate trot; finally
to a walk—for the ground was corrugated with narrow
gullies cut into the earth by the hill borne floods of innu-
merable rainy seasons. The gigantic boulders which strewed
the ground helped to create an impression that here was
the playground of the savage gods of a childish people.

THEN, SUDDENLY, devastatingly loud in
contrast to the silence which had hitherto encompassed
the place, a mass of rock halfway up the steep slopes of the
kopje separated itself from the hill and trundled down the

slope. Slowly at first, but momentarily gathering speed, an avalanche of smaller boulders following in its wake. The noise was comparable to that of an express train rushing through a tunnel.

"The lion roars," said Jim as, having halted the mules, the two men watched the downward rush of the rock.

"It is a warning to us, baas," Jim exclaimed when, after a series of grotesquely gigantic bounds the big mass came finally to halt and a cloud of dust was the only indication that Nature had been busy in her workshop. *"Au-a!* Truly it is a warning. The spirits of the *kop* are angry. They do not want us in this place. Let us go."

The Major laughed.

"For ages, Jim," he said, "the rains and the winds have been moulding the *kop,* cutting into the flaws. It is not the work of spirits, but of time."

"The baas is all wise," Jim muttered, "but he cannot explain why the rock fell today—at this moment—instead of yesterday, or tomorrow, unless it was to warn us. So I say again, let us go north and forget the debt Oom Paul owes us. *Wo-we!* The wealth of the world is ours for the taking— if the baas desires wealth. What need then to beg for the puny reward a Boer farmer can pay?"

The Major's lips set in an obstinate line. "Men call Oom Paul rich. It is just that he pay for services rendered. And so—I go to collect."

"What, baas? Has he gold?"

"Who knows. But what he has—that I will take. And he will still be in debt to me."

"No man will deny that, baas," Jim agreed with a sigh. "But still I do not like this place and I say it would be best to heed the warning of the spirits.

"Listen! They speak again!" As he spoke the veld air was split by a sharp report. Another followed—then another and another.

"The spirits speak," said Jim, but the grin on his face belied the tremor he endeavored to force into his voice.

"Truly, Jim," the Major drawled in English. "And they speak with high powered rifles." In the vernacular he added, "Since when, Jim, have the spirits spoken through the mouth of white men's guns?"

"The spirit of death has spoken that way," Jim said, "since man first made guns. And now at least it is clear, is it not, baas, that this is no place for us?"

Jim started to swing the mules round, evidently intending to return to the original course which would take them away from Lion's Head Kop.

The Major stopped him.

"We are not children, Jim," he said, "to run from a splitting rock or the noise of guns. It may be—" and his eyes lighted with the joy of anticipation—"that a game is being played in which we can take a hand. At any rate we go and see."

HE TOOK the reins from Jim and pulled the mules to a halt.

"We are children indeed," Jim observed dolefully as he watched the Major buckle a cartridge belt and take a rifle from the slings which hung from the roof of the wagon. "What does the baas mean to do?"

"I am going to climb up to the top of the *kopje,* Jim, to see what is to be seen."

"*Au-a!* Like children we are," Jim said again. "Curiosity rides us. A child once went into a leopard's cave to see what was to be seen. He never came out! Baas, I have no curiosity. Must I then also climb the hill to see what is to be seen?"

The Major laughed.

"There's nothing you'd like better. But no. You stay here, Jim, until I have reached the top. Then you will drive to the homestead of Oom Paul. I will meet you there."

"This is folly, baas," Jim grumbled. "Always when we separate there is trouble. *Au-a!*—" this as another burst of rifle fire sounded. "Whatever game is being played on the other side of the *kop* it is not for us to take a hand. Death is rushing through the air, baas."

"But not for us, Jim, I think. Maybe they are shooting at buck or baboons."

"And there are so many buck, so many baboons in this place," Jim said.

"At any rate, Jim," the Major retorted, laughing at Jim's sarcasm, "we have quarrels with no man in this place. What have we to fear?"

"It is folly to stand between two fighting warriors!" But he resigned himself to whatever Fate had in store for him.

The Major jumped down from the wagon, waved his hand gaily and was presently mounting the lower slopes of Lion's Head Kop.

He made light of the climb despite the furnace heat of the afternoon sun and the fact that the slopes were much steeper than had at first appeared. Steadily he climbed upward, bent forward, his keen eyes picking out the easiest line to follow; instinctively avoiding loose rubble, placing his feet so cleverly that he did not, even, dislodge one tiny pebble.

The black rock—it held imprisoned the heat of count-less cloudless, scorching days—seemed to burn through the soles of his boots and he once permitted himself to regret the impulse which had induced him to undertake the climb.

"Jim is right," he muttered. "The old boy is always right—nearly always. I'm a fool. I create hazards where none exist. I climb hills and ignore the easier trails. And all to no purpose."

BUT THAT mood quickly passed and he resumed his climb with the zest of a man setting out on his first adventure. That in part explains the Major's buoyant youth. He never outgrew his enthusiasm, despite a long career of adventure, and an almost daily risking of his life against wild beasts and men.

Jim, the Hottentot, was like that, too, despite the note of caution and pessimism which he always sounded when some new project was afoot. That was one of the ties which had kept them loyally together—master and man—during the years they had wandered up and down South Africa.

The Major was nearing the crest of the Kop now, skirting a deep scar in the side of the hill. A recently formed scar; a wedge shaped incision which had been made when the boulder had, a short while ago, torn itself away from the hill.

The Major paused to examine it, his eyes first attracted by shining bits of quartz.

"Fool's gold," he said with a laugh as he halted and waved to Jim, who was watching his every movement. The Hottentot, faithful to his instructions, gathered up the reins and drove off at a slow pace. Before he could get on the trail leading to Oom Paul's homestead, he had to make a detour round the *kopje's* base. A good two hours' trek, Jim calculated, if his memory of a previous visit was correct.

"Maybe we will never get there," he muttered.

This last was occasioned by another outburst of rifle fire. It was almost as if the movement of the wagon had been the signal for a resumption of hostilities between the unseen combatants.

THE MAJOR watched Jim drive off; then, very cautiously, crawling on hands and knees, he made for a place where a flat topped rock on the very crest of the *kop* afforded him a good observation post, with small risk of exposing himself to whoever might be on the other side of the *kop*.

This vantage point reached—the moment coincided with the burst of rifle fire which had alarmed Jim—taking every care to avoid exposing himself above the sky line, he swiftly scrutinized the scene before him.

The *kop* sloped steeply down to a vast undulating plain— treeless, but its red soil was masked by bush and luxurious grass. At the foot of the *kopje*—it looked as if it nestled against the rocky walls—was the homestead of Oom Paul. A low whitewashed, mud walled, thatched building—the primitive home of a somewhat primitive man—formed the living quarters.

Clustered about it were the huts of the native laborers. Just beyond was a fenced enclosure where cattle milled about. Here and there a half hearted attempt had been made at cultivation. All in all, it was a typical back veld Boer's homestead, the settlement of a nomadic man forced by age and the changing conditions to a life which was, comparatively, static. The home of a man whose forebears had been compelled to forego the refinements of living and who had come to the point where those refinements seemed useless and greatly to be scorned affectations. White South Africa is peopled by many of like nature. Simple primitives, bigoted, using Nature, but not understanding or appreciating her; accumulating great wealth in the shape of vast herds of cattle—and making no use of their wealth. A strange people; a kindly, hospitable people to those of understanding and who forebear to patronize. A brave people, too, and cunning fighters.

BEYOND THE homestead, gleaming like molten gold in the sunlight, flowed a wide river between precipitous banks. Its course was a winding one; it looked as if the slightest obstacle had diverted it from its path—but its onward sweep was toward a far distant sea.

"Something like the mind of brother Boer," the Major mused. "You can check 'em, you think you can turn 'em aside from their goal—but the check is only for the moment, their purpose remains unchanged." And then, with a shrug of his shoulders, he began to search for signs of human activity at the homestead below.

But he saw nothing.

"Everything looks very peaceful," he said. "But, then, things are not always what they seem.—Look at that, for instance."

That was a white puff of smoke which his supernaturally keen and veld wise eyes detected rising from one of the boulders which littered the veld between the *kop's* base and the homestead.

Other puffs rose from boulders to the right and the left of the first. Then followed a rippling sequence of crisp reports.

Thirteen puffs—thirteen reports.

"A baker's dozen of 'em," said the Major. "This ought to be interesting—very."

And he looked keenly at the rocks, distinguishing behind six or seven of them the forms of crouching men.

TWO MORE reports—fainter than the others; no louder than a child's handclaps—called his attention to the homestead. Two white feathery puffs of smoke floated still in the lazy air, but there was no sign of the men who had fired the shots.

"Wonder what it's all about," the Major mused. "Evidently the homestead is in a state of siege. And it's a lazy sort of siege. Neither side appears to be in a hurry. Maybe the attackers are waiting for the night before they get to close quarters, and the defenders 'll probably try to retreat under cover of darkness." He looked at the sun. "Well, there's at least three hours of daylight left and I rather fancy that I'm going to use a little of it. This seems far too interesting to miss.

"I wouldn't be at all surprised if those chappies down below were also tryin' to collect a little bill from old Oom Paul. And if they collect—thirteen of 'em—there's goin' to be jolly little left for me.

"Therefore—I must collect first. And so; I must move first. No time to lose."

And he moved—swiftly—along the top of the *kopje,* keeping well below the skyline, until he came to a point where the hill dropped steeply down to the river and, he conjectured, was masked from the view of the men at the foot of the hill and also from those who defended the homestead.

AND THERE he halted a moment, considering the best course to take.

"By Jove!" he exclaimed ruefully. "I've been a little—er—precipitate. I shouldn't have sent old Jim on to the homestead. I should have made him wait with the wagon and mules behind the *kopje.* And now the attackers will capture him and try to get to the homestead under cover of the wagon. Sure to. And that means I must hurry. I must get to the homestead first, and collect what I fancy is fair payment from old Oom Paul for services rendered. Quite!"

That thought seemed to spur him to instant action.

Slinging his rifle over his shoulder, he commenced the precipitous descent. He dropped from one jutting spur to another twelve feet below; he leaped over a gaping chasm, from teetering rock to teetering rock. And it was all done so gracefully, so effortlessly! It proclaimed, as nothing else could have proclaimed, the possession of iron nerves; of a superbly muscled and splendidly conditioned body.

The manner of that descent gave the lie to the Major's pose of vacuous inanity.

His last leap brought him to the foot of the *kopje* and to the very edge of the river's steep bank. He could hear the gurgle of swiftly flowing water some twenty feet below. But here the river was narrow and, flowing between undercut banks, invisible.

To his left, up-stream, there was a deep dip—a sort of gully running to the river—in the veld. There the banks were less steep and less than half the height of the place where he was standing.

But to go to that place to start his descent to the river bed entailed the risk of exposing himself to the attackers.

"Just the same," he concluded, "it's a risk I'm going to take."

ON HANDS and knees he started to crawl toward it, taking advantage of every scrap of cover, every sense on the alert. And that was just as well, because, suddenly, he was aware that someone was coming toward him.

Dropping full length behind a boulder, he peered cautiously around the side of his cover. He saw a man crawling toward his place of concealment. A tremendously gross man with a thick black beard. But for all his fatness, "Blackbeard" moved with the skill of a trained hunter, and the Major was lost in admiration of the way in which he took advantage of every scrap of cover.

"He must have heard me," the Major deduced, "and has come to investigate. Judging by the nasty look in his eyes and the way he grips his rifle, his investigation won't be a peaceful one. Therefore, I must not remain here for him to investigate. And that's a nuisance. And he blocks my way to the gully—therefore I've got to go down the bank here. And that's a damned nuisance.

"Of course I might hold him up. That would be easy, because I can see him and he can't see me. But what would be the use? His friends would come along—or at least my presence would be discovered—and my career as a bill collector be brought to a nasty end.

"And so—"

Watching his opportunity, the Major moved from his place of concealment to another rock nearer the bank; from that to another. And, presently, he was hanging by both hands from a ledge of rock which jutted out over the river.

Looking down, he saw that the river was barely fifteen feet below. It was an easy drop and one which could be made in perfect safety.

But still he hesitated.

"Old Blackbeard will hear the splash," he reasoned. "And even if I swung out and landed on that sand bank—I doubt if I could do it—he'll be able to read my spoor. No, that's not good enough. I've got to be killed—that's all there is to it."

For a moment he hung by one hand, with the other hand he removed his helmet and placed it on the ledge of rock, covering his gripping hand.

That done, he hung by both hands again and grunted loudly.

"It ought to look," he told himself, "as if I were standing on a rock peering over the top of the bank. I hope old Blackbeard thinks that. An' I wish the porky old blighter would hurry up."

He grunted again. With one finger he twitched his helmet slightly. His thoughts continued:

"It would be bally awkward if there were some men on the opposite bank. What a ripping target I'd make. But I fancy I'm safe there—I most fervently hope so." Then, "I imagine that a chap shot through the brain dies very silently. But I won't. My word, no. I rather think old Blackbeard would enjoy a little noise. I won't disappoint him!"

"Wish the old blighter 'ud hurry up. My arms are stretching most alarmingly."

He grunted again; once again he wriggled his helmet.

HIS REWARD came quickly.

A thick, guttural voice, alarmingly near, said, "I see you, *roinek,* and I have you covered. Put up your hands, quick, or I will send a bullet through your thick head."

"You go to hell, Dutchy," the Major retorted, affecting a gruff voice. "Two can play at that game. You chuck your rifle over here or I'll drill a hole in you. Quick now!" The Dutchman laughed confidently. He was well hidden behind a rock. His rifle was aimed at the *roinek's* helmet.

"Hands up, you old dirty neck," the Major continued hoarsely. "I'll count three. If you haven't surrendered by then you'll be a dead 'un with only yourself to blame. Now then. One—"

Before he could say "two," the Boer's trigger finger contracted, speeding a bullet on its way.

Almost coincident with the report, the Major uttered a loud, despairing wail, his fingers—they took the helmet with them—slipped from their hold and he dropped with a loud splash into the river below.

The Boer rose slowly to his feet, grinning triumphantly at two others who came running towards him.

"What is it, uncle?" they asked excitedly.

"A *verdoemte roinek*," Blackbeard replied. "Me he tried to hold up! The fool. He was peering over the bank there. He thought I could not see him."

"And you got him, uncle?"

"Could I miss at such a range?" the big man asked complacently. "Through the head I got him. You heard him cry as life rushed out."

"Was he from Oom Paul's place?" one asked.

"How should I know. If 'yes,' then there is one less against us. If 'no,' he has paid the price of interfering. I do not allow strangers to interfere with my affairs!"

The three went to the edge of the bank and looked down into the river.

ON THE edge of the sand bar, almost afloat and stirred by the river's flow, was the Major's helmet. The keen eyes of the Boers—men of the veld, all three—detected a hole in the crown just above the brim. The Major was not in sight. He was crouching under the ledge of rock.

"You did not miss, Uncle," one of the men cried exultantly.

"Almighty, no. I never miss," Blackbeard agreed.

Said the third man:

"But where is the *roinek's* body?"

"Where should it be?" Blackbeard retorted. "At the bottom of the river, or maybe the current has taken it down to the ford at Oom Paul's place. It will be a present for the *slim* old devil. But what matter? Let us get back to our post. Maybe those others—they are sly devils too—will steal a march on us. If we do not watch them they will forget the agreement—"

"If we give those others a chance they will forget the agreement—yes. Then let us forget it first."

Blackbeard chuckled.

"Truly! It would be easy to forget, Nephew. But now is not the time. Those others would not let us go our own way."

"They could not stop us—"

"A bullet in the back will stop a ma-an," Blackbeard pointed out. "And that is what we will get if those others see—"

"They will not see us," the younger man interrupted, "not if we follow my plan. Listen: We will drop from that rock down into the river below. Then we will make our way down stream—the water is not over deep—keeping under shelter of this bank. If those others should see us we will say that we plan only to attack Oom Paul from the rear. But they will not see us. And so we shall take Oom Paul by surprise. We will take what we want and be gone before those others can know what has happened."

BLACKBEARD AND the other man laughed.

"You are *slim*, Nephew," said Blackbeard. "Your plan is a good one."

"And you will follow it?"

"Truly. Now do you drop first from the rocks."

"Almighty, no, Uncle. You are our leader. Yours is the right to go first."

"No—you, Hans."

"Not I—let Pete go first."

"No, it is Hans's plan. He must go first."

And so they squabbled—giving evidence of mutual distrust.

Blackbeard ended the argument. "We will together drop," he said.

They wasted no more time then.

One, two, three—they dropped to the river below.

Once, twice, thrice—the long barrel of the Major's revolver rose and fell.

"This is hardly sportin'," he murmured as he dragged their unconscious bodies onto the sand bar. "But what else could I do?"

One of the men had a length of rope coiled about his shoulders. With this the Major bound the three together—but not so tightly that they could not, after much painful effort release themselves. He thrust improvised gags into their mouths; then, after arranging them so that they looked as if they were asleep, saluted them ironically, recovered his helmet, and hurried down stream; splashing through the shallows, under cover of the undercut bank.

"And three from thirteen leaves ten," he told himself. "That makes the picking a little better for the rest of us."

Then he frowned, adding, "For us? Oh, that's nonsense. I share with no one. And that means that ten more collectors are to be eliminated. Rather."

But the frown still persisted.

SHOTS OCCASIONALLY sounded and angry, guttural shouts of men. But it was not that which creased the Major's forehead and called into being that light of indecision in his gray eyes.

Actually, he was disturbed over the role in which he found himself. A little while ago he had confidently proclaimed his intention to collect a debt. But now, he was not so sure. At any rate, the joy had departed from his actions. If it had not been for the fact that he had undertaken to meet Jim at the homestead, it is more than likely that he would have given up the adventure.

As it was—

Well! The situation was forced upon him and, although he might try to decide himself with the thought that he was playing a lone hand, he knew that, in fact, he was one with the pack which was now besieging the homestead.

"There's nothing to choose between us," he concluded. "Their claim to old Oom Paul's wealth is probably every bit as good as mine. Maybe better, because, legally, I have no claim at all. It's a beastly nuisance. I seem to have plunged headfirst into a hornet's nest of trouble, and forced to turn my hand against—how many? Ten attackers, certainly, and goodness knows how many defenders. Long odds, what?"

He shrugged his broad shoulders, concluding resignedly, "An' there's nothin' I can do but carry on an' play whatever game is on the table."

PRESENTLY HE came to the ford. Here the banks on either side sloped down gently to the river. To the left a crude dirt road led to Oom Paul's place; to the right it wound a snake-like course to some far distant township.

A moment the Major hesitated, considering how best to proceed. His saturated clothes steamed in the sun's heat;

they were plastered with mud. He smeared some mud on his face and on his hair—his jet black, immaculately brushed hair! Then from his tunic pocket he took a monocle—that was his stalking horse, so to speak; the ambush which masked his quick wit—and staggered, like a man who is badly spent, up the road leading to the homestead.

His progress was unchallenged.

He passed by the stockade where the oxen milled about and lowed continuously, as if in protest at being penned up so early in the day. He passed a light, tent-topped, trek-wagon. Peering inside, he saw that it was all loaded, ready for departure; eight speedy looking mules were inspanned. He nodded, pleased at this confirmation of an earlier deduction.

He rounded the huts of the native laborers, surprised that they should be deserted, and so came to the rear of the homestead building.

He heard the sound of women's voices mingled with loud, gasping sobs.

He whistled softly; for the moment the look of futile inanity passed from him; he braced himself as a man does who prepares to face some great physical shock.

That phase swiftly passed and he walked boldly round the end of the long, whitewashed building, coming at length into full view of the veld and the *kop* which he had climbed.

His appearance was greeted by a fusillade of shots. Puffs of smoke rose above distant boulders; dust spurted up from the veld close to where he stood. A bullet thudded into an old brake block a little to his right. Another richocheted from a rock outcrop with a vicious *whee-ang*.

With every appearance of abject fright, the Major rushed to the door of the building and pounded heavily on it, imploring instant admission.

Other shots echoed over the veld; they seemed to carry with them the sneering, contemptuous laughter of the hidden marksmen.

Inside the house the Major heard whispering voices; the sobbing ceased.

"Let me in!" he shouted. "Let me in before they shoot me."

THERE WAS a fumbling noise behind the door; a hand pushed aside the piece of wood which hid the spy hole.

One brown eye regarded him steadily through the aperture.

"Quick!" he gasped.

The eye vanished; the piece of wood dropped down and closed the spy hole.

He heard a low voice say soothingly in the *taal*, "It is all right, *tante*. It is only a fool Englisher. He cannot, I think, help us, but, at least, he can do us no harm."

And another voice, a heavier, age hardened voice said, "Be on guard. Niece. If it is a *roinek*, be on guard. All *roineks* are liars."

This was greeted by a laugh. Then the bolts were pushed back, the door opened suddenly, and the Major sprawled headfirst into the room.

Recovering, he stared, mouth agape, at a tremendously fat woman, who covered him with an old-fashioned elephant gun. Grief now distorted her face which was heavily scored with laughter wrinkles; she tried to hide under a pose of stern suspicion the hearty good comradeship which was her normal attitude toward all the world. Yet, at the same time, she was no simple fool; it would not be easy to impose upon her. She was immensely capable— and shrewd.

"Put up your hands, *roinek,*" she now said. Adding, "You tell him that, too, Niece, in case he understands not the *taal.*"

"I understand," the Major said as he obeyed the command.

The fat woman beamed, then suspicion once again clouded her face.

"You do not look, Englisher," she said, "like a man who has the sense to speak the *taal.*"

The Major shrugged his shoulders. He wanted to see the other woman. The one who was behind him now. She was bolting the door.

"What do you make of him, Niece?" the old woman asked. "Do we trust him—or kill him?"

There was a soft rustle of skirts and the other occupant of the room came into the Major's vision.

SHE STOOD a few paces before the Major and scrutinized him closely. She was almost as tall and strong as he; yet gave the impression of soft daintiness. Her brown eyes were clear and candid; her wealth of honey colored hair hung down her back in two thick plaits; her complexion was perfect; her figure—vaguely masked by the shapeless gown she wore—superb.

"By Jove!" the Major exclaimed. "You are beautiful." Then, embarrassed, as he always was when dealing with women, he stammered apologies.

"Don't spoil it," the girl said with a soft laugh. Turning to the old woman, she added in the *taal:*

"He is quite safe, *Tante!* There is no guile in him."

The old woman nodded shrewdly.

"You may take down your hands, *roinek,*" she said heavily. Adding, as the Major obeyed, "Now tell us who you are?"

"My name," the Major said slowly, "is Aubrey St. John Major. But I am generally called 'the Major.'"

"And what are you doing here, Mister man who is generally called 'the Major'?"

"I came to collect a debt Oom Paul owes me," the Major replied, surprised that the woman—she was Oom Paul's wife—did not recognize him.

"My ma-an," said the old woman, "was a hard ma-an—but just. He always paid his debts. And now he is dead—I myself, will his debts pay. You shall present your bill, *roinek,* at the proper time—and it shall be paid. But now! Almighty! Now I mourn my ma-an's death. Now I wait to punish those who murdered him."

THE MAJOR started. Almost he had forgotten those others who waited out there behind boulders. Hardly once had his eyes left the girl's face. He had been stunned by her surprising beauty.

But now he became instantly alert—yet still hiding the quickness of his brain beneath a pose of vacuous inanity.

"My word!" he exclaimed. "You say Oom Paul is dead?"

The old woman nodded.

"Truly—my ma-an is dead. Those *skellums* killed him. My sons they killed too. They—"

Suddenly she dropped the heavy gun to the ground and, covering her face with her apron, sobbed loudly.

The girl murmured soothing words of comfort; then, going to the window, beckoned to the Major.

"You see!" she said softly when he had joined her.

Looking in the direction of her pointing finger, the Major saw five huddled figures sprawled behind an improvised breastwork.

"There you see," the girl said, "Oom Paul and his four sons."

The Major's jaw dropped.

"And they are dead?"

"But of course. What else? For a while I fought beside them. When they died I propped them up and fired from behind them. But, at last, the good *Tante* called me into the house. She could stand it no longer. And so I dragged them down behind the cover and went to comfort *Tante*."

"But I don't understand," the Major gasped. He was looking out over the veld toward the *kop*, wondering why Jim was so slow putting in an appearance; wondering why those five silent figures—experienced veld men, all of them—should have exposed themselves to the fire of their enemies.

"Who are those men out there?"

"Scum!" she replied bitterly. "Oom Paul's kin—but scum just the same. They envied his wealth, the fruits of his industry. Yesterday they sent a messenger demanding that Oom Paul divide his wealth and his oxen with them. They claimed Oom Paul owed them much money. If he did not share with them—truly they had never worked, the lazy, devil-possessed *skellums*—they said they would take it all. His brothers and their sons sent him such a message.

"And Oom Paul and his sons, they beat the messenger and sent him away empty handed. That was at yesterday's sundown. This morning they opened fire on us. Their first volley wounded Oom Paul; their second killed one of his sons. And all through this day they have fired when any of us showed ourselves. One by one they got my other uncles and, at last, Oom Paul. Me—they did not fire at. A very small thing to their credit. And now—"

She spread her hands in a helpless gesture.

The Major frowned.

"But I still do not understand. Why did Oom Paul and his sons expose themselves after the first volley? They could have sheltered behind the house, or in the house. There was no need for them to have died."

"I know," the girl admitted. "It was that which puzzled me. But Oom Paul—he was very obstinate. No one dared go against him—would have it that way. In some things today, until he died, he was like a madman. He insisted that my uncles build that breastwork. He made them gather all the old brake blocks which were lying about. I think," she smiled wryly, "Oom Paul must have been collecting old brake blocks for years. And it was when my uncles and Oom Paul—he was my grandfather; *Tante,* in there, is my grandmother—were getting brake blocks that they were killed."

The Major nodded—but it was not a gesture of understanding. He was still greatly puzzled.

"They must be very bold, those men out there," he said, "that they dare to murder—"

The girl laughed shortly.

"They run no risk. Who dare arrest them? They are loyal burghers. Three of them are Field Cornets. They will say that they came to collect a tax and that Oom Paul resisted them. And that, in a sense, is true. Oom Paul never paid a tax. He had beaten other men who were sent to collect. He was a hard man, my grandfather, and his death will cause no one sorrow—except to *Tante* and me. We loved him because we knew him so well. And so those men out there will escape punishment for the evil they have done. Truly!

They will be thanked by the burghers. And they will take to themselves all the wealth that was Oom Paul's."

THE MAJOR glanced round the crudely furnished room.

"And was Oom Paul so wealthy?" he asked.

The girl shrugged her shoulders.

"They say so," she said. "But never have I seen any proof of it. He has *only two ox teams;* he has always lived simply; he went nowhere; he spent nothing. And yet—"

"And yet?" the Major prompted.

"He has all his life been very cunning. He has dealt heavily in oxen. He has bought and sold land. He has loaned money at high interest—yet, now he is dead, we are penniless."

"Perhaps the *Tante* knows where he has hidden his wealth."

"She knows nothing. I thought perhaps he had banked his money, but I have been all through his papers and have found nothing to give me a clue."

"Then maybe those others know—"

She shook her head.

"They can know nothing. If my grandfather had money, the secret of the hiding place has died with him."

"And now what?"

The girl shrugged her shoulders.

"We wait—my grandmother and I—until those jackals summon up enough courage to come to us. We wait until they come within sure range of our guns. Then we will make them pay. Truly we will make them pay."

"But you cannot kill them all, dear miss," the Major protested. "Ten cunning men—and darkness is coming."

"Thirteen men," she amended. "And we are cunning too."

"No—only ten," the Major said, and told her of his encounter with Blackbeard.

SHE LOOKED at him curiously.

"You are not altogether a fool, I think. And there's much about you I would like to know—but not now. Not now."

The Major bowed.

"Agreeing I'm not a fool—won't you take my advice?"

"And that is?"

"Offer no resistance to those men out there. Believe me, that is the best."

She looked at him scornfully. "That is a coward's plan," she said. "That we could have done long ago. Oom Paul had the mules inspanned so that we could go. But we would not leave him then. We will not leave him now." Turning away from him the girl joined her grandmother, who had recovered from her outburst of grief. The old woman had retrieved her gun; her gnarled hands closed determinedly about the stock.

The Major looked at them thoughtfully, then turned to the window again.

He saw that there was no hope of attempting to persuade the two women to surrender and thus avoid fruitless bloodshed. The pioneer spirit ran too strongly in them both for them to follow such a course. Their men folk had been killed and they meant to avenge them at all costs. And the outcome, the Major knew, would be a very terrible one. Death for the old woman. Death, and perhaps worse, for the girl.

The sun was very low now. In an hour, at the most, it would be dark. And still Jim did not appear. The Major worried a great deal about Jim.

"They've captured him, most like," he mused. "Perhaps they've killed him. If they have—"

AND THEN he had other things to think of. Mounted men suddenly came from behind the distant rocks and rode at an easy canter toward the homestead.

"Wonder why I didn't see their horses," he mused. "Probably they were down in a ravine—not that it matters.

"And now what?"

With a cry of alarm, his face distorted with an appearance of fear, he sprang away from the window and looked wildly about the room.

"They're coming," he said. "Where can I get out of here?"

The girl laughed coldly and pointed to the front door.

He shook his head.

"No. They'll see and shoot me if I go that way. Is there no back way?"

She pointed then to a small window at the rear. It was shuttered; otherwise he must have seen it.

"It is small. But perhaps you can get through. Truly you are *very* small."

He winced at the scornful contempt in her voice.

"This is not my affair," he retorted.

He paused behind the two women, snatching a large cloth from the table as he did so.

The next moment he had flung it over their heads.

The old woman's gun went off with a deafening roar. The girl's revolver spat spitefully.

They struggled, but the cloth hampered them and the Major, grabbing one of the *reims* which hung from a nail driven into the wall, bound them securely with the tough rawhide rope.

Then he removed the cloth from their heads.

The two women looked at him angrily; the old one white with the anger which rendered her speechless.

"And I thought you could be trusted," the girl said, and spat at him.

"Listen," he said. "I came to collect a debt. And I'm going to collect. You say Oom Paul had no money. I say it is hidden in the flour bags he had loaded on the wagon. And the wagon was all ready for you to get away, the mules inspanned, as soon as darkness came. Yes! You are clever. But I am clever too. So—good-by, dear miss."

He bowed, laughing mockingly.

He unbolted the front door, flung it wide open, and looked at the oncoming horsemen—they were very near now. He could see that their rifles were slung across their backs. Running from the house, he rounded it and sped to where the mules waited so patiently.

He heard shots—and grinned triumphantly.

HE CLIMBED up into the wagon, and gathered the reins into his hands. But, instead of driving off, he sat there waiting.

He heard the thunder of galloping hoofs; saw a cloud of dust rise above the homestead as the riders reined to an abrupt halt.

He heard harsh voices.

Then as two horsemen appeared around the end of the building the Major, with every appearance of frantic haste, swung the mules round and commenced to move down the trail leading to the ford.

The horsemen spurred up to him.

Covering him with their rifles, they commanded him to halt. He obeyed them.

One dismounted and climbed up onto the wagon and looked shrewdly at its contents.

"What game do you play, *roinek?*" he asked gruffly.

"Oom Paul owed me some money and I've collected," the Major answered sullenly.

"Almighty! Do not lie, *roinek*. You mean you are trying to steal Oom Paul's treasure. But we are too clever for you. Get down. We will see what Andries has to say to you."

"Listen," the Major said hurriedly. "Why lie? I'll speak the truth. Yes; I found out—I made the women tell me—where old Oom Paul hid his money. It's in there—in the flour sacks underneath that pile of rubbish at the back of the wagon." He spoke loudly so the other man could hear him. "Well! I know what your game is. You too are after old Oom Paul's treasure. And there are a lot of you. It will not be very much when it is divided amongst ten. And Andries—he is your leader, not?—he will take a big share. But divided between us three, equally—"

The man in the wagon looked at his companion.

"The *roinek* speaks wisely, not?"

The other nodded.

"*Ja!*" he said. "But why share with him? Hurry, before Andries comes."

"But listen—" the Major commenced to expostulate.

A heavy fist struck him in the chest, knocking him from the wagon to the ground.

THE NEXT moment the wagon moved off at a fast pace, the horseman riding closely behind it. Down to the ford, over the river, up the other side and over the veld they galloped.

The Major sat up, laughing softly.

Three men came running to him, questioning him excitedly.

"They've gone off," he gasped, "with Oom Paul's money. They robbed me—"

The men dragged the Major before a thin, red whiskered man who was sitting on the top of the improvised breastwork.

His face became inflamed with passionate anger when he heard of the double dealing of four of his followers.

He shouted orders.

Two men came running from the homestead.

"The women will not speak, Andries," one said. "Shall I use the *sjambok?*"

Andries silenced him.

"That *skellum* Hans and his brother have got the money. After them, before they lose themselves in the darkness."

THE MEN hurried, but they had all unsaddled, and precious time was lost before they galloped after the fugitives.

"You'll let me have my share," the Major shouted.

A curse was the only response.

Thereat the Major sat down on the breastwork and laughed until the tears ran down his cheeks. Presently he sobered and went into the house and unbound the women.

The old woman glared at him; the girl's eyes were speculative.

"I was right after all," she said when he explained what he had done. "You are to be trusted unless—" she hesitated—"unless you are playing the game for yourself. Unless you hope to find out from us where grandfather's reputed wealth is. Are you?"

The Major met her gaze.

"To tell you the truth, I'd forgotten all about it," he said.

The girl nodded.

"We couldn't tell you, anyway," she said.

Rifle shots sounded faintly and the old woman laughed grimly.

"Almighty!" she exclaimed. "Already our vengeance has begun. They are killing each other. That was a *slim* plan of yours, *roinek*. But vengeance won't put life into my men. *Aie!* Vengeance is empty comfort."

The tears came again, a noisy flood of them.

The Major, in response to a gesture from the girl, tiptoed out of the house. Just as he did so, Jim the Hottentot, looking very shamefaced, drove up.

"You are all right then, baas?" he exclaimed in tones of relief.

"Truly, Jim. But where have you been?"

"*Au-a*, baas! For once I was blind. Into a mire I drove. The mules were embogged—they could not pull out the wagon. I had to unload—"

"It is just as well, Jim. Had you come earlier I could not, perhaps, have done what I have done."

"And what have you done, baas."

"Kept a woman from shedding blood, Jim."

The Hottentot raised his eyebrows.

He pointed with his whip at the bodies of Oom Paul and the old man's sons.

"But blood has been shed, baas. Did you—?"

"Nay, Jim."

"Shall I outspan, baas?"

"No, Jim. We must trek on; even after darkness we must trek. Those others have gone on, they will not return. But—"

HE HASTENED into the house, having suddenly remembered the three men he had left bound on the sand bar.

Already they might have freed themselves.

He explained matters to the two women.

"I will take you," he said, "to the *dorp*. You cannot stay here."

They agreed.

"But," said the old woman. "My husband and my sons. I cannot let them stay out to be food for the hyenas. Bring them in here."

The Major nodded.

With Jim's help he carried the bodies into the house.

"Now leave me for a little while," said the old woman. "You go too, Katje."

They left her, the girl climbing up into the wagon, while Jim and the Major conversed in low tones.

"And you have received payment for the debt which was owing, baas?"

"Why talk of that now, Jim?" the Major said shortly. "I was wrong—rumor was wrong. Oom Paul had no money."

He climbed up into the wagon and sat beside the girl.

Jim laughed softly.

"It is in my mind," he said to himself, "that my baas did not think of the debt once he got to this place."

The door of the house opened and closed again.

The old woman came to the wagon and, assisted by the Major and Jim, climbed into it.

"I have bid farewell to my man," She said stolidly. "And now I am ready to go. But it is hard to go thus—a pauper, having nothing."

The girl, Katje, tried to comfort her.

"I have nothing, I tell you," the old woman wailed. "Almighty! My word I gave to this *roinek* that I would pay the debt owing him. And now I cannot keep my word."

"You can," the Major said. "Long ago, for a little service I did, Oom Paul offered me a brake block. Because I was very young—truly I did not know how necessary a brake block is—I refused it. But now—

"Put one of those brake blocks in the wagon, Jim," he ordered.

And as the Hottentot obeyed, he continued:

"There—the debt is paid. Think no more of it, *Tante*."

A moment later they drove off at a fast canter, heading toward a distant township.

IT WAS three weeks later. The Major and Jim were outspanned at the foot of the *kop* which overlooked the homestead of Oom Paul.

The Major was seated in a deck chair at the opening of his bell tent, watching Jim, who was indulging in the veld-traveller's spring cleaning. In other words, Jim was clearing out the wagon, putting its contents into two piles.

As he worked, Jim looked frequently at his beloved baas, wondering at his somewhat pensive expression.

"It is because of the woman," Jim told himself with a sage nod. "Ever since the baas said farewell to her he has been like this. *Wo-we!* Like a moonstruck youth he has acted. But it will soon pass. Now we are on the veld again he will remember that the sun is warmer than a woman's smile, the stars are brighter than her eyes. *Au-a!*"

From the wagon he took an old brake block—that same one the Major had taken as payment for the debt Oom Paul owed him. With an expression of disgust, grunting under its weight, Jim put it on the pile of stuff to be discarded.

"No, not there, Jim," the Major said sharply. "I keep that."

"Wherefore, baas?" Jim grumbled, kicking the block. It was about two feet long, six inches by six.

"Why keep it, baas?" Jim asked again.

"It is a memory, Jim," the Major said.

"It is best, sometimes, to forget," Jim replied sulkily.

But he moved the block to the other pile.

The Major rose and went into the tent.

PICKING UP an ax, Jim struck the block with it in a fit of childish temper.

Struck again and again.

Then, "baas, baas!" he cried.

As the Major came running to the call, Jim pointed to the block which his blows had split in two, exposing six holes which had been bored through the block with an inch auger. The holes had then been rammed with sovereigns, and plugged with wood and mud.

Jim capered about excitedly.

"The baas's debt is paid," he cried. "*Wo-we!* It is wealth."

"It is even more than wealth, Jim. It is opportunity."

In a very little while they had loaded the wagon, the mules were inspanned, and they drove swiftly to the homestead of Oom Paul.

IT WAS now a place of desolation. It had been looted by Oom Paul's kin; the floor of the living house had been dug up in their search for the murdered man's wealth.

The brake blocks which had formed Oom Paul's breastwork were scattered about—almost hidden by the rank grass which had sprung up.

These blocks—one or two of them the Major split, discovering them to be loaded with sovereigns like the first—the Major and Jim loaded onto the wagon.

"That is all, baas," Jim said, grinning happily. "Truly the debt is now paid in full."

"Not yet, Jim."

"No, baas? Then what now?"

"You shall see in time."

A few minutes later they were heading for the distant township where Katje was working to support her aged grandmother. There was only one course for an honest man to take; and the Major, despite rumors to the contrary, was essentially honest. Besides, only Katje, herself, could pay to him the debt her grandfather incurred.

And the Major hoped to collect.

THE MAJOR SETS
A TRAP

THE NATIVE knew that death was very
near, but he faced the knowledge with the fatalistic,
Spartan-like composure of his race.

He was terribly thin, emaciated almost to the point of
starvation. His naked body was plastered by mud, reddened
by blood from his wounds and caked hard by Africa's sun.
One arm, terribly torn, dangled helplessly downward; his
breathing was painful, each indrawn breath was a gasp of
pain.

He was lying full length along the branch of a thorn tree,
clinging desperately with his one arm, staring down with
fever-reddened eyes, at the fate which awaited him should
he lose his hold and fall to the ground.

And even if his failing strength enabled him to outlast
out the death which waited so patiently below, death was
just as sure, ultimately. A few hours more of life—that was
all. The vultures which perched in nearby trees knew that,
and waited with ghoulish patience.

The African bush is never over-kind to humans; to one
incapacitated, deprived of all means of defense, it is hell-
ishly cruel. The bush scavengers are patient up to a point;
but they rarely wait for the very end.

Four of the obscene birds flew heavily over to the tree where the native was. They alighted on a branch immediately above and craned their naked necks inquiringly downward. They croaked derisively.

The native shouted feebly and moved his legs up and down.

The vultures took flight again, and on the ground below two cats—a lion and his mate—which had been crouching motionless, almost invisible in the shafts of sunlight which shot through the bush, became galvanized into action.

They leaped upward, snarling viciously, but just failed to reach the native's refuge.

He spat at them and their snarls increased to deafening roars at the insult. The air vibrated with their clamor and the vultures, croaking protestingly, took flight, circling ponderously over the place.

Presently the lions, sensing the futility of their leaps, subsided. Once again they crouched silently, yellow eyes upturned. Once again the vultures settled. The branch immediately above the native creaked under their weight.

The native was very still, his body limp, his eyes closed. It seemed that his last gesture of defiance had completely sapped his strength.

A vulture hopped down on the branch where he lay.

IN THE African bush sound travels far. The roars of the lions reached the ears of a white man and his Hottentot servant who were driving their light trek wagon at a leisurely gait along a winding apology of a road.

The white man pulled the eight sleek mules to a halt.

"Lions, Jim!" he exclaimed.

"Yah, baas," the Hottentot replied wearily. "And that means we turn once again from the trail. *Au!* That has been our life since we first came together, baas. Never do we keep to the broad road; never do we get to our journey's end. Always we turn aside: to pull a man from a bog; to rescue fowls from their folly; to take upon ourselves the grievances of others; to—"

The white man stood up on the wagon seat and looked over the sea of bush in the direction from which came the roars of the man-eaters. His gray eyes narrowing somewhat as he scrutinized the bush, he said in the vernacular, "Ah—look, Jim. There are vultures."

"But of course, baas," the Hottentot replied with a hint of sarcasm. "The lions are at their kill. When they are full, then the vultures feast— But what of it? It is all one to us. We are not going to turn from the trail because of the roar of lions?" He added abjectly, as the Major dropped down on to the seat, picked up the reins and swung the mules off the road, heading them in the direction of the lions, "But we are! I knew it. It is as I said."

"And why not, Jim? What need of haste?"

"No need, baas. No need. Yet it was only a little while ago the baas said he desired to return to the diamond town. A little while ago the baas said nothing would delay him. But now he turns aside because lions roar."

The Major was concentrating on his driving. Here was no road at all and it required all his skill to avoid wrecking the wagon.

THEY WERE silent for a little while. The bush thinned; the ground was soft, and their progress was comparatively silent.

"The wind blows from them to us, Jim?"

"Yah, baas," the Hottentot agreed. A little while later he put a tentative hand on the Major's coat sleeve.

"Baas, it comes to me that if we continue on this course we run into danger."

"Danger!" the Major scoffed. "Danger from lions—from vermin? We are neither of us untried hunters."

"True, baas. But this—this may be a trap."

The Major laughed aloud.

"Folly, Jim! Fool's folly you speak. Trap! Who would want to trap me here where I am unknown? Where I have no enemies?"

"The baas is modest," Jim grumbled. "Where is not the 'Mah-jor' known. As for enemies—*wo-we!* Evil is always the enemy of good. And where can we go and find not evil?"

The Major pulled the mules to a halt. "The heavy rifle, Jim," he said curtly. "I go on from here afoot. You will stay with the wagon."

Silently, making no more protests, Jim handed his baas the heavy Express rifle and with a gay wave of his hand, the Major jumped down lightly from the wagon. The next moment he had vanished from sight.

Jim grinned.

"*Wo-we!*" he exclaimed, "the baas is a great hunter. As strong as an elephant, he moves with the speed of a springbok, with the silence of a snake. *Au-a!* He is a man amongst men. And I—I am Jim, his servant."

And then Jim's ugly face set in stern lines as he listened intently; and his eyes searched the surrounding bush. He was not to be trapped by the ambushes which Nature sets in Africa.

But, despite his self-control, he started violently when, presently, the vicious report of a high-powered rifle split the air. It was followed instantly by another shot, and a series of coughing grunts and the blood-curdling roars of lions.

Jim tensed; his lips moved rapidly as he whispered a charm to protect his baas. Lions are vermin; they are gross cowards; but because of the uncertaintly of their reactions, because it is impossible to guess their movements, they are always dangerous.

The sky beyond was now blackened by vultures which soared reluctantly upward, their croakings indicative of disappointment.

PRESENTLY THEY appeared for a little while like black astigmatic spots against the cloudless blue sky. Then—they vanished.

Some of the tenseness departed from the Hottentot.

"That," he mused, "is like my baas! There was death. Now there is life." He rubbed his strong, muscular hands together; he cracked, one by one, his finger joints.

But then more shots fired in quick succession. A pause; then another shot. Again Jim's heart was filled with fear.

He picked up the reins and shouted hoarsely to the mules. They responded readily—had he not trained them with the skill that seems to be part of a Hottentot's natural equipment?

And at last Jim pulled the mules to a blowing, sweating halt, on the edge of a clearing, with a loud cry of relief.

He jumped down from the wagon and ran to where his baas stooped over the motionless body of a native.

He almost tripped over the body of a dead lion; its mate was only a few feet distant. Jim barely glanced at them or at the ground; but his supernormally keen eyes had noted the spoor and his hunter's sense enabled him to read the story written there.

His baas, he realized, had been very near death. The lioness had reached almost within striking distance before she had succumbed to the heavy bullet which had bit into her brain.

"Baas," Jim cried, expressing in that one word all the affection he felt for the white man, and an understanding of the danger he had faced.

The Major looked up. His gray eyes were very stern.

"This one," he said, indicating the prostrate native, "was on the branch up there. He fell as I made the second kill. I think death is very near."

Jim knelt down beside his baas and examined the native carefully.

"He looks, baas," Jim said, "as if he had been in the Fork."

"The Fork, Jim?" the Major exclaimed.

"Truly, baas—" as he spoke the Hottentot with sensitive, understanding fingers, was probing the native's hurts. "He was a slave. Maybe he ran away from his masters. Look, baas!" And the Hottentot pointed to the half of a broken, old-fashioned handcuff, rust red, which was on the man's left wrist.

The Major nodded understandingly.

"What think you, Jim?" he asked. "Will he live?"

The Hottentot shrugged his broad shoulders.

"Who knows, baas. I think yes, if his will tells him to live. His belly is empty—we must fill it slowly. And—" His finger tips were exploring the native's ribs— "These bones are broken. *Wo-we!* You can feel them creak. But they can be mended; his arm can be mended. But as to whether he will live or not I cannot say. And I think, baas, it were better that he died than that you should have risked your life to those evil ones."

The Major made a gesture of impatience, then he and the Hottentot got speedily to work.

They washed the native's wounds in water which they first boiled over a fire. They bandaged his arm, covering it with a healing ointment—an evil-smelling compound of Jim's mixing. They bandaged his ribs tightly.

When the native opened his eyes and stared weakly about him, eager to ask questions, but restrained by fear, they fed him a little of the nourishing soup which Jim warmed up over the fire.

Then they carried him to the wagon and made him comfortable there on a pile of blankets. A few minutes later the trek was resumed. But at a very sober pace. They made wide, sweeping detours to avoid crossing rough ground where the jolting of the wagon might cause the injured native pain.

They talked very little.

Once Jim said, "Shall we camp here, baas, and go on to the kraal in the morning."

"I think not, Jim," the Major had replied. "We will get the sick one to his people without delay. In the morning we trek south."

"I think not, baas," Jim replied lugubriously. "It comes to me now that many days will pass before we trek for the diamond town. And I like not this place. Evil is loose in the bush hereabouts, baas."

"Foolish croaker, Jim," the Major said banteringly. "I have killed all the evil."

"Two lions you have killed, baas," Jim replied. "But there are other lions—there is greater evil."

IT WAS after sundown when they came to the kraal built in the heart of the bush; a kraal surrounded by an unusually stout stockade of thorn bush and another inner one of stout poles. Between the two a deep, stake-armored ditch was built, and the narrow entrance was carefully camouflaged.

And yet it was a very small, poverty-stricken kraal. Its residents could have little wealth to tempt stronger neighbors. Having that in mind, the elaborate stockades puzzled the Major. He was puzzled, too, that none of the kraal's inhabitants had shown themselves; that they made no sound. Not even a dog barked.

"They are asleep," he said to Jim.

"Or dead, baas," the Hottentot replied grimly.

Swiftly, with the ease of experienced veldsmen, the two men outspanned the mules, hobbled them and turned them loose to graze. In a very little while, before darkness triumphed over sunset's red afterglow, the Major's white bell tent was erected, his bed made and shrouded by a mosquito net. Just outside the tent the pleasant, aromatic fumes of the smudge fire drifted lazily on the still air, routing all flying pests. There stood a small table spread with snowy linen. The silverware on it gleamed in the white light of the lamp which hung from the overhanging branch of a tree.

The Major lounged in a deck chair near by. He had changed his trekking clothes had bathed, shaved and was now clad in a suit of spotless white duck. A gold-rimmed monocle gleamed in his right eye. That and the way his jet black hair was brushed back in an immaculate pompadour, made it seem impossible that he could be the same man who had, only a little while ago, stalked and killed two lions. He looked the utter opposite of the popular conception of a big game hunter: A gilded popinjay?—yes. A man of action?—most decidedly no!

He smoked, delicately blowing rings, and watched Jim prepare the evening meal. Jim, too, had bathed and changed. But the white duck trousers he wore and the spotless white shirt, failed to transform his appearance. He was still the savage; the black child of black Africa. The clothes of civilization failed to disguise the strength of his powerful chest and his abnormally long arms.

Nevertheless, he presently served his baas with the facility and gravity of demeanor of an English butler.

HAVING EATEN, the Major rose from his chair, lighted another cigarette and paced restlessly up and down.

"It is strange, Jim," he said, in answer to the Hottentot's grunt of inquiry, "that curiosity has not driven them out to see who we are and what our errand."

"Maybe their fear is greater than their curiosity, baas. Wait until morning, then they will swarm about you, offending your nostrils with the stink of their unwashed bodies."

Long association with the Major had made Jim over contemptuous of kraal-dwelling natives and their uncleanly habits.

"I am going into the kraal, Jim," the Major said. "I do not like this silence."

"Wait until morning, baas," Jim pleaded, "and there will be noise enough." The Major shook his head.

"I go now, Jim. You stay here to guard the wagon and tend the sick one."

"At least, baas," Jim pleaded, "take your gun with you."

"I have my voice, Jim. Is that not enough?"

"It is enough, baas, if the men who dwell there will listen to you."

There was no answer, and the Hottentot continued, speaking to himself. "And truly I have known the baas's voice turn an *assegai* from its mark. I have known the baas's voice put an end to a fight between two warring *impis*."

The Hottentot, thus self-comforted, forgot the half-formed fears and busied himself making everything snug for the night. He caught the mules and tethered them to the wagon wheels. He washed the dishes, replenished the fire and saw that there was enough fuel on hand to last through the night.

That done, he satisfied his own gargantuan appetite, brushed his teeth with a twig broken from a *mapani* bush, then squatted on his haunches before the fire.

FOR A long time he remained thus; apparently emotionless, looking as if he were graven from Africa's soil.

After a while a spirit of uneasiness stirred him to restless movement, and he rose to his feet.

"I do not like it," he muttered. "All this time the baas has been gone—and no sound comes to my ears. *Wo-we!* He has entered the kraal of the dead—and death has taken him." He paced restlessly up and down. *"T'chat!"* he exclaimed, having come to a decision. "Then I go there too. But not empty-handed." He chuckled grimly. "No. My voice holds no charm like the baas's; so my hands must bear charms."

He took down the lamp and climbed into the wagon, intending to arm himself with knobkerries and *assegais.*

As the lamp illuminated the wagon's interior the injured man opened his eyes and groaned. With his uninjuried hand he beat against the floor board, signalling for attention.

Impatiently, the Hottentot went to him, shielding the light so that it did not dazzle the sick man's eyes.

"I am thirsty. I am hungry," the sick iman whispered hoarsely.

Jim grunted. He was in a hurry to go after his baas, fearing that the Major had met with some ill fate. Yet, because he knew his baas would have so desired it, he efficiently ministered to the sick man's needs.

"Au-a!" that man gasped at length with a sigh of relief, holding on to the Hottentot's arm when Jim would have gone. "Stay a little. There is much I want to know."

"Let me go," Jim retorted roughly. "There is much I want to do."

But the other did not relax his hold and Jim, not wishing to use force, stayed. "Well?" he questioned.

"Strength comes back to me. I remember—"

"With strength comes a woman's wagging tongue," Jim growled.

But the other ignored him. "I remember a white man appearing suddenly in the bush," he said. "He killed the lion. The lioness charged him; but he did not move. *Au-a!*" He was a man."

"He is my baas," Jim observed.

"So? Then you should be proud, Hottentot. The lioness charged him—and he killed her. The rest I do not remember. Now call your baas to me that I may thank him."

"*Wo-we!* My baas is no dog that he should run because you call," Jim exclaimed angrily. Then, sadly, "I think my baas has gone to the land of the Spirits."

"What mean you? Did the lioness kill him."

"No, fool. Nothing mortal can harm my baas. He is all wise; all powerful. But, listen: At sun-under we came to this place and made camp not more than six spear throws from a kraal. Yet none came from that kraal to give us greeting. No dogs barked. In it, there seemed no life. And after all had been done as we, who are no common travelers, are accustomed to do, my baas went into the kraal. Into the darkness he went. And—*Au-a!* Since then a long time has passed and no sound has come to my ears. *Au-a!* And I waste time talking idly to you. I must go to my baas."

"Wait!" The other's voice was imperious; his fingers closed more tightly about the Hottentot's arm. "Tell me where we are? Describe this kraal to me."

And Jim the Hottentot obeyed, giving, in a few trenchant sentences a masterly word portrait of the kraal and the country immediately surrounding it.

"And toward the place of the sun's rising—" he was concluding when the native interrupted him.

"Quick!" he gasped. "We must go to that kraal—which is *my* kraal."

"I go alone," the Hottentot said. "You cannot walk."

"You must carry me then. *Au-a!* If you go alone you will meet death, Hottentot. Carry me—unless your strength is less than a woman's. If that is so I must walk.

"Now hurry. Hurry!"

Jim grunted agreement.

A FEW minutes later, carrying the native before him in his arms, the lantern hanging from his hand, he went up to the kraal.

At a whispered order he halted before the narrow gateway through the double stockade.

"What now?" he asked.

"Sound the call of a bell bird—thrice," the other replied between grunts of pain.

"It is a child's game," Jim grumbled, but he sounded the dismal note of a bell bird.

"And now what?"

"Wait—listen!"

Behind the stockade a voice challenged softly. "Who seeks entrance to the kraal of Chivamba now that night has fallen?"

And the man in the Hottentot's arms answered, "It is I, Chindi, Chivamba's son, who awaits entrance."

"Chindi is dead—or at least has gone from us. And yet—it is his voice."

"Fool. I am not dead. And I have come back to you. The white man you hold saved me from death; he and his black dog, a Hottentot, who now carries me in his arms. Talk no more—you, whose voice is the voice of Bombva—but let me enter. My bones are broken, my spirit weakens. Let us enter before great evil is done to the white man who saved me."

"Aye, hasten," shouted the Hottentot, unable to restrain himself any longer, "and be assured if any harm has come to my baas I will tear down this place and give your bodies to the hyenas."

"The dog barks loudly," the voice replied with a chuckle. "And now I open the way for you. If you have lied you will find it leads to death."

There was a noise of poles being removed; of thorn bush being pulled to one side. And then, "Enter!" said the voice.

As Jim, stooping a little under his burden, went forward, four armed natives pressed about him. They took the lantern from his hand and silently examined the features of the man he carried.

"*Au-a!*" one exclaimed. "It is indeed Chindi come back to us. Give him to us, Hottentot. It is our right that he should be our burden."

"I carry him," Jim replied. "He is now hostage for my baas's safety."

"Let the Hottentot have his way," Chindi interposed feebly, when the others would have used force, "and let us hasten to the hut of the chief.

WITHOUT FURTHER delay they escorted Jim through a maze of thorn hedged passageways until they came finally to a large hut. This they entered.

The hut was lighted by flickering torches which paled before the white glare of the lamp, held by one of the natives escorting Jim.

A thin age-shrunken native—the thatch of his head and his straggling beard, snow white—sat on a carved stool in the center of the hut. Other gray-beards sat on his right and left.

They all stared incredulously at the man the Hotten-tot carried and then the old man exclaimed brokenly, "Chindi—my son—is it really you?"

"Aye. I am no ghost," Chindi answered. "But that I would be, were it not for the white man and this one who carries me. Where is the white man? Has any harm been done him?"

"No—not yet."

"Nor must not. Bring him here. The Hottentot holds my life in his hands as hostage for his baas's safety."

"I have sworn an oath—" the old chief said slowly.

But Chindi interrupted impatiently, "And is my life of less value than an unwise oath?"

"It would be easy to take you unharmed from the Hottentot and—"

"Not easy," Jim boasted.

"And *his* life is forfeit too."

"If harm comes to the white man or the Hottentot," Chindi said stoutly, with a final surge of strength, "I will die. And that is my oath."

There was a moment's pause. Then, "Fetch the white man," the old chief ordered. And to Jim, "Now let me have my son, Hottentot."

"Not until I have seen my baas and *know* he is unharmed. Not until I have your word that no harm shall come to us."

The old chief nodded.

"My word I give. By the son I thought dead, but who lives, I swear that no harm shall be done you. In a little while the white man will be here; then you shall give me my son."

And so, for a time, the pose was held. Jim in the center of the hut holding Chindi in his arms; the eyes of the graybeards and of the warriors riveted on him. Joy at the return of one they had thought dead was suppressed by a racial stoicism; but not even the custom of ages could kill the light of pleasure which shone in their eyes.

And Chindi—he succumbed again to the weakness born of long days of brutality and starvation. His eyes closed; his body sagged limply in Jim's arms.

PRESENTLY THERE was a sound of scuffling feet outside, and the Major entered, blinking at the blaze of light.

His hands were tightly bound behind his back, his clothing was torn and covered with filth. His left eye was partially closed and discolored, but in his right eye the monocle still gleamed mockingly.

Jim, with a low cry of rage, lowered the unconscious Chindi to the ground and rushed to his baas. He snatched an assegai from one of the natives and cut the Major free.

"Now, baas," he shouted savagely. "Now we will punish these fools who dared to lay hands on you."

"Softly, softly, Jim," the Major chided. "There is no great harm done. And there is doubtless a reason for it all."

The Major looked, as he spoke, at the old chief, who nodded his head sagely before replying.

"Ample reason, white man," he said. "But now—*Au-a!* Get you both to your wagon and leave me alone with my son—my only son."

He added orders to the armed natives, bidding them escort the strangers to their camps.

"No," said the Major, resisting Jim's efforts to drag him away, "there is work to be done here."

He knelt down beside Chindi.

"You should not have moved him," he said chidingly to the Hottentot. "He was very weak; and the weakness has conquered him. Go to the wagon and bring the medicine box."

Jim hesitated. Having seen his baas restored to freedom, he did not want to leave him alone again. He glowered at the natives who crowded round him, looking down in helpless sorrow at the son of their chief.

And suddenly Jim's normal buoyant optimism returned to him. Here was nothing to fear. This was no kraal of death dealers; it was a kraal of men who were themselves gripped by fear. A fear which might urge them to ill-considered deeds of bloodshed in the darkness of night; but which now, when light had been brought amongst them, were as harmless as fangless snakes.

"Hurry, Jim!" the Major said impatiently.

"I go, baas," Jim replied. "You—" he addressed one of the men who had escorted him to the hut— "show me the way through the thorns. And run, fool! My baas does not like to be kept waiting."

IT WAS six days later, and the Major's camp was still pitched outside the kraal of Chivamba. At first Jim had sulked. He did not like the place. The beer the women brewed was vile.

"Why do we stay here, baas?" he asked over and over again.

"I think these people need us, Jim," the white man had retorted.

"Yah! They needed us so badly," Jim said with heavy sarcasm, "that they were ready to kill us when we first came to them."

"I wait to find out why that was, Jim. Besides, I do not go until Chindi's bones give promise of mending."

So the days had passed, and gradually Jim's impatience to trek lessened and his contempt for the people of the kraal changed to pity; the men were so lethargic, so oppressed by fear. The women—he wondered at the absence of comely maidens—looked haggard and moved listlessly about their daily tasks.

Jim completely won the confidence of these natives, except that they would not, or could not, tell him what was the shadow which oppressed the kraal.

They were sitting around a fire now, listening to the tales the Hottentot told, of the adventures with beasts which had befallen his baas.

There was an old iron pot on the fire in which a viscous liquid seethed and stank most abominably.

A vagrant breeze blew the pungent scent across to where the Major was seated in grave debate with the elders of the kraal.

He coughed, rose to his feet and suggested that they all move to the windward of Jim's unholy brew.

The old men acted on his suggestion, though visibly amused at the white man's fastidiousness.

The Major halted a minute in the outer fringe of Jim's interested audience.

He interrupted presently, with, "The Hottentot would have you believe, that I am everything and he nothing. I tell you that he forgets to give to himself the credit that is due."

"*Au-a!* Baas!" Jim exclaimed. "I am only your dog. When you order it, I bark. That is all."

The Major laughed, and the boys echoed him.

"We know!" they chorused. "The Hottentot is a great hunter, white man. But he lies often. That is obvious. When he would have us believe that he is always afraid—then we know he lies."

The Major nodded, laughed again at Jim's pretended outburst of indignation.

"He has told you of the times I saved his life. But, *wo-we!* Has he told you of the times he saved mine? Ask him that. If he will not speak, I will tell you when I have finished with the graybeards."

"Baas!" Jim protested.

The Major held his nose and stooped over the stinking mess in the pot.

"*Gnap,* Jim?" he asked.

"Aye, baas. They have been chewing for me all yesterday and today we boil it with resin and fat. Tomorrow we will spread it on the boughs of some trees in a certain place we know of. *Au-a!* And to think of it! They knew not how to make it."

"There are doubtless many things they do not know," said the Major.

And to the boys, the Major said: "Pay heed to what the Hottentot says and what he does, for I now tell you that he is a man, and no finer hunter lives."

THE MAJOR laughed as Jim tried to silence the demands of the boys for stories of his own achievements. But, as he met the eyes of the chief, he became gravely serious.

"*Au-a!*" the Major exclaimed. "It is an evil story you tell me about your kraal. But the end is in sight. I will speak of the matter to the white police."

Chivamba laughed harshly.

"To what end, *inkosi?* They will do nothing. They can do nothing. When you go to them with the tale I have told you, they will laugh. They will ask you what proof you have. They will tell you that they can do nothing—even if the story be true—because the evil ones live beyond the river."

The Major nodded thoughtfully.

"I shall give them proof," he said. "I shall make them act. But now tell me, why did you take me that night I first came to you?"

"I had sworn an oath, *inkosi!* Those evil white men had taken my son—as they had before taken many of our young men and maidens—to sell as slaves. *Au-a!* I have told you all that! So I made an oath that I would kill the first white man who came to this kraal." Chivamba shrugged his shoulders. "That is all."

There was silence for a little while. Then, "But why do you stay in this place? Why not move your kraal?" the Major asked.

"Where can we go, *inkosi,* where evil can not reach us? Besides, perhaps they will leave us alone now. We have no young maidens left and but few young men."

"But your son? Because he escaped they may come searching for him."

"No, *inkosi.* They think him dead. Besides he is of no value to them now."

"Aye—I know it."

The Major's blue-gray eyes set sternly as he thought of that story, visualizing a long line of shackled natives, herded by brutal white men, marching to a life of cruel serfdom; leaving a trail of blood to redden the black soil of Africa. Visions came to him of men and women falling from exhaustion; he saw them kicked and beaten to their feet; saw them stagger on—only to fall again. And this time they failed to rise and were left, shackled hand and foot, to whatever death might come first to them.

THE MAJOR said suddenly, "And there are other kraals hereabouts who have lost their young men and maidens as you have lost yours?"

"Truly. There is the kraal of Tomasi, of—" and Chivamba named some ten kraals in the vicinity.

"Then listen," the Major said abruptly. "You will bid the graybeards of those kraals to come here."

"They will not come, *inkosi,* at my bidding." The old chief made a gesture of contempt. "They are dogs. Between us all there is an enmity. In order to curry favor with the evil ones they have helped them. And so the hand of every kraal is against its neighbor."

"Fools! And so you play the white man's game," the Major said bitterly.

Chivamba shrugged his shoulders.

"And you helped the white men against your neighbors?" the Major accused suddenly.

"Of course, *inkosi.* Life is as sweet to me as to them."

"Yet if you had stood together from the first it may be this evil would not have come to pass."

"True, *inkosi.* We see that now. Our sorrow has taught us that."

"Then let your sorrow teach you to become friends again." The Major paused a moment or two, mentally considering distances and the time it would take him to do what he wanted to do.

"Now listen," he said. "Today I leave you—"

"Au-a, inkosi!" the old men chorused regret.

"Aye, I go today. But in twice seven days I will come to you again. On that day I want to see here all the people of those other kraals. They must come secretly. No whisper of it must get to the ears of those you fear."

"But how can I do this, *inkosi*. How make friends of those who have become enemies?"

"Give a big feast. I will leave with you the wherewithal. Promise much feasting. Full bellies kill enmity."

"I will do what I can, *inkosi*."

"You must do all that I say," the Major countered sternly.

"Now this further: You and all your people will leave this kraal and live until the day of my return in the bush. You will persuade the people of those other kraals to do likewise. In that way you will escape the white men should they come over before my return; Is it understood?"

"*Yah, inkosi.*"

"One other thing: Chindi is still a sick man. You will deal with him as I have shown you. When the pain is great and an evil spirit seems to dwell within him, you will give him the sleep medicine I will leave with you. But only as much as I show you. To give less will be of no avail. To give more will mean death. It is again understood?"

"Yah, *inkosi!*"

The Major rose briskly to his feet.

"Jim!"

"*Yah*, baas?"

"Inspan. We trek at once."

"*Au-a*, baas! And tomorrow I was going to show these *umfans* where to spread the lime. I was going to bring laughter to their eyes by showing them how vultures and hyenas can dance when they find themselves smeared with *gnap*. We—"

"We are going to mix another birdlime, Jim," the Major interrupted impatiently. "And maybe we will snare vultures and hyenas of a sort."

IT WAS nearing sundown of that same day. Three white men sat on the ground, their backs against the mud wall of their native built hut, watching a wagon, drawn by eight mules, come slowly up the road leading from the river's ford to the high ground on which they had built their huts.

Their appearance was indescribably vicious, their souls being as ragged and filth-smeared as their clothing. Africa had conquered all three. And they had been willing victims.

Said one, ejecting a stream of tobacco juice from the corner of his mouth. "Nothing to get windy about, Carlos. That ain't no police outfit."

"And if it was," said the tall, thin, sandy-haired man, leering at the fat, porcine appearing man they called Carlos, "what of it. They ain't got no right over here. They can't do anything to us. If they tried to get funny, a bullet in the gizzard 'ud stop 'em. And there'd be no awkward questions asked either. Police! Hell! You can't frighten me with talk of police from that side. And as for the comic opera beauties on this side—they get their palm oil! So why worry?"

Carlos tugged thoughtfully at the waxed ends of his mustache. He was the dandy of the three. A broad red sash girded his enormous stomach. The braces which supported his dirty duck trousers were silk-embroidered. A large diamond gleamed in his shirt front; his hair was plastered with a strong smelling pomade; the fingers of his soft hands were laden with rings.

The red-headed man swore; the other groaned. A livid scar ran from his left eye; the knife which had caused it had sliced off the top of his ear. But he hid that defect by allowing his hair to grow long and hang down over his ears. But he could not control the habit he had of rubbing the top of the injured ear. He did that now.

Carlos continued. "You may swear, and you may groan. But I say—as I have said so many times—it would be the best for us to move our house back from the river. A long way back."

"What the hell for? We command the ford where all the niggers cross. Besides—"

"I know—I know all your arguments," Carlos interrupted. "But I confess that I am afraid. I am most stupendously afraid that some day a policeman will forget that the river is a boundary river, and then—"

"He won't live long enough to remember he made a mistake," Red said brutally, and drew his forefinger across his throat.

"To hear you talk nobody 'ud think you got your day's fun out of thrashing niggers with a *sjambok*," Squint sniggered.

Carlos mopped his red face with a scented handkerchief.

"Not fun, dear Squint," he objected, "but merely a painful duty. I have often wondered," he added vaguely, "if the *sjambok* would be more productive of results if I pickled it in brine—" He broke off, suddenly conscious—as were the other two—that the wagon was very near.

THEY ALL tensed slightly and sat with their hands on the butts of their revolvers.

But when the wagon came to a halt and the white man, who had been handling the reins, climbed cautiously to the ground, they visibly relaxed; smug, self-confident grins distorted their faces.

"Of a certainty," as Carlos afterward framed it, "we had no cause to be on guard in our dealings with this monumental example of the asinine inefficiency of England's aristocracy."

They rose and advanced together to greet the Major. Phrases of hospitality tumbling from their lips.

He stood waiting for them, tapping his highly polished riding boots with his riding whip; toying with his monocle; his lips apart—looking utterly nervous and brainless.

And Jim the Hottentot sat on the driver's seat, the long-poled driving whip in his hands, watching his baas with a contemptuous leer on his face. The three men noted that. It helped them to size up the situation; it confirmed the opinions they had already formed. Thus they became less dangerous.

"How do, stranger," said Red. "Not often we get visitors here."

"No—that it ain't," Squint echoed. "And now you're here you must stop a while. Tell your nigger to outspan. Our niggers'll be along presently to show him where to put the mules."

"That's bally good of you," the Major drawled. "But I hardly like to inflict my presence on you longer than is absolutely necessary. You see—"

"Oh nonsense, *senhor*," Carlos interposed. "You must honor us by accepting our humble hospitality. We insist. But pardon: our names. On my left you behold Senhor "Red' Haines, a very noble gentleman of— But where he comes from matters not. No? On my right is Senhor Squint. It was an act of indescribable heroism which earned him that scar; his badge of courage, I call it. And lastly, myself, Senhor Carlos d' ya Gomez. And all very much at your service."

The three men raised their helmets and bowed profoundly.

The Major answered with an even more elaborate bow.

"And my name, gentlemen," he said, "is Aubrey St. John Major. Very much at your service." He raised his helmet and bowed again.

"And now," Carlos puffed, so much bowing had winded him, "now we will go to the huts, *senhor.* We have time to salute the sun's setting—and then we will dine. Come!"

"Just one moment, please. I think it best first to state my business and then, if your offer of hospitality is still open, I will be most pleased to accept it.

"Business! *You* talk business? My God!" Red exclaimed with a laugh.

The Major looked offended.

"But, really," he expostulated, "I'm no end of a good business man. Really. Of course people think I'm a bally ass, an' all that—just because I wear a monocle an' talk like a silly ass—"

"Of course," said Carlos. "You must forgive Senhor Red. He has sometimes an unfortunate way of putting things. He meant to express his astonishment that so elegant a gentleman as yourself should sully your mind with details of business."

The Major simpered.

"But—alas! Gentleman must work in these days," continued Carlos. "Behold also me! And so you shall state your business, Senhor Major."

AND NOW the Major hesitated, looking anxiously at the three men. His jaw muscles seemed flabby; his slouching pose made him look less than his true six feet of height.

The dudish cut of his riding breeches and tunic coat hid the muscles of his splendidly proportioned body.

"You seem such top hole Johnnies," he said, "that I hardly know where to begin. Briefly, dear lads, I would have you know that I have come to scold you most severely. Oh very."

"Going to *sjambok* us most like," Squint said with affected gloominess, and shivered.

The Major looked distressed.

"Oh no. Not quite that—really. You misjudge me. Nothing quite so actively demonstrative, I assure you. No. I simply want to punish you with words. That is all. You see: I am a licensed labor recruiter, and I've just made a tour of the kraal over there—" He waved his hand toward the river—"In the hope of getting some of the laddies to work in the mines down South. And what do I find but that you have, as it were, swept the place bare. An' it's not fair, really it isn't. I'd invested a lot of money on this expedition, and it looked as if I'd have to go back empty—er—handed. You know you have no business to cross the river. You ought to remain in your own territory. 'Pon my word! I'm tempted to report you to the police."

"Oh—don't do that, *senhor!*" Carlos begged.

"You wouldn't send a hard working man to prison, just because he crossed a lousy river for a lousy nigger or two, would you?"

"I—wait a minute." He fumbled in his tunic pockets, produced another monocle which he put in his eye with a sigh of relief. "Blind as a bat without one," he explained. "And now—as to business; I'm almost finished. I have scolded you about poaching in my—er—exclusive territory. But that is not all, really." He shook an admonishing forefinger at them. "You have absolutely terrorized the Johnnies over there. Why, they even tried to kill me. Had a funny idea of revenge. Fortunately I was able to deal with them." He tapped his leg suggestively with his whip. "A *sjambok*," he murmured "is a most deucedly effective argument."

THE OTHER three looked at each other significantly. At last the dude had expressed his real self. Carlos recognized a familiar spirit, the soft exterior which covers a shell of cruel brutality.

Squint and Red eyed the Major with new interest. They understood him now.

Suddenly they linked their arms in the Major's and led him to the *skoff* hut. Carlos remained behind to talk with the Hottentot.

"You are fond of your baas, Hottentot?" he asked.

"*Wo-we!*" Jim growled. "I am no dog to lick the hand which whips me. The *sjambok* is his voice, and he talks constantly."

Carlos murmured sympathetically. Then, "So your baas's mission was a fruitless one over yonder. He goes back to whence he came and no *funa joins* go with him."

"True. But he comes again next moon some time. And then he will not depart empty-handed."

Carlos looked thoughtfully at the Hottentot.

"How so?" he queried.

"*Au-a!*" That one I call baas—"Jim spat—"He is in some ways *slim*. By luck he saved Chindi, the son of Chivamba, from death. And he has used that to further his own ends. And so Chivamba has promised to get together many men for the man I call baas when he comes again. And the baas has left with Chivamba much food and *puza*. Truly. My baas is all evil; but he is no fool, although men first seeing him, and understanding him, think it easy to trick him. If you have a mind that way—I say, beware. I say: Remember how like a dead twig a spitting snake can be."

Carlos nodded.

"To the man," he said casually, "who brought us word when this baas of yours returns to this district to take back the *funa joins* Chivambra gathers together there would be great wealth paid."

Jim said stolidly, "A handful of corn is great wealth to a starving man; a string of beads to a woman; a toy to a child. I am not starving, neither am I a child or a woman. What is great wealth, white man?"

Carlos laughed.

"Ten shillings for every *funa join* Chivamba delivers to your baas."

"*Au-a!*" Jim exclaimed softly, and beat his hands together. "That is great wealth indeed. *Au-a!* That would make me as rich as the headman of my kraal. I know the man who will bring you word." He cupped his hands together and held them out toward the white man.

"Give me something to bind the bargain," he pleaded.

Carlos took a handful of coins from his pocket, selected one and gave it to Jim, saying meaningly, "I too can use a *sjambok*, Hottentot. So do not play me false."

"Have no fear, white man," Jim said earnestly. "I shall play my part honestly. It is for you to take care. That baas of mine is—have I not already said it?—no fool."

Carlos waved his hand and hastened to join the others in the *skoff* hut.

EARLY THE following morning the Major announced his intention to trek immediately after *skoff*, and would not be persuaded otherwise, despite the protestations of the three who seemed to have found in him a kindred spirit.

"No," he said, this was at the breakfast table and in reply to their urgent entreaties that he stay a while with them. "I'm immensely flattered an' all that. But I must toddle along. I have a little business deal afoot. Perhaps next time I'm in this neighborhood you'll put me up for a week or so and we'll spend the days hunting and the nights listening to your interesting experiments, Senhor Carlos. Personally, I'm of the opinion that no nigger could survive one hundred lashes with a *sjambok*. Perhaps we can conduct a joint experiment next time I come. And I want to hear more of your theories, Squint, old top. They are immensely colorful, to say the least. And yours, Red. 'Pon my soul. The more I think of it, the more I dislike the idea of departing. But duty calls. And so—"

He rose to his feet.

"A parting drink, *senhor*," said Carlos. I have, anticipating your refusal to stay, already given orders that your nigger be given instructions to inspan."

The Major held up the glass Carlos handed him.

"To my perfect hosts," he said with a soft chuckle, "and a just reward for all our merits."

They drank standing.

CAPTAIN JAMESON of the Mounted Police at Paarburg, leaned back in his chair and laughed softly.

"I can't do it, Major," he said. "Even supposing I accepted all you have told me as truth, there is nothing I can do."

"Oh, but really," the Major expostulated, "here I trek hard for five days to bring you a report of slave raiding in your territory; I tell you stories of gross brutality, and you calmly sit there and tell me you intend to do nothing."

"And I repeat, Major, that there's nothing I can do."

"Oh bosh!" the Major exclaimed impatiently.

"Well—what would you have me do?"

"Send a strong detachment of men up there—"

"I can't spare a stronge detachment of men," the captain interrupted. "We've got our hands full here."

"Then send two or three."

"And what will they do?"

"Arrest the blighters who are causing all the misery. I tell you," the Major continued heatedly, "that I saw the mutilated remains of brutally murdered natives. I've got evidence of slave raids which make the accounts of Arab slavers read like the report of a Sunday school picnic. You must do something."

"There's nothing we can do, Major," the police captain said wearily. "It's silly going over the ground again. I've already told you once. Now I'll tell you again. I can't do anything because, in the first place, the men against whom you lodge these wild complaints are living beyond my jurisdiction. They are in Portuguese territory."

"I told you that I had planned things so that they would conduct a raid—"

"That's all very well, Major. But even supposing they came across, they wouldn't meekly submit to arrest; and I have no doubt, supposing they did, that they would claim to be engaged in a peaceful recruiting mission and we'd be having international complications of the sort which I have recently been instructed to avoid at all costs.

"All this, however, is quite by the way. The chief reason for my inaction—always overlooking the fact that I should be loath, under the circumstances, to act on your unsupported statements—is the fact that I cannot spare a single man. And there you have it."

THE MAJOR was silent for a moment; his face, an expressionless mask. But inwardly he was a volcano of rage. He was not accustomed to having his word doubted. Despite his reputation as an I.D.B., he had always been ready to cooperate with the police—and they with him—in matters of this sort.

He said coldly, "And is it permitted to know why you can't spare a man—or four men, for the matter of that—from the routine duties of a place like Paarburg?"

The police captain chuckled.

"Don't be so damned innocent, Major. You know as well as I do—"

"It seems useless to give you my word that I don't," the Major observed icily.

The police captain winked.

"Well the fact is—I'm sorry you're so ignorant about a matter which so vitally interests you—that diamonds have been recently found here. As a result we are crowded with honest diggers and all the riff-raff of the Continent. Hence, you will understand my inability to appear enthusiastic when a notorious illicit diamond buyer comes to me with stories of slave trading and urges me to send a detachment of men away on a long trek to arrest the alleged traders. Have I made myself plain, Major?"

"Oh quite," the Major drawled, adding incredulously, "And there are diamonds, you say, here—in Paarburg?"

"Oh, quite," mimicked the other.

"Bai Jove," the Major murmured. "Then I must toddle along. Expect to be no end busy. Suppose it's no use trying to persuade you that I'm telling the truth about those slavers?"

"Not a bit."

"No—I see it isn't. Oh, well. Toodle-oo!"

As he left the office a young, fresh-faced trooper came in and saluted smartly.

"You sent for me, sir?"

"Yes. Did you get a good look at that fellow who went out?"

"Not more than a passing glimpse, sir. He looked like a silly ass, stage door Johnnie."

"You may take it from me, he's not," the captain said dryly. "He's one of the cleverest men in South Africa. There's nothing he can't do or doesn't know. And he's suspected of being an I.D.B. That explains his presence in Paarburg, I think. If we could catch him it 'ud be a big feather in our cap—so many others have tried and failed— and it would completely discourage the lesser lights of the I.D.B. fraternity from operating here. Well, I'm giving you the job, Pearson, of watching the Major. Don't let him out of your sight while he's in the *dorp*. Dog his steps. Don't try to trap him. He's too clever, and too decent for that.

"But *get* him and I'll listen more favorably next time you come to talk to me about my daughter."

Pearson's face flushed with pleasure.

"I'll get him, sir," he said confidently.

TROOPER JAMES Pearson was very busy during the remainder of that day. And yet, despite the fact that he had abilities of no mean order, he lost touch with the Major. The monocled dude seemed to have vanished into thin air. After several hours of fruitless searching in the many drinking shacks and canteens which had sprung up almost overnight, he decided to go out to the Major's camp which was pitched on the veld some four miles from the *dorp*.

And there was no secrecy about the Major's camp. It was on the open veld, visible for miles round. Perhaps in that was its secrecy, for no one could approach it unseen.

Pearson found Jim the Hottentot in charge, and at once commenced to ingratiate himself with that individual. A course which he found extremely easy.

The Hottentot, it appeared, was nursing a grievance—real or fancied—against his baas, and readily succumbed to Pearson's clever flattery and his promises of reward.

"Truly, *inkosi*," he said as he vigorously stirred the *gnap* he was boiling in an old pot, "my baas is playing the diamond game. He always plays it. He has gone now to buy stones from black dogs who steal them from their masters. By an' by he will come here, his pockets full of stones. If it were possible for you to hide somewhere you could take him—the stones on him."

"I could hide in the wagon, Hottentot. Or in the tent."

Jim considered that.

"No—*inkosi*. That would not do. The baas is very *slim*. He always looks in the tent and wagon when he returns. No, that is no way."

"But we must find a way," Pearson urged. "Think, Hottentot. What can we do?"

"There is nothing we can do, *inkosi*," Jim said glumly. "And soon my baas will be on his way back, and he will see you from afar. Then he will not come. Or if he comes he will have hidden the stones somewhere. *Au-a!*" Jim put his ear to the ground. "Already, I think, I hear his footsteps."

Pearson turned and looked in the direction of the veld; but that was also toward the setting sun, and he saw nothing.

"Think quickly, Hottentot," he urged. "There must be a way."

"There might be a way," Jim said slowly, "if—"

"If what! Go on, fool."

"If the *inkosi* was to take off his policeman's clothes—all his clothes—and blacked his body; and wore an old hat of mine to cover his hair, and a blanket to cover his body. And if he sat beside this pot, stirring the *gnap*, sitting in the smoke and stench of it. Then I think it would be possible for him to remain and my baas not suspect his presence. I would say that you are a witchdoctor I know of. And my baas would not look at you too closely. The smell of *gnap* sickens him.

"That is the only way I know of. The *inkosi* will pardon. Of course he could not so debase himself."

THERE WAS silence for a little while as Pearson considered the likelihood of such a plan's success. Then he said quickly, "I will do that, Hottentot. Help me."

They worked fast then but nearly half an hour passed before Pearson was disguised sufficiently to please the Hottentot.

"It is not good," he grumbled, "but it will do if you keep your blanket close about you; if you remain in the smoke which comes from the cooking *gnap*."

"*Faugh!*" Pearson gagged. "The stink will make me sick."

"Then be sick before my baas comes," Jim said brutally. "And at least you should be thankful that no mosquitoes will bite you as long as you remain there."

He chuckled softly to himself.

Presently Pearson said weakly, "What is this stinking mess, Hottentot?"

"It is bird lime, *inkosi*. It is a stuff I spread where birds settle; and they stick fast in it.

"And now you must keep quiet and not talk, for the baas comes. And—*Au-a!* Your voice is the voice of a white man. *Wo-we!* Keep your blanket closer about you. I can see places where the skin is not blackened: I can see the fire light on the gun you have buckled about your waist."

The minutes passed very slowly to Pearson. The stuff the Hottentot had smeared on his skin had dried and itched tormentingly. The grease stained old felt hat he wore flopped about his eyes and the stench of the *gnap* was intolerable.

But he stuck to his pose, as gallantly as any knight of old; for success would win for him his lady.

At length, when his senses were almost bemused by the fumes of the *gnap,* his head swimming, came a promise of relief.

"The baas comes," whispered the Hottentot. And then Pearson heard a strong, tone-true baritone voice singing one of the Freebooter ballads.

A few minutes later and the Major strode up to the fire and stood there, legs apart, staring whimsically across the fire at the blanketed form of Pearson.

"And what have we here, Jim?" he asked.

"A witch doctor, baas." There was a tremor in the Hottentot's voice. Excitement, Pearson judged. Laughter, of course, he never considered. Jim continued, "He makes great medicine, baas. He is a famous medicine maker."

"Must be," the Major remarked dryly, "if he can sit in that infamous stink."

He laughed. Then he said, "My pockets are full, Jim. And tonight we trek. We must be far from here before the police come asking questions."

AND THAT was Pearson's cue.

He let the blanket fall from his shoulders.

"Put up your hands, Major," he said curtly and rose to his feet, his revolver aimed at the pit of the Major's stomach.

The Major's jaw dropped, his monocle dropped from his eye as he stared incredulously at Pearson. His hands shot above his head as if jerked by invisible strings.

" 'Pon my word," he stammered. "What does this mean?"

"Only," Pearson said with a short laugh, "that I'm going to search you. No—not here, but before witnesses. I'm going to bind you first so you can't play any tricks. Then I'm going to take you into the *dorp*."

"Splendid," the Major said. And he began to laugh wildly.

"I don't see anything to laugh at," Pearson said curtly.

"Oh, but you don't see what I see, old dear. 'Pon my soul, you're absolutely priceless. What are you? A Christy minstrel or what?"

"I'm a policeman—"

"Oh, nonsense! You'll be telling me next that that's the new undress uniform the Corps is wearing. Very undress, I should say."

Pearson flushed under the stain. He was acutely conscious of his ludicrous appearance. But elation at the success of his ruse steadied him.

"Never mind about that. My appearance served its end long enough to get you off guard. You're under arrest on suspicion of possessing illicitly bought diamonds. And that's all you have to worry about."

The Major laughed again.

"And are you going to escort me to the *dorp* dressed like that. Really, you know, you're not decent."

"I've got my uniform here. Get it, Hottentot."

"I do not understand," Jim replied. "What does the *inkosi* mean?" Jim appealed to his baas.

"You see," the Major bantered. "You have no uniform. Of course not. You are not a policeman. You are not a white man. At least I have no proof that you are. And you come to my camp, dressed like that—doubtless with some evil purpose in mind—and threaten me with a revolver. And so—"

The Major let his hands drop to his side.

"Put up your hands, Major," Pearson said hoarsely. "I can prove what I am at the proper time. But never mind that now. I have you covered, and your Hottentot. I don't know what funny game you're playing. But it won't work. Put up your hands."

"Oh—rather not," drawled the Major. "Of course, if you were really a policeman I should never think of resisting—er—arrest. That is a most serious offense in my opinion. But I'm certainly not going to surrender to a half-naked, filth-smeared lunatic. Oh, rather not."

The Major thrust his hands into his pockets.

"Shoot, old lad, if you're a mind to," he said.

PEARSON WAS in a quandary. Apart from shooting he did not know how to enforce his authority. And he dared not shoot. The situation did not justify that. Had he been in uniform and the Major had acted as he was now acting, he would have fired without compunction. But something told him that had he been in uniform, then the Major would have dealt with him in a different way.

His head swam; that beastly stink was nauseating. He moved away from the reek, moved toward the Major and instantly mosquitoes attacked his naked body. He slapped at them ineffectively.

"I am tired of the game, Jim," the Major said. "Inspan, and we will trek."

"Do not move, Hottentot," Pearson ordered. But again he felt helpless when the Hottentot ignored him and busied himself in carrying out the Major's instructions.

What could he do? He was young, and, in a measure, inexperienced. The Major and the Hottentot had called his bluff. Worse! He realized now that the predicament in which he now found himself had been deliberately planned. But why? Why?

The mosquitoes tortured him. The sun had set, and the temperature dropped. He shivered. He clenched his teeth in an endeavor to fight back the overpowering feeling of nausea induced by the fumes of gnap.

The revolver trembled in his hand.

"Steady, steady, old lad!"

The Major's voice seemed to come from a great distance.

He was vaguely aware of footsteps behind him. But before his fingers could act on the message sent to him by his brain, before he could squeeze the trigger of his revolver, a thick, heavy blanket was thrown over his head.

He struggled feebly, then succumbed to the weakness which possessed him.

His next conscious knowledge was the fact that he was lying on the floor of a wagon which was being driven at a mad pace over the veld. He tried to move and discovered he was bound hand and foot.

He shouted.

The Major answered him.

"Not so much noise, old top, or I'll have to gag you."

Pearson spluttered with indignation.

"I demand that you release me. I—"

"Can't do it, old lad. You're *non compos mentis,* you know. Oh quite. We found you wandering on the veld, stark naked, stark raving mad. But you'll be better soon. Yes, you'll be better soon. Perhaps by the time the stuff you dyed yourself with has worn away you'll be quite sane." He chuckled and continued, ignoring Pearson's ravings. "But that will be some time. Jim makes splendid dyes. Guaranteed not to wash off. But they wear off. Dear me, yes."

Pearson at last made himself heard. "You'll pay for this. Abduction of a police officer is a serious crime."

"Very, I should say," the Major agreed. "But a most amusing one, under the circumstances. You'd never be able to live it down once the facts were known. And how the girls will laugh. Women have such a distorted sense of humor, I always think."

Pearson groaned.

"Where are you taking me? What's your game?"

THERE WAS a grave note in the Major's voice as he replied. "I'm giving you an opportunity of performing a much greater duty than that of endeavoring to trap an alleged I.D.B. I'm going to show you that there are things far more deserving of protection than bits of dirty stones. I.D.B. Hell!—Pardon my profanity, but I get hot when I think of the injustice of it. I.D.B.— Bosh! You, dear laddie, are going to stop I.N.B."

"I.N.B. What do you mean?"

"Illicit nigger buying, laddie. Slavery."

"That sounds big," Pearson sneered. "But you can't expect me to swallow a wild story like that. I demand that you release me at once."

"If you are not very careful," the Major said wearily, "I shall do just that. Now listen. Whether you like it or not, you are coming with me; and you are going to play your part as it should be played."

"How long will this business take?"

"Two weeks."

Pearson groaned.

"I'll be arrested for desertion when I get back," Pearson said moodily.

"You won't—my word you won't. You'll get a commission instead."

"They'll send a search party out after me!"

The Major chuckled.

"I hope they will. It'll make things easier." He added bitterly. "But they won't. Diamonds are more important sometimes, than human lives."

SQUINT, RED and Carlos chuckled contentedly as Jim, the Hottentot concluded his story.

"And you say, Hottentot," questioned Carlos, "that this baas of yours treks tomorrow with one hundred men who go to labor at the mines?"

Jim nodded emphatically.

"Aye—ten times the count of my two hands. They wait now in the place I spoke of. The old graybeards and the women are drinking and feasting. The men who go to the mines—they are chained. Hand and foot, they are chained."

"And only the white man guards them? He has none to help him?"

"He guards alone. And he is sufficient. I have said the young men are chained; the old ones are helpless—or soon will be helpless—having drunk much strong puza."

"Hell! Come on. Let's get 'em," Red growled.

"He may be lying," Carlos said absently. "Niggers are treacherous dogs." In the vernacular he said suddenly, "Why do you betray your baas, Hottentot?"

"*Au-a!*" Jim spat contemptuously then drank deeply from the bottle of rot-gun gin the white men had given him. "Did I not make a bargain with you last time I saw you? Besides, look what that baas of mine did only this morning."

With a dramatic gesture he tore off his shirt and, turning, showed the men his naked back.

"*Por dios!*" Carlos exclaimed.

"And I, know how to revenge myself," Jim growled. "But are you answered?"

Carlos nodded.

Meanwhile Jim, the bottle was now nearly empty, reeled drunkenly about, singing hoarsely and waving his hands.

"We can't take him to guide us," Red said with a curse. "The fool's blind drunk."

"We don't need a guide," Squint observed. "I know the place he means. And we know there's been a lot of niggers hanging about the place lately. That proves the Hottentot's story to be true. We'll leave one of our niggers here to look after him. An' hurry. No good hanging about here talking. If we look slippy, we'll have all the niggers safe in our hands over here afore sundown."

SIX BIG, brutal looking natives, armed with repeating rifles, now came from their huts.

One was told to remain on guard over the Hottentot. When he scowlingly objected, Red went into one of the huts and brought out a bottle of gin. This somewhat mollified the huge Negro, but it was evident that he would much have preferred to have joined in the raiding party.

He struck out fiercely as Jim reeled past him, and the Hottentot dropped to the ground and the big man sat on him.

The others laughed as they moved off.

"I'll have my fun with this one," he said. "It is a pity he is so drunk. But I will sober him."

And Jim sobered very quickly. The raiding party had barely passed out of sight in the bush on the opposite side of the river when he heaved mightily, throwing his captor sprawling on his back. Before the big man could recover, Jim had pounced on him. His strong hands closed on the big man's neck, choking him.

For a little while the other struggled; then he suddenly went limp.

Jim dragged him to a foul-smelling, wooden hut and locked and bolted the door.

Then Jim ran for the river, crossed it at a point high above the ford and vanished into the bush.

"I THINK, Pearson, old top," drawled the Major, "you'll admit that I did the right thing in bringing you to this place."

"By God, yes, Major," Pearson exclaimed. He was in uniform now, his face cleanly shaved, his buttons glistening like gold. He looked what he was, a fine representative of white man's justice in black man's Africa.

"By God, yes," he repeated, and he looked round at the natives who crowded the little clearing, and who looked on him as their protector.

For over an hour he had been listening to their tales of the men who lived across the river. Tales of brutality, of murder and rapine. He had seen men and women who had been mutilated but who still lived to bear witness against the men who had tortured them.

The bare recital of their wrongs had filled him with a determination to bring the degenerate white men responsible for it all to justice. And this determination, destroying the callowness of youth, improved his manliness. He felt now that he was more nearly a fit companion for the real man who hid himself behind an ambush of futile inanities; the man he had learnt to admire during the past few days of their trek together.

"And is there anything else you'd like to hear?" the Major asked.

"Is there more?" Pearson asked incredulously.

The Major nodded.

"You haven't heard half the story yet. But the rest is all of a piece with what you've heard. More raiding, more tortures, more kraals destroyed. I think there's no need of your listening to any more of that. The point is, are you convinced that these old graybeards are telling the truth?"

"Absolutely."

"And you're ready to do your bit in capturing the men responsible for all this misery?"

"Absolutely! But how! It's got to be done by strategy. There are three of them, and their natives are armed, you say. And we've got to get them in this territory—otherwise they'll get off when they come up for trial. Although—" he concluded thoughtfully— "I could say that I arrested 'em over here. It 'ud be my word against theirs and—"

"I've arranged for them to come over here," the Major said softly.

Pearson began to see difficulties, his police training began to assert itself over his natural reactions.

"I don't see how I can arrest 'em just because they're in our territory. And I've no real evidence—not police—caught evidence against them. All I know is what you've told me, and what they've told me." He nodded toward the natives. "Of course, I believe all you've told me. I believe all they've said. But will the judge? And I can't arrest three white men without something more to go on. I'd have to investigate the complaints and—" he shrugged his shoulders, concluding lamely: "It all seems rather hopeless."

The Major said sharply, "Just what sort of evidence do you want, Pearson?"

"Well—if I could see them slave raiding with my own eyes—"

"I've arranged that you should, old lad."

Pearson stared at the Major.

"Is there nothing you cannot do?"

"Oh—quite a lot, old chap," the Major said airily. "But never mind that. I suggest now that you talk to these poor devils. Tell them that you have come to save them and to punish the evil doers. Tell them that many more police are coming and will soon be here. Otherwise they won't have the guts to carry out my plan, and they'll go scampering into the bush at the first sign of trouble. And tell 'em also that they must do exactly as I tell them. They'll obey you blindly. Wonderful what a uniform means to women and natives."

"They don't need me to tell them to obey you, Major. They would follow your lead, no matter where you went!"

"Think so? Oh you're spoofin'!" exclaimed the Major, pleased at Pearson's tribute. "Well, get up on the tail-board of the wagon an' talk to them. Then I'll chin a while with them. We haven't a great deal of time to spare."

They walked toward the wagon, followed by a surging gesticulating crowd of natives.

"What makes you so sure, Major," Pearson asked, "that they'll come over here?"

"Have you ever noticed," the Major drawled, "that if you spread bird lime on the branch of a tree, birds are sure to alight on that branch."

"Yes. But I don't see—"

"Don't you?" the Major interposed. "Well—" his gesture embraced the natives swarming about them—"I've spread my bird lime."

IT WAS an hour later.

The clearing in the bush now presented a scene of great dejection. The young able-bodied men sat sullenly in long rows; the women huddled together behind them, wailing dolorously. There was a clank of chains whenever one of the men or women moved; they were handcuffed and leg-ironed together.

The graybeards, together with several toothless old women were seated about a large fire in the center of the clearing, singing drunken snatches of ribald song.

And the Major! Somehow he had contrived to invest himself with the truculent air of a swaggering bully.

He strode up and down the long line of manacled natives, shouting curses, aiming blows at them with his *sjambok.*

Having passed down the whole length of line, the Major halted; and standing with feet wide apart, his hands on his hips, he laughed softly.

"I think they're absolutely top-hole," he said. " 'Pon my word, they make me feel like a bally Simon Legree. How does it look to you, Pearson, old dear?"

And Pearson, he was safely ensconced in the upper branches of one of the trees which fringed the clearing, answered, "It's real, Major. Almost too real. It's all I can do to keep from shooting you."

"You'd better keep your finger off your trigger, old lad," the Major said dryly. "And you'll see what the real thing is like when those devils come. And even then—no shooting until you get the signal. I don't want my little play spoiled by stage fright. An' besides, if you go off half-cocked it may result in these poor devils being handed over to the fate from which we're trying to save 'em. Not to mention the fact that we're likely to die a particularly nasty death if anything goes wrong."

Pearson answered soberly, "I know my lines, Major. And I won't speak until I get my cue."

"I'm sure you won't, Pearson. And so—you'll get the evidence you want: the unholy three'll get it in the—er—neck; these bally Johnnies'll get a new lease on happiness. And I—"

He paused.

"Yes," Pearson prompted. "Just what do you get, Major?"

"Why," the Major appeared confused. "Do you know—I never thought of that."

He spoke gravely to the natives. They grinned confidently at him, and he turned away, assured that they would play their part.

His keen ears caught the sound of someone hastening through the underbrush.

"I think it's Jim," he muttered, "but better take no chances."

AND—AS IF he had donned a mask—he became once again the swaggering bully. The dolorous wailing of the women broke out afresh; the men became even more abject; the old graybeards' songs grew more ribald.

Jim, his scanty clothing dripping water and plastered with mud, ran from the bush to his baas.

"They come, baas," he panted exultantly. "The three white men and five black ones. All armed. I swam the river below the ford—there were crocodiles, baas—so that I could get here before them. They—"

The Major interrupted, "They must not see you here, Jim."

The Hottentot nodded. He moved away from his baas, and the next moment he had vanished from sight in the undergrowth.

The Major stood for a moment, tensed, considering the plan he had evolved; considering this drama that he was staging. He had written a hard part for himself, and he knew that it must be played thoroughly if his plan were to succeed; if he were going to get those others off their guard and convince them of their own security.

Just a moment longer he stood there; then his hands went out to the watching natives in a gesture which begged forgiveness for the things he had to do.

Their lips moved; the expression of their faces assured him that they understood.

One stalwart said, his voice so cleverly modulated that the words only just reached the Major's ears, "We understand, *inkosi*. It is a game which must be played. Strike hard—and we will howl."

The Major nodded. Then he ran up and down the line of men, shouting threats, kicking, cursing, lashing about him indiscriminately with his *sjambok*.

The lash curled about naked bodies.

The natives howled for mercy. But no mercy was shown them. The Major was like one gone mad.

SUDDENLY A harsh, mocking laugh freed him from his torture.

He sighed with relief as he turned with a start in the direction of the voice.

The man Carlos, rifle levelled at the Major, came from the bush. A big native, also armed, was with him.

Simultaneously, Red and Squint, both accompanied by two armed natives, converged on the Major from different sides of the clearing.

"The dogs were getting mutinous," the Major said in a dull, monotonous voice.

Carlos smiled. He recognized the symptoms; he, too, had experienced the reaction which sets in after an orgy of brutality.

"I had to thrash them," the Major continued. "They were getting mutinous."

"But of course, *senhor*," Carlos said affably. "I understand. We heard you were having trouble with the niggers. And so we have come to assist you."

The Major stared at Carlos.

"I don't understand," he said slowly.

Carlos laughed.

"Yes, we have come to help you, *senhor*," he repeated.

The Major was recovering his usual jaunty air; a drawl crept into his voice as he replied, "But I don't need any assistance, old tops. I can quite easily manage alone any little mutinous outbreak, though I offer you my hospitality."

As he spoke he hooked his thumbs in his cartridge belt. His right hand was very near his revolver belt.

"We would be only too happy to accept your hospitality, *senhor*," Carlos began smoothly, "were it not for the fact that we have important business—"

"Oh stow the gab," Red interrupted coarsely. "Let's get going."

He shouted an order, and the five armed natives, grinning with anticipation of the joy of unbridled license, ran to the line of chained natives and kicked them to their feet.

They treated the women in the same way. Carlos and Squint ran to their support.

"Hi! Stop it," the Major shouted frantically. "What are you doing to my niggers?"

"They're your niggers no longer, mister," Red scoffed. "We don't like the way you treat 'em so we're going to take 'em across the river, where they can live happily ever after."

"By God, you're not!" the Major shouted.

The Major fumbled with the flap of his revolver holster.

"Here—none of that!" Red growled, drawing his own revolver and levelling it at the Major's head. "Put up your hands."

The Major obeyed, cursing.

Red took the Major's revolver from its holster, and stuck it in his own belt.

"You ought to practice a quick draw, mister," he sneered. "Now you back against that tree and I'll rope you to it. Not too tight. I'll fix it so as you can get free all by yourself in an hour or two."

Red passed a rope round his waist and chest, and knotted it securely. But he had left the Major's hands free.

MEANWHILE CARLOS, Squint and the five natives were creating an atmosphere of hell as they got the natives in line for the journey across the river.

Their brutalities were devilish. The air was filled with the wailing of women and the pain-filled cries of strong men.

Here and there men in the line slumped forward, unconscious; kept from falling by the chains which shackled them to their comrades.

Carlos ran pantingly to where the Major was bound. He bowed mockingly.

"A thousand thanks, *senhor*," he said, "for your stupendous generosity. We are ready to march now. In a few hours we will be safe in our so humble homes." He spat in the Major's face. He turned to Red.

"Ready, Senhor Red?" he said.

Red nodded.

"Here's something for luck, dude," he growled, "and to teach you not to try an' play a man's game. You ain't cut out for nigger running."

He lashed out with his clenched fist at the Major's face. Yet, somehow, his blow missed and his fist crashed against the unyielding trunk of the tree.

Squint and Carlos laughed unsympathetically. The Major drawled, "The quickness of the head deceives the hand, eh, old dear?"

"Bring me a *sjambok*," Red roared, "and I'll cut the devil's heart out!"

Carlos handed one to him.

Squint objected, "It ain't wise to go heatin' up a white man, Red. Besides, we're ready to go. An' the sooner I'm over our side of the river with this batch of black ivory, the better I'll like it."

"You go on," Red growled. "I'm going to give this hyena a taste of the *sjambok*. I'll catch up with you."

Carlos sighed.

"I'd like to stay and see it, but duty forbids. I wish you a pleasant time, *senhor*. Red's hand is very heavy."

He shouldered his rifle and placed himself at the head of the long line of captives. Squint was at the rear. The armed natives were stationed at intervals between the two white men.

"March!" shouted Carlos.

Sjamboks cracked. There was another outbreak of dolourous wailing, louder shouts of pain, and the line moved slowly forward.

IN A little while they would be swallowed up by the bush; embogged in the quicksands of white man's brutality.

Red, his back turned to the Major, watched them; he slammed his *sjambok* tentatively.

Squint called.

"I'll bet you he faints afore he's had thirty cuts."

"He won't stand ten," Red growled.

"He won't stand one!"

At the Major's mocking voice, Red turned with a curse. Then his mouth gaped open, for he was looking into the muzzle of a revolver.

"I keep this one out of sight," the Major drawled. "And I can draw it very quickly. You'd be surprised."

Red's hands shot above his head.

"Carlos! Squint!" he shouted. "Rescue!"

The line halted. White men and black turned to look at the tableau.

"I almost believe," the Major said softly, "That I could do the whole thing unaided. But perhaps not. I don't think your sty companions would risk a penny to save you."

"Drop to the ground, Red," Squint yelled. "So's I can have a shot at him!"

"Don't do it," the Major warned, and Red stood still.

"Let's go, Carlos," Squint shouted. "Red asked for it. He got himself into a hole; let him get out of it himself."

"Of course," Carlos shouted his reply. "Sorry—Senhor Red and goodbye."

"Blast you!" Red screamed. "Come here. Shoot this damned dude."

The Major laughed.

"I told you they'd do nothing," he mocked as the line began to move again. "But I can't let them get away—"

"Carlos!" Squint shouted. "I'm going to put a bullet into Red, or he'll be setting the dude free an' joining forces."

"A good plan, Squint. Put the dude out of his misery, too. Then we'll be very safe."

"I can't have that," the Major said, and sounded the Go-a-way cry of a gray lourie.

Things happened quickly then.

But first Squint fired and the bullet plowed its way through Red's body. Another grazed the Major's ribs and flattened itself against the tree trunk.

Before Squint could fire again, before Red's lifeless body had slumped to the ground, Trooper Pearson dropped to the ground, revolver in hand shouting, "Hands up, Carlos—and you, Squint! Hands up. I arrest you—"

But the rest of the formula was lost in the loud, exultant shouts of the captured natives. The chains dropped from their legs and arms, and they savagely attacked the two white men and their native followers. For a little while all was helpless confusion; a tangle of struggling men and women who were eager to avenge past brutalities.

IT WAS a one-sided fight. Squint and Carlos and their five armed bullies were taken completely by surprise. They had been so sure that their captives were securely chained; the Major's exhibition of brutality had convinced them that there was no trap. The natives had looked as innocent of guile as a lime-spread bough must look to a bird.

But the chains were a mockery. Vital links had been cunningly filed so that they snapped in two at the slightest pressure, freeing the supposed captives to attack their torturers.

The policeman cut the Major free. Jim came running to join them and the three men used all their strength—physical and moral—to separate the maddened natives from their prey.

At last it was done, and Trooper Pearson was able to complete the formality of arrest.

Two of the armed natives had been killed; the others were badly hurt—but nothing serious.

Squint groaned with the pain of four broken ribs; groaned louder as he thought of the murder trial he would have to face.

And Carlos—he was a broken man who whimpered with terror whenever a native looked at him. In that first heated onslaught of the natives, he had met a punishment which far transcended anything a white man's justice could inflict on him.

The freed natives were jubilant. The policeman was going to take them to the great white kraal that they might give evidence against the evil men. He had promised them plenty of food; had hinted that the government would give them cattle.

For them the night had passed.

And Pearson—he was inflamed with the pride of a Crusader, and though he now gave the Major all the credit, it was easy to see that, with the passing of time, his own part in the business would assume a greater and greater importance.

"And you, baas," Jim asked. "What is there in it for you? At least," he chuckled, "it brought to me the weight of my baas's hand. *Au-a!* My back still smarts from the sting of the *sjambok.*"

The Major nodded gravely.

"It was part of the game I had to play, Jim. And those others, who felt the lash at my hand, in time they will forget the lashes were given only because of the game which had to be played. They will count them to my brutality."

"*Au-a!* And if they do," Jim said, "What matter. We know."

THE NATIVES who had been released now came up to where the Major was standing.

They pushed one of their number forward. He was their spokesman. In his hand he carried a blood-stained *sjambok.*

"*Inkosi,*" he said, and his deep voice throbbed with the intensity of his emotion. "We are your dogs, for was it not your hand, and the plan you made, which delivered us from great evil. Aye. Because, too, of you, the kraals which were divided against each other have reunited. When this matter is over we plan all to live in one great kraal. *Au-a!* We are your dogs, *inkosi!*"

"I scored your backs with a *sjambok*," the Major observed.

"*Wo-we!* It is of that I would speak, *inkosi*. Many of our backs are scored with the lash, *inkosi*. To us they are scars of remembrance. We shall never forget what they stand for. And our children shall not forget, nor our children's children. But some of our backs are unmarked, *inkosi*. You did not reach us all. And so—" At a signal a number of the men turned round and knelt on the ground, their heads slightly bent—"Mark us all, *inkosi*. And start with me—before your arm grows tired."

He handed the *sjambok* to the Major and then knelt at the head of the line of kneeling men.

The Major's hand trembled. His voice was soft when he said, "That I cannot do; and it is not necessary that I should scar your backs for remembrance. So take the *sjambok*. It is red with your blood. Let it be sufficient for a memory of this day."

He turned away, murmuring:

"I think that this affair has given me more than any other thing. It has given me a people's gratitude. Eh what, Jim, old horse?"

And Jim replied very gravely, "Golly damme yes. If I don't see you, s'long hullo."

WATER

"**SOMETIMES, JIM**," said the Major. "I think I am a fool."

The Hottentot nodded his head sagely and spat out the smooth pebble which he had been frantically sucking in the hope of inducing saliva to flow.

"Yah, baas," he agreed fervently.

The Major laughed, but the effort caused him some pain, for his lips were cracked and bleeding.

The two men were seated on a flat slab of basaltic rock which, despite the fact that it was in the shade of a towering hill, was unbearably hot.

"Yah, baas," Jim said again in a voice which would brook no denial. "This time you are indeed a fool. Three days ago—but truly it seems many years ago since we left the carriers in order to take a quicker way to the place by the great lake—I said it was folly to leave the well trodden trail; and again when we climbed over hills, where a *dassie* could not get a footing, in search of blood-red stones I said it was folly."

"True, Jim," the Major replied, stretching his long legs and looking reflectively at his brown polo boots. "We seem to be in a bad fix, Jim. Perhaps it was folly to seek a new

road and even greater folly to look for the blood-red stones in this maze of hills."

The Major looked around at the hills which hemmed them in on all sides. To the north they towered, higher and higher, row beyond row; and the last row of all was dominated by a gigantic mountain whose top was snow crowned.

At last the Major rose wearily to his feet and stood for a moment looking down at Jim. From the breast pocket of his tunic he produced a monocle which he carefully screwed into his eye.

"Come along, old top," he said, and with an easy, effortless gait he led the way along the barely discernible track which ran down the side of the hill.

Painfully, his naked feet cut and bleeding, scorched by the heat of the rocks, Jim limped slowly after him.

They had no guns, for Jim had lost them.

On and on they went, clinging like flies to the smooth walls of the hill. The long morning hours slowly passed. For an eternity, it seemed, the sun hung motionless in a cloudless sky directly overhead and then hurried to its setting.

Both the Major and Jim showed the strain under which they were laboring. They were facing death at every step; their thirst had increased until the desire for water was an indescribable agony. Their faces were drawn, their eyes bloodshot; their tongues felt like swollen pieces of blotting paper. There was no moisture in them. And despite the heat and the immensity of their efforts, of their physical exertions, they could no longer sweat.

For a little while they sat down, dangling their legs over the ledge of rock, breathing heavily, seeking to recuperate their strength. Presently the Major arose to his feet.

"Come on, Jim," he said wearily. "There is an end to all roads. All trails lead somewhere—and so must this one."

And on they went, the Major in the lead.

Gradually, almost imperceptibly, the downward trail became easier, the path wider. Now they were able to walk abreast.

And soon it seemed as if they had come to the bottom of the hill. The rocky nature of the country changed almost immediately. They passed through the fringe of a forest of black, leafless trees onto a flat plain of dark brown and green marshland, covered with patches of mimosa trees and grass.

IT WAS nearly sunset when they saw, through a vista in the trees, the bright blue waters of Lake Tanganyika, contrasting wonderfully with the dark red cliffs and the pale purple, feathery surface of the forest on the hills rising to the east. The surface of the water was flecked and streaked by dark catspaws made by the trade wind which blew north.

"Water and so much water," the Major murmured as he halted to take in the beauty of the scene.

"I could drink it all, baas," said Jim, hurrying on.

Leisurely the Major followed him, conscious of the overpowering heat, tormented by the clouds of mosquitoes which suddenly arose about him. He, too, felt the desire to break into a run as Jim had done and plunge into the cool waters of the lake. But....

"Slow, Jim. Go slow," he ordered, and dutifully the Hottentot obeyed.

The sun had dropped behind the western hills. Purple shadows flitted over the surface of the lake. The trail leveled off.

Jim started as a wild scream echoed through the air. Two more followed.

"What was that, baas?" he exclaimed, terror of the spirit world completely possessing him.

The Major laughed.

"It was only a bird, Jim; a fish eagle, that was all."

"You may call it a bird, baas," Jim replied, "but I say that it is the voice of the evil spirits which inhabit this place. And I say further that that is not water that we see before us. It comes to me now that we two shall never drink again."

There were more screams, human ones this time. Shots were fired and then, just as they came in sight of a wattle and daub hut, a native burst out of the door which hung on broken hinges, shouting with terror and vanished from their sight. More shots sounded from within the hut and a white man's voice screaming curses.

The Major and Jim came to a halt and looked at each other wonderingly.

"My thirst is great, baas," said Jim, "but it can wait a little while. There is death in that hut—and now it comes out!"

Again the hut door opened and a white man emerged. He wore a suit of dirty, tattered pajamas. His feet were bare, his flaming red hair hung down over his forehead; his face had known no razor for many days. He stood in a crouching attitude just outside the door of the hut staring wildly about him. In his right hand he flourished a smoking revolver which he aimed at some object now to the right, now to the left.

"You devils," the Major heard him rant. "I'll kill you. I'll kill every one of you. You will put out my lights, will you? Hell! I'll roast you alive."

"He is bewitched, baas. Come away."

The Major shook his head and advanced cautiously a pace or two.

"It would be best, baas," Jim said, "to run."

"It would be easier," said the Major, "if I knew whether he has fired all the shots. I think he has. I may be wrong." He shook his head doubtfully, then he called: "We are friends. Won't you let us help you hunt them?"

The man's wandering attention was held. He leveled his revolver at the Major.

"I see you," he gasped. "I see you swine. Put out my lights, would you?" The revolver spat flame. A bullet passed dangerously close to the Major's head.

"Run, baas," cried Jim. "We can hide from him in the reeds." And before the man could fire again they were running desperately through the tall grass which grew in the thick black mud of the lake's foreshore. And after them ran the redhead. Their own progress was comparatively silent, save for the *plocking* sound made by their feet in the mud. The redhead made as much noise as a rogue elephant. He thrashed about, floundering in the mud, shouting at the top of his voice. Several times it sounded as if he had fallen full length to the ground.

"If we can double back and get him when he falls," the Major gasped, "there would be an end to this."

"And if we fail," Jim replied grimly, "that would also be an end. No, let us go on, baas. Soon we will come to water and at least we will drink."

THEY WERE running now in a fairly wide pathway which doubled and twisted on itself. Their feet sank deeper into the mud at every stride and presently a thin scum of water appeared on the top of the black surface. Jim wanted to halt, to drink, but the Major urged him on. The water deepened. Then another turn in the trail brought them to the edge of the reeds; beyond were the wide, sparkling waters of the lake.

"There is only one way, Jim," the Major murmured. "We must retrace our steps and make our peace with the mad one."

"Best," Jim murmured, "that we lure him on to this place and let him become food for the crocodiles."

The Major shook his head. He led the way back along the trail for a little distance—far enough at least to minimize the danger of attack from the crocodiles—and stepping off the path hid in the thick reeds which fringed it. He gathered up a double handful of the black, evil smelling mud. Jim followed his example and the two men waited patiently.

Presently the redhead came into sight, lumbering down the path, shouting bloody threats. He was smeared with mud from head to foot. His eyes held a wild, fanatical light. As he came opposite to the place where the two men were hiding he halted suspiciously, then shouting, "I've got you," he fired twice into the reeds on his right.

Before the echo of the shots had died away the Major and Jim acted. Shrewdly they threw their handfuls of mud. It struck the redhead in the face, blinding him, half choking him. He slipped backward in the mud. His revolver dropped from his grasp and before he could do anything to protect himself the Major and Jim closed with him. He struggled violently and seemed likely to overpower them until Jim brought up his head sharply under the redhead's jaw. After that he struggled no more.

"What now," Jim asked, looking down at the unconscious man.

"We will carry him to his hut, Jim. Maybe we will find there things which will tell us all that has happened and why." The Major looked for the man's revolver but it had sunk out of sight in the mud. Then he bent down and raised the man by his shoulders and Jim took his feet.

AND SO they came at last, just as the sun disappeared below the horizon, to the hut. They pushed open the door and put the still unconscious man on the crude, disordered bed. That done they looked eagerly round the place, remembering once again their colossal thirst. From the center pole of the hut hung a bulging water bag. On the table close by were two glasses.

The Major filled them, thinking that he had never heard sweeter music than that made by the water as it flowed out of the canvas bag. He sat down in the one rickety chair that the hut contained. Jim squatted on the floor at his feet. They toasted each other silently, then slowly sipped the water with the caution that comes as second nature to experienced hunters. The glasses empty, the Major filled them again and again. In silence they drank.

The Major was staring round the hut, noting its filthy disorder, endeavoring to deduce from it the life which had been led by its owner, the man whose labored breathing now filled the hut.

The Major took the hurricane lamp down from its peg with an air of fastidiousness and lighted it, dispelling the dark gloom which had so quickly followed the setting of the sun, then he again turned his attention to the contents of the hut.

In one corner was a pile of mold-covered trade goods. On a broken down desk made from a packing case was a dusty ledger. Glancing through it swiftly, the Major read from it a record of failure; the story of a man who had opened a store, full of ambition and of a determination to wrest wealth from Africa's begrudging soil, but who had, with the passing of time, been beaten by the heat, the insects and the intense loneliness. An item dated several months previously registered the receipt of a case of gin. After that there had been no entry.

The story was plain to read and a not uncommon one.

The Major rose to his feet and gave the hut a still closer scrutiny, discovering, to his satisfaction, a revolver and a fair supply of ammunition which had been buried beneath a pile of debris.

He loaded the revolver, filled his pockets with extra shells, and thrust it into his belt.

"Feel better now, old top," he said to Jim in English. "Ready for anything, if you know what I mean."

Jim didn't, but he remarked sagely:

"When do we eat, baas?"

"We have work to do first, Jim. We are men—not pigs. It is not seemly to eat surrounded by filth, Come."

He took down the hurricane lantern and led the way outside the hut.

"*Au-a!* What a man," Jim grumbled. "A hunger like mine does not recognize filth."

At the rear of the hut was a broken down lean-to. There they found a broom, soap and a large tub full of water. There was, too, a primitive cookstove, a pile of dirty crockery, a hip bath and cooking utensils.

"Now, Jim," the Major said briskly, "we will work."

THE LIGHT of a full moon flooded in through the open doorway of the hut, paling the yellow gleam of the hurricane lamp.

The Major was seated in a chair smoking contentedly. He was clad in a suit of thin cotton pajamas which he had discovered in a tin uniform case. They fitted somewhat too snugly, safety-pins served as buttons—but they were clean.

From the lean-to back of the hut sounded Jim's voice and the clatter of dishes. Jim was washing up the dinner dishes.

The Major chuckled softly as his eyes roved idly round the hut.

"Dear old redhead," he muttered, "won't know the place when he wakes up." Then he frowned and, rising to his feet tiptoed over to the bunk where the owner of the hut still snored profoundly, and bent over the sleeper, examining him intently. There was nothing at all the matter with him.

The Major returned to his chair with a sigh of relief.

"No!" the Major mused again, "I fancy that redhead will be surprised when he wakes up. I wonder if he'll be a talkative chappie. There is so much about him I want to know so badly that I am tempted to read his letters."

The Major picked up and examined tentatively three letters which he had found unopened. Two bore postmarks that were comparatively recent ones. The first, a Devonshire one, the second had been mailed at Cape Town. The third was unstamped, it had not passed through the mail.

"A woman's handwriting, I think," the Major muttered. "And so I can't open the bally things."

Again he was silent. Relaxing, he sought some ease from his bodily fatigue.

Outside, Jim was crooning a soft lullaby. The redhead's snores were tempered now to a deep inhaling and exhaling of breath. Mosquitoes *pinged* savagely in an ever-increasing cloud.

The moon rose higher. Its light flooded the hut. Long minutes passed. Jim came to the door of the hut. In his hands were the Major's brown polo boots. They were polished, the spurs on them glistening in the moonlight. Jim placed them on the ground just inside the doorway.

"Is all well, baas?" he asked, indicating the man on the bed with a nod of his head.

"Yes, Jim," the Major said.

Jim grunted relievedly.

"Why do you not sleep, Jim?" the Major asked.

"Shall I sleep while my baas keeps watch? No. I go now to wash the baas's clothes. Then maybe I will sleep."

Again the Major was left alone with his thoughts, begrudging the slow passing of time. His eyes closed, his head sagged forward. For a little while he slept.

The scream of a fish eagle followed by a frantic cry of *"Baas, baas!"* awakened him. He jumped to his feet and, revolver in hand, rushed outside the hut. He heard the harsh hissing noise of an infuriated crocodile. Apart from that there was no sound.

He went to the lean-to at the back of the hut, but there was no sign of the Hottentot. He tried to quiet his fears, telling himself that Jim was down at the lake washing his clothes. Then he thought of the crocodiles which guarded the lake and his fears increased.

The wind suddenly died away. For a few moments there was an almost unbearable silence. Then the clouds were split by a jagged streak of lightning, followed almost instantaneously by a heavy peal of thunder, and the rain fell. A heavy, tropical downpour which immediately soaked through the Major's thin clothing.

The bushes and trees bent before its fury and the Major, head down, ran swiftly to the shelter of the hut. He peeled the wet clothes from him, dried himself with a coarse towel which he draped about his middle, and sat down again in a chair.

JIM'S DISAPPEARANCE had hit him hard. But there was nothing that he could do but wait; wait until the redhead returned to consciousness. And then almost simultaneously with that thought, the redhead at last awakened. Indeed, that man was now sitting up in his bunk, his eyes wide open, staring wonderingly.

"Better now, old chap?" asked the Major cheerfully.

The other looked at him, a truculent expression in his eyes.

"Who the hell are you," he asked savagely, "and where did you come from?"

"Me?" the Major laughed. "My name's Aubrey St. John Major. Call me Major, it's so much easier, and I come from…" He waved his hands. "Where haven't I come from?"

"I am asking you," the other growled, "and I want an answer." But, despite the confidence in his words, his voice trembled and his eyes watered. It was an effort for him to remain in a sitting position. He swayed to and fro.

"Better lie down," the Major suggested easily. "You will be a lot more comfortable that way, and we will be able to talk better."

The other glared angrily. His lips formed a heated denial but he obeyed, nevertheless.

"That's better," the Major continued, soothingly. "And now suppose you tell me your name and the matter of introduction will be completed."

"It's Tom Saunders," the other said dully. He added, "Where in hell am I?"

"In your hut, old lad. Where else?"

"You are lying to me," Saunders said. "My hut—God!" He made an expression of disgust. "My hut's like a bloomin' pigsty."

"It was," the Major agreed. "It most certainly was. But we took a few liberties with it. You were sleeping peacefully and we did not wish to awaken you. So we cleaned up a little. You must have been ill a long, long time. I took the liberty to glance through your day book. It didn't tell me much. Just what started you drinking? Loneliness, heat, fever, fear or what?"

"I don't see that it's any of your damned business what I do or why I do it."

"But it is, I assure you," the Major countered. "I arrange to meet my native carriers here—and I am ready to take my oath that they were loyal—and they desert with all my provisions. I come down to your hut. A native runs out into the bush, you after him. You chase Jim, the Hotten-tot, he is my servant, you know, and myself down to the lake. There we were, as the saying goes, between the devil and the deep sea.

"Well, we knocked you out, brought you back here, cleaned up you and the hut, had *skoff*—and now Jim the Hottentot has disappeared. And I want to know why. I want to know the explanation of everything. And if you can't give it to me, who can?"

Saunders sat up again.

"You say you had a nigger with you?"

The Major nodded.

"And he has disappeared?"

"Oh, quite! Vanished into thin air."

"And did you," the words seemed to come reluctantly, "did you hear nothing before he went?"

The Major considered thoughtfully before he replied.

"A fish eagle screamed and Jim called, *'Baas, baas!'* and I ran out of the hut to his assistance. But there was no trace of him."

SAUNDERS DROPPED back on his pillow with a heavy groan.

"That's it," he muttered. "That's the cause of everything."

"What do you mean," the Major asked sharply. "What is the cause of everything?"

"The cry of the fish eagle," Saunders replied. His eyes closed; for a while he seemed to sleep.

The Major frowned thoughtfully; his long fingers, which suggested abnormal power, beat a rapid tattoo on the table. He looked at Saunders shrewdly.

"So you're afraid of a scream," he commented sarcastically. "The scream of a fish eagle."

"Have it that way if you like," Saunders assented. "A fish eagle. Yes. The damned bird used to sit on a rotten log and scream for hours at a time. Day after day; it got on my nerves. The rest didn't matter—the loneliness, the mosquitoes, the stinking things that fly at night, the fever… Hell! I didn't mind any of them things. When niggers threatened to get out of hand—I could deal with them. I can handle niggers. And when Lopez got nasty—I knew how to handle him."

"Lopez! Who is Lopez?" the major questioned.

"He was my store assistant. A dirty little Portuguese half-caste."

"You couldn't trust him?" the Major prompted.

"Partly that—especially after I found the— But never mind about that." For a moment angry suspicion seemed to possess Saunders. He continued with a clumsy effort to conceal the fact that he had been on the point of giving away a closely guarded secret. "I got rid of him after I found the—the cunning devil was poisoning the minds of the niggers against me. He hung about for a time. He tried to poison me; he tried to stick me with a knife. But I was too clever for him. He went away at last. He's running a store up the lake a bit."

"But about the fish eagle," the Major prompted gently. "It got on your nerves, you say."

"Hell, yes," Saunders agreed. "You know how it is. I found myself waiting for it to come and scream. Couldn't do anything all day but sit and wait for it. I used to stuff my ears with cotton—then pull the stuff out just in time to hear the first scream! It drove me mad—mad I tell you." He lapsed into a moody silence.

"And so the scream of a bird got on your nerves, eh?" the Major prompted. He knew it was like turning a knife in Saunders' tortured nerves. But he had to know more. He had to find out what had become of Jim, and Saunders was his only avenue of information—until morning, at any rate.

"Yes," Saunders said slowly. "It was that blasted eagle that got me. It used to perch on a rock down there a-ways and scream. God, how it used to scream!"

"Why didn't you shoot it?"

"I did. I blew the blasted bird into a thousand small bits. But it made no difference. It's a ghost bird. Nothing can kill it."

"Don't talk like a bally ass," the Major said lightly.

"You don't know what I've been through," Saunders moaned. "I've lost everything—yes, everything. Things disappeared mysteriously. My niggers ran away. They left the villages hereabouts. No one came to trade. No one came near me.

"I'd be sitting in my hut of nights and the light 'ud slowly go out. I'd hear things moving about the hut. That blasted eagle 'ud scream. Then by the time I'd struck a match I'd be all alone—but something would be gone from the hut."

"What, for instance?" the Major asked softly.

"A chair, a book, pictures… Oh, what does it matter."

"Not much," the Major agreed. "Most nerve-racking, I should say. Things fluttering about the hut, and the scream, an' the darkness. My word! An' the light went out slowly, you say?"

"Yes!" Saunders gasped, his eyes strangely dilated. "Just as it's doing now. Look!"

As he spoke the lamplight flickered, became very dim, then went out completely, leaving the two men in total darkness.

"My word!" the Major exclaimed softly. "This is spooky. Quite!"

A wild scream echoed through the night. The next moment the Major was fighting for his life, fighting to free himself from the hands which, reaching out from the darkness, had closed about his throat.

IT WAS a losing fight he waged. The hands seemed imbued with maniacal strength; they formed a steel band about his throat, and that band slowly constricted.

He went limp, his knees sagged. Red fire seemed to dance before his eyes; his ears were filled with a deep, booming noise.

Subconsciously he was aware of a cold blast of air, and his body was lashed by a wind driven rain.

The pressure about his neck was relaxing; either that or it had tightened to the utmost extent, putting an end to all pain, all consciousness. He thought he heard a wild cry of *"Baas, baas!"* A cry which came to him through unfathomable depths.

He returned slowly through a desolate waste of waters. He groaned wearily. His head rolled limply from side to side. He opened his eyes and looked up into the familiar face of Jim the Hottentot. He looked past Jim and saw that he was still in the hut of the man, Saunders. It was lighted by flickering flames of a crudely made torch. On the floor not far from him was the huddled body of the trader. The man was lying on his back, his mouth sagged open. Blood oozed gently from a wound in his forehead. Near the closed door was a native, bound hand and foot, who glared balefully before him.

With an effort the Major sat up.

"Better now, Jim," he said thickly, and added in tones of excitement, "But what happened?"

"Au-a! baas," Jim began, "I was cleaning the kit outside the hut and I heard a noise in the bush. I went to see—but cautiously, baas. And then that thing which you call a bird, but which I say is an evil spirit, screamed. For a moment I forgot caution. A heavy something struck me on the head, and for a time I knew only utter darkness. When light and life returned to me, baas, there was water all around me. Truly, baas, I was on the face of the waters, in a canoe hollowed out of an old log.

"There were two men, baas, in the canoe. They wore masks. Birdlike masks which they thought made them appear to be evil spirits. Then there was a swirl in the waters and a crocodile rushed at us. And those two men cried out in fear as they beat upon the waters with their paddles. And then fear left me entirely. I could deal with men who were afraid of crocodiles.

"It was very easy, baas. I lurched with all my force to one side of the boat and it turned over, throwing the three of us into the water. They floundered about, baas, shouting and splashing mightily. I think fear made them forget they could swim. I righted the log which was a boat, climbed into it and waited. A paddle drifted near me. I picked it up. Then one of the men screamed for a last time. I think a crocodile took him, baas. The other one, the one you see over there, he swam to the boat and clung on to it, begging for his life. But I did not trust him, baas. I hit him on the head with my paddle and before he could sink I grabbed hold of him and hauled him into the canoe. And then, after binding him, I rowed back to the shore. The rest you know, baas."

The Major opened his eyes and looked at Jim.

"But I do not know, Jim. What is the rest? Who was it who fought with me in the dark? What happened to the redhead yonder?"

"It was the redhead you fought with," Jim replied. "I hit him on the head with a paddle."

The Major nodded. Rising to his feet he went over to the table and examined the lamp. The air holes were choked with the bodies of insects.

"Everything," he said slowly to Jim, "can be explained. When the light went out I thought evil spirits had breathed upon it. But not so. The flies put it out. Jim. Their dead bodies stopped up the holes so that it could not breathe."

"But what make you of the scream?" Jim asked.

"Surely men can imitate the cry of a bird," the Major answered dryly. "That is no great mystery, Jim."

"Truly not, baas," Jim replied, looking rather shame-faced. "I had not thought of that."

THE MAJOR bent over Saunders, and seeing that he was slowly struggling back to consciousness, picked him up and put him on his bunk. Then he turned to the native Jim had captured.

"What is the meaning of all this folly?" he asked sharply.

"I know nothing, white man, except that I obey the commands of the Keeper of the Red Ones," the native answered sullenly.

"And who is this 'Keeper?' What is his name?" the Major asked sharply.

"No man has seen him," the native answered. "His voice is but a scream in the night."

"A scream!" the Major exclaimed sarcastically. "The scream is many words. It tells you to go here or there; it tells you to do thus and so. It tells you to take a man prisoner and carry him away over the water. *Wo-we!* What folly. Do not lie to me, do not tell me that all those words are contained in a scream."

The native's eyes blazed fiercely.

"The desire of the Voice which cries in the night is made known to us by the servant of that Voice."

"And who is that servant?" the Major asked.

The native made no reply.

"Who are the Red Ones?" the Major asked.

"They used to hang about the neck of the juju whose form is like that of the Voice which screams at night."

The Major raised his eyebrows.

"Then they are not men?" he said. "They do not live?"

"No, they are not men, they do not live. But the blood of all the world is imprisoned in them."

"And these Red Ones," the Major continued, "you say they *used* to hang about that one's neck. Then where are they now?"

The native looked towards the bed. The trader had returned to consciousness and was now staring at the three men with a cunning expression in his eyes.

"Ask that one," the native said fiercely. "He knows where they are, for he took them unto himself."

And that seemed to give the trader his cue for speech.

"Yes," he shouted fiercely. "I took them, I hold them and they are mine. And none of you devils, for all your tricks, will get them from me." In the fury of the moment he sprang from his bunk. Jim and the Major had all they could do to hold him for he fought with a berserk fury.

Finally they overpowered him and to guard against another outbreak tied him firmly to the bed. He lay there, glaring malevolently at them.

Shrugging his shoulders the Major philosophically conceded defeat.

He cleaned and lighted the lantern. That done he sat down again in the chair and stared moodily before him.

PRESENTLY HIS eyes were drawn to the three unopened letters. He took the envelopes up in his hand and toyed with them absentmindedly.

"What a fool I was not to think of this before," the Major said. And he considered for a moment the one which was unstamped, which was addressed simply to Tom Saunders. A moment he hesitated then he slit it open. The note it contained had been evidently written hurriedly and in pencil. It read:

> *Tom:*
>
> *I am heartbroken. Even since I arrived here you have been drunk, maudlinly drunk. So drunk that you did not know me. Perhaps you are not to blame altogether. Perhaps Africa is too strong for you. Perhaps the greater part of your drunkenness is the delirium of fever. I only know that I am frightened and that I cannot stay here any longer and so I am going away back home. For a little while I shall stay with Mr. Lopez and his wife. If you recover in time, and if you still care enough, you will find me there. Goodby,*
>
> Your Despairing Wife.

The Major whistled softly.

"My word!" he exclaimed. "This rather complicates matters." Then sharply to the native he said, "Where is the store of the man Lopez?"

"I do not know," the man replied tunelessly.

"Is he a servant of the Voice?" the Major next asked, and again came the reply, "I do not know."

The Major went over to the bed and looked down at Saunders.

"Get hold of your senses," he said sharply. "Forget your own fears, forget everything except the fact that your wife is in danger."

Saunders chuckled.

"You can't trick me that way," he said. "I know what you are after. You want the Red Ones. But I'll never tell you where they are. They are mine. I found them and I am going to keep them."

"I tell you," the Major repeated gravely, "that your wife is in danger."

Saunders laughed.

"My wife—hell! She's safe, safe in Devonshire; where the air is soft, and the sun never burns and a man can sleep nights. You can't make me talk by wild tales like that."

"Fool!" the Major exclaimed impatiently. "When did you hear from her last? Have you read these? If you haven't, read them now." And he gave the man the other two letters. The one with the Devonshire postmark first.

LIKE A man in a trance Saunders opened it and read slowly. Then, his hands shaking with excitement he held out his hand for the other, the one which bore a Cape Town postmark.

"My God!" he murmured again and again as he read.

"Is there more?" he asked in a trembling voice.

When he came to the end, the Major gave him the last one. Saunders read it, and he rolled over on his face and sobbed. For a little while the Major left him to his misery.

Presently the noise ceased and Saunders rolled over again on his back.

"Cut me loose," he demanded.

"Why?" the Major asked.

"Because, damn you, my wife is in danger!" Saunders shouted.

"But what do you intend to do if I cut you loose?"

"Go after her."

"And where?"

"To Lopez's." Saunders' voice was filled with the agony of anxiety. "If my wife's gone there… Don't you see what that means? A white woman alone with that devil!"

"She was alone here with you," the Major remonstrated gravely, "and you were not much comfort to her."

Saunders groaned. He moved his head slowly back and forth.

"I know, I know," he muttered. "I failed her. But I didn't know she was coming. I didn't know she was here. I was mad. But now I am sane, so cut me free at once."

"Are you so sure you are sane?" the Major asked. "In any case what can you do tonight? Perhaps your wife is safer where she is. She says she has gone to stay with Mrs. Lopez."

"Hell!" Saunders snapped. "Lopez hasn't got a wife…. And I think I am beginning to see things now, beginning to understand why he liked to see me drinking. He knew when I was drunk he could do what he liked here. And after he had left, after I had kicked him out of the place, the drink had got hold of me and I could not stop. And I am beginning to see, I think, the connection between the scream of that blasted fish eagle and the things that disappeared. He was breaking down my nerve. I am beginning to think he was the fish eagle. He thought he'd drive me mad and then he could come and search for the things he wanted. But never mind about that. Cut me free, I tell you. I've work to do." And Saunders struggled to free himself from the ropes which bound him.

"Gently, gently, man," the Major said calmly. "Don't you think it would be best first if you explained things a little."

"I am telling you nothing," Saunders snapped.

"Don't you trust me?" the Major asked.

"Yes," Saunders said finally. "I reckon I can trust you. I do trust you."

"Then that's that," said the Major as he cut the bonds which bound the other man.

"And now let's go," Saunders said, rising to his feet and stretching himself. "I know where Lopez's place is."

The Major shrugged his shoulders.

"All right, MacDuff," he said. "Lead on, we will follow."

Saunders sprang to his feet and took the hurricane lantern up in his hand. Then, for the first time, he seemed to be conscious of his own and the Major's scanty raiment.

"Haven't you more clothes?" he asked. The Major turned to Jim.

"Where are my clothes, Jim?" he asked.

"I washed them, baas. They are hanging in the lean-to."

"Go and get them," Saunders ordered. "We will take them along with us. We will dry them on the way."

And as Jim went to do his bidding, Saunders put on some clothes which were in the tin uniform case. He threw over a pair of khaki slacks to the Major.

"These will have to do for you," he said, "until your own are dry."

The Major nodded as he pulled them on. Then he put on his boots.

"I am ready now," he said, as Jim reappeared. "But what are we going to do with this fellow?" He indicated Jim's prisoner.

"Let him stay until we come back," Saunders said roughly.

The Major considered this.

"No, we can hardly do that," he said as, stooping over the native he loosened that man's bonds so that he could, by exercising considerable patience, in time release himself.

"Now," said the Major, "we are ready to go."

SAUNDERS, LANTERN in hand, led the way out into the darkness and the devastating deluge of rain. Down to the lake he went, the Major and Jim following carefully in his tracks. They slipped in the mud, water rose to their ankles, to their knees.

"I say, old top," the Major called. "You are not planning to swim the bally lake are you?"

"Come on, and don't talk like a fool," Saunders shouted back.

They seemed to be following a pathway which led through forests of reeds. Deeper and deeper the water got.

Suddenly Saunders came to a halt and pointed to something in the water.

The light of his lantern shone on a large dugout.

"Get in," he said. And they did.

The crazy craft rolled heavily, threatening every moment to capsize, but Saunders was an expert with the paddle and they forged slowly out from the shore.

Their progress was halted abruptly, the nose of the dugout crashing into something which loomed weirdly in the darkness.

"A rock!" the Major exclaimed.

"No, a steamboat," Saunders replied tersely.

Somewhat clumsily—the Major was no seaman—he boarded the boat. Jim followed and the dugout drifted away.

"Come on," said Saunders, and led the way along the untidy deck to the engine room aft.

The place was an indescribable chaos, and stunk like a charnel house. Enormous cockroaches swarmed everywhere. The engine, a primitive affair, looked to have reached the point of total disintegration.

There was a lantern hanging from a beam, and Saunders lighted it.

"I can use your nigger down here," he said, "making and tending fire. She gets up steam easy—easier than she holds it."

Then he picked up an ax and rushed up on deck. A few minutes later he returned.

"I've cut the anchor loose. You go and take the wheel. Keep the wind at your back; that's all you've to worry about."

The Major looked at Jim. The Hottentot's face was a ghastly, greenish hue.

"I say," he began.

"Get out," Saunders roared.

Just then the boat heeled and the Major, his hands to his mouth, rushed up on deck.

Recovering presently he tottered about, with difficulty keeping his balance, searching for the wheel. He found it at last and clung to it as the one solid thing on that dilapidated craft.

Experimentally he turned it now this way, now that. As far as he could judge it made no difference at all to the course of the boat.

TIME PASSED very slowly. The rain ceased, the clouds disappeared. Once again the moon's light ruled. The wind increased.

They were now out of the lee of the shore and the tub felt the full forces of the howling gale. She bucked like a wild steer; she teetered precariously on the crests of gigantic waves; she wallowed sluggishly in every trough.

She had full steerage way and the Major, feeling the wheel kick in his hands, laughed enthusiastically.

The lake was rising. Every now and then an enormous form of a wave appeared over the moonlit waters and stalked majestically after the boat until its crest toppled over into white foam, rushed under the stem, driving the boat ahead.

They were now drifting blindly on the great lake which seemed to be drawn out into long lines of hissing foam between which were the dark hollows of waves.

Saunders came up on deck and staggered to the wheel.

"She is going. I have got her going!" he exclaimed exultantly. And the Major could feel the vibration of an engine protesting against the work it was being forced to do.

"She'll do for a while," Saunders said, "if the propeller doesn't jar off." The racing of the screw as the boat nose-dived down the black side of a gigantic wave shook her from stem to stern.

The Major looked up at Saunders. The trader was very tired. Sweat made grotesque patterns on his smoke-blackened face. His eyes held a haunted look of fear; a fear that all this was labor in vain; that he would be too late to save his wife.

"It'll be all right," the Major said encouragingly. Saunders made no reply.

"Can't you tell me something now?" the Major continued.

"What do you want to know that you don't already know?" Saunders asked gruffly. Anxiety, his heavy labor, had sweated fear and madness from him.

"Not much. Just what are the Red Ones, what is the Voice?"

"The Red Ones," Saunders laughed harshly. "I thought they were going to bring me happiness. They were going to enable me to go home and join my wife and live like a prince. Instead of which they brought nothing but misery. They are rubies, man. They used to hang around the neck of the big juju, near the village where Lopez now keeps a store."

"You mean you stole them," the Major asked sternly.

"No," Saunders replied. "I know better than to monkey with a nigger's superstitions. No, I bought them. And the niggers were glad to make the deal. I gave them all my trade stuff. In place of the necklace of red stones, which have no value in the eyes of the niggers, the juju is now covered from head to foot in beads of all colors—red, green, yellow and gold. The niggers are satisfied with their bargain, and so is the juju. But Lopez! He reckons he ought to have a half share. That was the beginning of the row between us, and I am beginning to see now that Lopez has been at the back of all my trouble. He's been trying to frighten me into giving up the stones. And now he's got my wife. That's all."

Now you get down below and keep the fire going. I want all the steam she can carry."

The Major nodded and went down below.

WHEN THE lantern's light paled before the light of breaking day a dull thud shook the boat from stem to stern and she no longer moved. There was a sharp crack and a shout of pain. At the same moment the engine ceased its groaning labor.

"We're aground, Jim," the Major cried and rushed up on deck, followed wearily by Jim.

The Major stared in amazement. There was no water visible. It looked as if they had been sailing for many hours over dry land; it looked as if they rested now in the center of a green meadow land. Actually the boat had pushed her way along a narrow lane in the reeds which fringed the shore—had pushed on until not even her shallow draft could take her further. She was aground now in black, evil smelling mud, and the reeds, springing up again, had hidden her passage; the projecting spur of land round which they had passed hid from sight the waters of the lake.

All this the Major saw in one comprehensive glance. He had no time for more. His thoughts now were for Saunders. That man sprawled headlong on the deck, his legs pinned by the mast, which, rotten at its base, weakened by the night's gale, had been snapped by the boat's jarring halt.

Quickly the Major and Jim levered off the spar and examined the man's hurts.

The Major whistled softly.

"What is it?" Saunders groaned as he tried to rise.

"Broken thigh bone, I'm afraid, old top," the Major replied. "You're *hors de combat* for a while, I'm afraid. Oh, quite."

With that skill acquired by a man who spends his life where doctors are few and far between, the Major set the broken bone and strapped on splints.

"I fancy that's a pretty neat job," he said when he had finished. "And now, old top, where are we?"

"Inland, not two miles from here," Saunders replied, "is Lopez's place. Hell!" he groaned. "To think I should get so near and then be knocked out like this."

"Cheer up, laddie," the Major said airily. "I'm fit. I think I know how to deal with Mister Lopez... Do you think he'll be expecting us?"

Saunders shook his head.

"He probably thinks I'm too drunk to know or care. I might as well be. But you—you'll go on?"

"But of course. Why not? Lady in distress, and all that. There's just one thing: you told me the truth about the rubies?"

Saunders nodded emphatically.

"Then things should be easy," the Major concluded. "I've only got Lopez to deal with. It 'ud be a somewhat difficult matter if I had tabus and what not to contend with. The wily heathen are somewhat jealous of their Gods. Oh, quite. And not even a return of things stolen always appeases them. I suppose from the little you've told me, Lopez has got his heart set on obtaining those rubies. Perhaps it would simplify matters if I offered them to him in return for Mrs. Saunders. But, perhaps not. He's a half caste, isn't he? And half castes have strange ambitions at times."

Saunders groaned and cursed bitterly.

"Oh," the Major continued swiftly. "I don't think we ought to anticipate the worst.

"Well! I'll toddle along. Don't like wasting time. Jim'll look after you. I hope to be back with Mrs. Saunders by noon. If I'm not—well, Jim'll take care of you."

He took off his polo boots and lowered himself over the side, then, boots in one hand, revolver in the other he looked up to grin goodby.

"Wait, baas," Jim cried and disappeared for a moment. When he reappeared he held the Major's clothes, carefully wrapped up, which he had washed and which had dried over night in the boiler room.

"Splendid fellow!" the Major chortled as Jim lowered the parcel to him. "I hope I'll be able to wash before I don them."

"Hottentot," Saunders called. "Give this to your baas."

He gave Jim a large chamois leather bag which he had worn on a chain about his neck and Jim handed it on to his baas.

"And Major," Saunders shouted, pain in his voice. "The stones are nothing to me. I give them all for my wife."

"Splendid, lad," the Major shouted. "I think perhaps, you will have both."

He put the bag, after a swift examination of its contents—it was full of good-sized, beautifully colored rubies—into his pocket.

"Goodby," he said again. "I'll be back, with luck, at noon."

"Take care, baas," Jim pleaded. Adding in his own peculiar English, "If I don't see you, so long, hullo."

LOPEZ SCOWLED triumphantly at the white woman who stood so defiantly before him. Her clothes were smeared with mud and clung limply to her buxom figure. Her black hair streamed in disorder over her shoulders.

"And so," Lopez said softly, his enunciation very precise, "you would try to escape from me, yes? You like not this place of mine?"

The woman tried to spring forward but her feet were tied, and she fell heavily to the ground, unable to break her fall with her hands by reason that they were tied behind her back. Lopez gave a curt order to the two natives who had stood behind the woman. They turned her over, lifted her up and seated her on a stool which was placed in the shade of the hut.

"Yes, you are a fool," Lopez, continued, "to try to run from me."

He snapped an order at the natives and they quickly retreated out of sight. Lopez was silent for a little while.

There was much that was laughable about Lopez, much that was detestable, and not a little which called for pity. He was an undersized little rat of a man. His color was almost white, a dirty yellowish white, his skin greasy. His short, black, curly hair was daubed with grease in a vain attempt to straighten its kinks. It was his tragedy that he wished to be taken for a white man.

He said slowly, addressing the woman:

"I will never let you go. You will stay here with me until you die, but perhaps before then you will decide to marry me as white folks are married. We will go to the mission."

"Fool," the woman spat the word at him. "I am already married and my husband...."

Lopez laughed.

"Your husband. I can deal with him. He is a fool; he is a gin soaked idiot. Willingly you left him to come to me."

"You said you were a white man," the woman inter-rupted. "You said you had a wife, and I believed you."

"Willingly you came to me," Lopez repeated, "now, because I will it, you will stay."

"My husband," the woman began again, "will come for me."

"Your husband will do nothing. If he is not dead already he will soon be. I have played upon his fears. The cry of a bird has driven him mad. That and gin."

The woman was silent.

"And so," Lopez continued, "as I have said before, all that your husband had will soon be mine. Yes. When he is dead, you and the red stones will be mine. I will be rich."

"You are a fool," the woman said. "A fool to think that I would ever go with you anywhere. I would die first."

"Maybe," Lopez replied casually, "that choice will be put before you. We will see. But I am in no hurry. Here we are safe from interference. No white men ever come this way. One man there was who wandered about in the hills. But I have dealt with him. His carriers are my men. Even should he come to this place by some strange chance, he can do nothing."

AND THEN he gave a start of surprise, for coming towards him from the thick jungle growth which surrounded the village, was a white man, guarded by two natives with spears.

Lopez rose to his feet, his mouth sagged open, his eyes protruded from their sockets, for this white man presented a remarkable figure. He was very tall and broad. A monocle gleamed in his right eye. His face was shaded by a white pith helmet freshly blancoed. He wore a white shirt, open at the neck, wrinkled but clean, and his riding breeches were of a dazzling snowy whiteness.

Lopez ran into his hut. When he emerged again he flourished a revolver.

The natives with their prisoner came to a halt.

"Look here, I say," the Major began indignantly. One of the natives jabbed him in the ribs with the butt of a spear and his words ended in a frightened squeak of protest.

"Where did you get this man?" Lopez asked.

The native grinned.

"He was washing in the pool. He is a fool. We caught him as easily as a snare catches a foolish hen."

"It was well done," Lopez commended casually. "And was this white man alone?"

"All alone, master."

"And unarmed?"

"Unarmed, master."

"My word," the Major exclaimed indignantly in English. "Those johnnies are the most frightful liars. They sprang on me all unawares. I was afraid, give you my word. Thought they were cannibal laddies—an' all that, you know."

"They are," Lopez said in a voice that was pregnant with meaning. "And so you understand the vernacular of my people?" He looked at the Major with closer interest. "Then you are not as big a fool as you look."

"You're damned insulting," the Major spluttered.

Lopez waved his hands in an airy gesture.

"That is my privilege. I am, you see, master of the situation. But, go on. You were saying that my servants are liars."

"My word, yes. They leaped on me—what chance had I to struggle—as I was, er, bathing. And they took my revolver from me. Then they brought me here. It's a wonder they permitted me to dress. It took me no end of a time to persuade them that I could not go about—er—naked. Tabu, and all that, you know… But, pardon. I see there is a lady present." He took off his helmet and bowed gracefully to the woman.

She was sobbing quietly. At the first appearance of the Major her confidence had been restored, she had hoped for a rescue. But now that she realized that he too was a prisoner, and, apparently, a dudish fool, the splendid courage which had hitherto buoyed her up, suddenly departed.

"Look here, you know," the Major continued. "A joke's a joke an' all that. But you're carrying things a bit too far. 'Pon my word, you are. The lady is bound hand and foot. You treat me like a bally prisoner. It won't do, you know. I shall write to the papers about it. I—"

"Silence, fool!" Lopez snapped. "Speak only to answer the questions I ask you. Which one of these men took your gun?"

The Major pointed to the one on his left.

"That one, I think. But I'm not sure. They're so alike, aren't they? And you'll make him give it back to me, won't you?"

ONCE AGAIN the Major lapsed into silence, as if intimidated by Lopez's scowl.

"Kigara," said that man, addressing the native the Major had indicated. "This white man says you lied. He says he had a gun which you took from him. Now give it to me."

He held out his left hand.

The native scowled.

"Quick!" Lopez demanded.

Slowly the native fumbled under the gaudy blanket which was draped over his shoulder. Slowly he withdrew his hand, and in it was a revolver. He aimed deliberately at Lopez.

"This," he said thickly, "is mine. Too long have we done your bidding—you, who are neither white nor black—receiving kicks for our pains. And now we, Juma and I, have decided to go our own way."

As he concluded his defiant speech, Lopez fired and the native sprawled face forward to the ground, life escaping through a small hole which the bullet had drilled in his forehead. The other native, shouting threats, leaped forward, brandishing his spear.

Again Lopez fired. The heavy bullet spun the native round, and he sprawled in a huddled heap upon the body of Lopez's first victim.

The Major sprang for the revolver which Kigara still held in his lifeless fingers.

But as he bent down to pick it up, Lopez called mockingly:

"Touch it, white man, and you follow the same trail those two fools have taken."

The Major saw that the half-caste covered him. So shrugging his shoulders, he straightened up.

"That was murder," he remarked casually.

Lopez smiled as he picked up the revolver.

"But, no. I shot only in self-protection. The dogs would have killed me. For long I have suspected them of desiring to mutiny. But now... I think they will be loyal now."

He raised his voice, shouting orders and in response several natives suddenly emerged from their huts and dragged the dead bodies away.

"Now we can talk," Lopez continued, when the natives had disappeared and there was no sign of the recent tragedy save that the ground was slightly discolored where the murdered men had dropped.

The woman moaned faintly. Her eyes were wide open. She seemed to be stunned by the tragedies.

"YES," LOPEZ repeated, after a short pause, "now we can talk."

"Talk," the Major exclaimed. "And why should I talk to you? Except to demand my revolver and a little courtesy from you. How dare you—"

"I dare do many things," Lopez interrupted him. "I am master here. Two, three hundred warriors obey my commands."

"Really?" the Major exclaimed. "And do they all obey as readily as those two who are now dead?"

Lopez's eyes flashed.

"I have dealt with them," he said with an assumption of dignity.

"And the others? It is not like thoroughbreds to obey the commands of a—pardon—mongrel."

Lopez's finger trembled on the trigger of his revolver. Then he laughed, harshly.

"They obey," he said, "because death would come to them if they did not. And," he added vindictively, "you will die presently. Now answer my questions."

"Why should I, if you intend to kill me?"

"Life is sweet. While you talk, you live."

"By jove! What a Solomon you are. Well, what do you want to know?"

"Who are you? Why did you come to this place?"

"Ah! Wouldn't you like to know? Well, to cut a long story short, my carriers deserted. I got lost in the hills—and here I am."

"You speak truth?"

"Well, naturally, dear old soul."

Lopez looked puzzled; he did not know what to make of the Major's airy persiflage.

"And now that you are here, what do you expect?" he asked slowly.

"That's easy to answer," the Major said blandly. "Proper treatment, hospitality, you know. And I want this lady released; you appear to hold her a prisoner."

"She came to me willingly," Lopez interrupted.

"It's a lie," the woman exploded. "At least, I didn't understand. I am in a strange country. I thought he was a white man, a gentleman. And my husband, he...."

"I understand, dear lady," said the Major softly. "Of course our dear Lopez is not a white man. But he is, I think, a little mad."

As he spoke he moved cautiously toward Lopez. But that man was too cunning to be caught off his guard that way.

"Back," he said, and his finger pressed on the trigger of his revolver.

The Major retreated to his original position.

"As you will," he said. "But suppose you tell me what you intend to do with us. You seem to hold all the cards—if you know what I mean."

"You," said Lopez thoughtfully, "I am going to kill when it pleases me. Perhaps now; perhaps tomorrow. Perhaps I will give you to my natives. They like to torture before they kill. But you will die. Yes. As for the woman—I am not sure.

I may use her to trap her fool of a husband. I want to know where he has hidden the red stones. *Au-a!* And I want to punish him. He dared to kick me."

"A vindictive soul, aren't you?" the Major observed.

"Vindictive—yes. But maybe I will forget my vengeance. And, after all, of what value are red stones. I have the woman. She shall become my wife in the white man's way."

"Yes—you are mad. Quite mad," the Major said. He looked at the sun. "I think," he continued thoughtfully, "That it will be noon in three hours."

Lopez started.

"What has that to do with things?"

"Not much. And yet I had rather set my heart on doing things before noon."

Lopez grinned.

"Then I will be kind. I will let you live until noon."

The Major bowed.

HE LOOKED around the untidy kraal. No natives were in sight. Men, women and children were all in their huts, or hiding in the jungle growth beyond. He noticed that Lopez's hut was built apart from the rest and almost encircled by a stout stockade.

"You're afraid of the natives, aren't you?" he said.

"I can manage them," Lopez replied truculently, but fear glistened for a moment in his eyes.

The Major smiled.

"Suppose," he said, "the woman's husband offered to give you the red stones in exchange for his wife. Would you accept the offer?"

"Why should I—when woman and stones can both be mine?"

"Something in that," the Major agreed.

He put his hands in his trousers pockets and, withdrawing them, made a low, clucking noise.

A number of scrawny fowl came running up to him. He appeared to throw things to them and the fowl scattered, pecking in the dust, as hens foolishly will, for the food they thought he had thrown to them.

"This is almost a case of casting pearls before swine," the Major drawled.

"What do you mean?" Lopez asked.

"Only," the Major said, "that I'm casting rubies to hens. It's a pity. But they're no good to me, if I must die at noon. And one thing, I'm not giving them to you. Oh, rather not."

Again he made the scattering movement with his hands.

"And it's such a pity," he continued. "They're such beauties. Found them back yonder in the hills. Look!"

He thrust his hands again into his pockets and withdrawing them, held them out to Lopez.

In the palm of each hand glistened a number of rubies.

With a catch of his breath Lopez came several paces nearer.

"You fool!" he exclaimed. "And you throw them to the fowl."

"Why not," the Major replied airily. Again he made the scattering movement of his hands.

Three or four stones dropped close to Lopez's feet. Hens flew squawking after them. For a fraction of a second, greed conquered Lopez's caution.

Cursing, he waved one arm to keep away the fowl as he stooped to pick up the glittering gems.

And, at that moment the Major acted.

He sprang forward, his right arm flashed, his fist crashed on Lopez's jaw, and for a time the half-caste had no further interest in life.

COOLLY, THE Major picked up the rubies which had been the cause of Lopez's undoing and put them in his pocket with the others which he had appeared to cast away.

His next thought was for the woman.

Quickly he released her, answering her flood of questions and explanations.

"It's quite all right, dear lady. In a short while we will rejoin your husband. He met with a little accident—nothing to worry about—or he'd be here with me now.

"Really, yes," he insisted, answering her look of doubt. "He has quite recovered from his—er—illness. Oh, quite.... And now you must sit still in the hut and be very quiet. We are not out of the woods yet."

The woman went meekly into the hut. Somehow this man she had considered a helpless fool inspired confidence.

The Major acted swiftly.

In a very few moments Lopez was bound hand and foot. A gag was thrust into his mouth just in time to silence the curses which rose to his lips with a return of consciousness.

Then, possessing himself of the two revolvers, the Major seated himself on the stool and rested his feet on Lopez's body.

Not until then did he seem conscious of the fact that natives had swarmed from the huts and were now surrounding him menacingly.

He looked up at them confidently, assured of his ability to deal with them now that the renegade half-caste was rendered harmless. The Major understood Africa's black people; and with that understanding went sympathy. That explains to a great degree his constant success in dealing with them. Rarely was he reduced to a display of force; speech, governed by knowledge of their psychological make-up, was nearly always sufficient.

And so now his attitude toward them was that of a stern, but very just parent.

"Au-a!" he began in a clear voice. "You have done many evil things—and for that there must be punishment."

There was a gasp.

This white man, alone, dared to speak to them of punishment! But, quickly following the resentment, before resentment could be manifested by force, came the thought that the white man was not perhaps alone. Perhaps he had a strong army in hiding, waiting for his command to rush on them and put them to death.

So they waited in uneasy silence. A few scuffled their feet. Many glanced furtively behind them as if expecting to see a force advancing on them from the jungle.

"Yes. You must be punished for the evil you have done," the Major continued. "But, because this one, who is truly all evil—" the Major prodded Lopez with the toe of his boot—"was your master, his shall be the greater punishment. Tell me: Why did you obey this worthless one?"

"Au!" an aged native, the headman of the kraal, exclaimed. "He came to us with many loud-sounding promises. He gave us plenty of the white man's drink. He carried the sticks which killed. In this way and that he made himself a chief among us. Yet—I speak truth, white man—we hated and feared him."

The Major nodded; then spoke:

"He has killed two warriors today. For that I take him to the place of the white man. He must answer to them for the killings."

A deep murmur went up from the men.

"Give him to us," some cried, "and we will save the white men much trouble."

The Major shook his head.

"That I cannot do," he replied. "White man's justice is not so easily set aside.... Now tell me one other thing: Have you any grievance against the white storekeeper?"

"None. He was always our friend until the madness seized him."

"You," the Major said sternly, "at the bidding of this one, caused that madness. But he is now cured of that madness. And now, that all may be set right, pay heed to my words...."

THE SUN was at noon when Jim the Hottentot saw many men advancing through the reeds toward the boat. At their head marched the Major. The four natives immediately following him carried a hammock slung on a pole, and in that hammock a woman reclined. After that walked a man, a rope about his neck, his hands tied behind his back. Warriors with spears guarded him on either side.

Then followed an army of natives. Each carried a load of wood.

"All well with the white man, Jim?" the Major called as he neared.

"Yah, baas. He sleeps now. And you, baas?"

"All's well, Jim."

The Major climbed on board, the woman followed.

"My husband?" she demanded anxiously. "Where is he?"

The Major led her aft to where the trader lay under an awning Jim had rigged.

And there he left her, returning to supervise the stowing of the fuel the natives had brought and to make sure that his prisoner, Lopez, was safely secured.

That same night most of the Major's carriers came to the boat, with their loads, with lengthy tales to tell which they hoped would justify their desertion.

Lopez's men had given them gin; had told them that their baas was dead; had promised them great wealth if they would throw in their lot with him. And so forth....

The Major dealt very gently with them.

"After all," he said to Jim, who hotly advised the Major to punish them severely, "the fault was not theirs. And they have been punished. They have trekked further than they need have trekked. And—" he looked up at the wind clouds which flecked the sky—"they will be punished some more when the boat begins to roll. And now they shall haul her out into deep water!"

IT WAS nearly a week later. A police patrol had come to Saunders' place and had departed with the half-caste, Lopez.

Saunders—carried in a hammock—and his wife went with them. The trader had had enough of Africa. The rubies would make him richer than many years of successful trading.

"And now we must trek, too, Jim," said the Major.

"Where, baas?"

"North, I think, Jim. There is a land we have never seen."

Jim grinned happily and turned away to give directions to the carriers.

"Wait, Jim," the Major said. "I think we can let the carriers return to their kraals."

Jim stared in amazement.

"The baas said?"

"Why walk, Jim, when we can travel in comfort?"

The Major's eyes were fixed on the steamboat which rode lightly at anchor on the lake's blue waters. She had been fixed and painted.

He felt confident in his ability to sail the boat, sufficiently well, at least, to run her to the northern end of the lake.

But—

"Baas," said Jim, "if you go that way, you go alone."

"What folly, Jim," the Major exclaimed. "If we go in the boat there is no labor—"

"*Au-a*, baas!" Jim exclaimed. "If we go in the boat, I die a thousand deaths. So, too, will you. And so I say, if we must go north let our feet take us."

"But, Jim," the Major expostulated, reluctant to give up a cherished plan, "if we go afoot the trekking is hard. We will have to go back into the hills, And there will be no water—"

"Water!" Jim interrupted forcefully, having a lively memory of the night of storm. "I care not if I never see water again."